LOVE LETTERS
TO A
SERIAL KILLER

LOVE LETTERS
TO A
SERIAL KILLER

TASHA CORYELL

BERKLEY
New York

BERKLEY
An imprint of Penguin Random House LLC
penguinrandomhouse.com

Library of Congress Cataloging-in-Publication Data

Names: Coryell, Tasha, author.
Title: Love letters to a serial killer / Tasha Coryell.
Description: New York : Berkley, 2024.
Identifiers: LCCN 2023036919 (print) | LCCN 2023036920 (ebook) |
ISBN 9780593640272 (hardcover) | ISBN 9780593640296 (ebook)
Subjects: LCSH: Serial murderers--Fiction. | True crime stories--Fiction. |
Serial murder investigation--Fiction. | LCGFT: Thrillers (Fiction) | Novels.
Classification: LCC PS3603.O7984 L68 2024 (print) |
LCC PS3603.O7984 (ebook) | DDC 813/.6--dc23/eng/20231103
LC record available at https://lccn.loc.gov/2023036919
LC ebook record available at https://lccn.loc.gov/2023036920

Printed in the United States of America
1st Printing

Book design by George Towne
Interior art: ripped grunge paper © Natasa Adzic / Shutterstock

To anyone who has ever felt unappreciated

LOVE LETTERS
TO A
SERIAL KILLER

PART ONE

1

Undisclosed Location

I didn't plan to fall in love with an accused serial killer. Nevertheless, my wrists and ankles are bound to a chair, and I can blame only myself.

I'm in a nondescript white room with fluorescent lights and gray carpeting lined with geometric shapes. Across from me there's a window that reveals that it's still daylight and that I'm somewhere above ground level but gives no clues of my overall location. The ropes chafe where I strain, rubbing my skin raw. My bladder is regrettably full. If I'd known that I was going to find myself in a kidnapping situation, I would've used the bathroom.

"Hello?" I cry out.

I suspect that no one can hear me, because my mouth remains uncovered and I was not put here by a stupid man. My suspicions are verified when no one arrives.

"Please, I have to use the bathroom," I say.

The silence is more disturbing to me than anything else.

I'm not as frightened as I should be, though I am frightened, which is a relief. I always appreciate when I feel the emotions I'm expected to feel in any given situation, like when I bake a cake and it looks like the picture from the recipe when I pull it out of the oven.

Beneath the fear is undeniable excitement. If I wanted to be kind to myself, I would identify it as adrenaline that I need to help me survive, but I'm not sure that I deserve kindness. Even as I'm afraid, there's something thrilling about being tied to a chair, like a scene from a movie. There is no question about who the protagonist of this story is.

I'm worried that when my body is discovered, I will be found undeserving of mourning. That's the catch of martyrdom on social media. First, they lament your death, and then they count all the reasons why you deserved to die.

I want to believe that I'm a good person. I vote in every election and care about the environment. I have a Black Lives Matter sticker on the back of my laptop and send money to various groups whenever there is a national tragedy.

All of these things will be outweighed by the great wrong that I've committed in falling in love with an accused serial killer.

"Don't tell me you didn't want this," Meghan would say if she could see me. "No one does what you've done if they don't find being tied up and about to die at least a little hot."

Meghan isn't wrong. I find no pleasure in the prospect of death but enjoy picturing the mourning of the masses. I want my name remembered, unlike the hordes of other women who have been brutally murdered and then forgotten. At the very least, I want a podcast in my memory.

I hear a noise outside the door.

"Please! Help me!" I call out.

Despite the urgency of the situation, I can't fully believe that my death is inevitable. What is the world if I'm not in it?

Too late, I realize that the sounds are not those of a would-be rescuer and instead are the familiar footsteps of the man who brought me here. I strain at the ropes again, a futile act. I take a deep breath and prepare to die.

2

Before falling in love with a serial killer, I worked in communications for a nonprofit. It was a job that I got following a monthslong search after graduating with my bachelor's degree. I graduated into the recession and suddenly all of that "promise" that I'd always been told I had dissipated into thin air. "You can do anything" turned into comments from my parents suggesting that I apply to work at Target or Starbucks, which I did. They turned me down because I had no retail experience. No one cared about my English and political science double majors with a German minor. They just wanted men who could write code.

The job offer from the nonprofit in Minneapolis was a godsend. It allowed me to move out of my parents' house in the suburbs and live as the pseudo-adult I'd always dreamed of being. I figured that I could stay in the position for a couple of years and eventually move up the ranks until I had the type of job that I actually wanted. As it turned out, there was no moving up. The people already employed in the upper ranks of nonprofits took turns switching positions like a game of musical chairs. I scrolled hopelessly through real estate listings, fantasizing over houses with yards big enough for a dog, aware that I had somewhere between seventeen and a hundred dollars in my savings account at any given time and would never be able to afford a down payment. I bought shirts that cost five dollars and went out for brunches that cost twenty-five because brunch was the main and only joy in my life.

Needless to say, I was unmotivated in the office. I spent my days scrolling social media when I was supposed to be working. I followed celebrity gossip sites to find out who was sleeping with whom. I read articles about politics (bad), about how the U.S. treated immigrants (bad), how it treated women (bad), and how it treated members of the LGBTQ community (bad). I kept a document open on my computer called "Work in Progress" in which I intended to write the next great American novel and which was perpetually blank.

At night, I drank too much and went on dates with men who would never love me. I don't want to say that not loving me was an equivalent crime to killing women. In a legal sense, there wasn't any wrong committed at all. No contracts had been signed, no living spaces shared, no kids wounded in custody agreements that weren't fair to anyone. It was only my heart, that stupid clichéd thing, that had been stabbed, bruised, and strangled until I was willing to embarrass myself for even the tiniest drops of affection.

Before I opened myself up to William, before I knew the names Anna Leigh, Kimberly, Jill, and Emma, and had memorized the ways in which he was accused of hurting them, I dated

Max Yulipsky. There was no real future with Max; I knew that from the start, a knowledge that never stopped me from willingly bending over and spreading my legs.

Max ghosted me on a Thursday, though I didn't know that yet. Max was always like that, ethereal and hard to reach. It was one of the things that drew me to him. Max was in a punk band called the Screaming Seals that rarely practiced and wasn't very good. That was another thing that I liked about him. It was endearing the way that he got onstage and played his little heart out in songs that were less than two minutes long and could've been written by a high schooler. I had one of their exclusive band T-shirts that was printed in the basement of the house that Max shared with his two roommates and featured an image of a seal wearing a bandana. I wore the shirt only on the nights that Max didn't stay over, because I didn't want him to know how much I cherished it.

For his day job, Max worked at a shop that sold specialty cheeses and sandwiches that I couldn't afford. Sometimes he brought me small pieces of cheese in plastic wrap and I allowed myself to cut tiny slices off in the evening as a way to taste him when he wasn't around. I still had cheese left when Max disappeared. If I had known it was the last cheese, I would've made it last longer. I would've kept it in the fridge until it grew moldy and then I would've eaten it anyway. To risk food poisoning for a person was a true sign of love.

But Max and I didn't use words like "love" or even "relationship."

"I'm not looking for anything serious," he murmured into my ear the first time we made out.

"Me neither," I said as I unzipped his pants. It was a lie that I'd uttered so many times that it no longer felt like a lie. Talking with men was more like reading a script than confessing from the heart.

Because I lacked sincerity, I assumed he did too. Surely, we would grow closer and closer until we were inexorably linked, and he would be forced to admit during the throes of passion that he couldn't stop thinking about me and wanted to be together forever. Instead, when we finished lovemaking, or fucking, or whatever term didn't make him uncomfortable about the carnal acts we'd just committed, he said things like "Do you think McDonald's is still open?" or "Can you make eggs the way that I like in the morning?"

The last date we ever went on was to a semi-vegan restaurant pop-up in a rapidly gentrifying area of town. It was October and the trees were grasping at their last bursts of color before turning skeletal for the winter.

"How can a restaurant be semi-vegan?" I asked Max. "Isn't the whole point of veganism that you're all in or, I guess, more accurately, all out?"

He smiled at me. He was wearing a homemade Fugazi T-shirt with a hole in the armpit. I wanted nothing more than for him to love me forever.

"That's what I love about you, Hannah. You're always thinking," he replied. I glowed at the use of the word "love."

Afterward, I asked Max if he wanted to go back to my place and he brushed me off.

"I have a lot to do tomorrow," he said.

I didn't remind him that he worked at a cheese shop.

"Come on," I replied in my most alluring voice, pushing my body against him. I wanted my flesh to be irresistible. It wasn't.

"Sorry," he said, pushing me away. He smiled when he said it, but it was crooked.

The rejection might've bothered me less if I thought we were each other's equals. Max still drove the car that his parents passed down to him when he was sixteen, even though the whole structure creaked every time he put on the brakes. He didn't have health insurance and when I asked, he said he couldn't remember the last time he'd gone to the doctor for a checkup. I assumed the same was true about the dentist, especially considering that he'd turned down my offer of keeping a toothbrush at my place.

"That's a little too serious for me," he said.

Max once explained to me that he couldn't get a real job because to get a real job was to sell out and he was dedicated to his punk band. *What,* I wanted to ask, *is the pinnacle for a punk band? Once you've achieved everything you've dreamed of, what are you holding?* Rather than say any of that, I murmured something about talent.

"I'm not like you, Hannah," he said at the end of the conversation. "I can't just get any old job."

The comment stung. It was true that I'd abandoned the creative pursuits I'd had as a child—theater, art, and writing—in favor of a forty-hour workweek. But if nothing else, I wanted to believe that I was doing good through my job at the nonprofit.

"Making change from the inside!" I'd said enthusiastically when I got the position, before I realized how the inside slowly devours a person until they're doing nothing at all.

I consoled myself with my health insurance that had a deductible that was too high, insurance I used to briefly attend therapy with a woman that I could describe only as being akin to a scolding teacher. I knew too that there were steady drips of money going to my retirement account, though I'd never learned to comprehend what those numbers meant. And on the days when those things weren't enough, I took solace in the occasional taco bar that appeared in the break room, stuffing chips in my mouth until my stomach hurt.

Max didn't have any sympathy for me. To him, it was the life that I chose, like there had been any kind of choice involved in the matter.

It took me a week and a half to realize that Max ghosted me. In the meantime, I wore my band T-shirt, nibbled on cheese, and refreshed his social media feeds looking for clues as to his whereabouts. When he posted a graphic for an upcoming Screaming Seals show, I stupidly decided to attend, thinking that the mere sight of me would be enough to trigger arousal.

I put on my favorite little black dress, plucked from a closet full of little black dresses. I straightened my hair into submission and drew cat eyes with my eyeliner, thinking that it made me look a little punk. I invited my best friend, Meghan, to attend the show with me and she arrived at my studio apartment with her boyfriend.

"He's going to be the designated driver," she said apologetically, an admission that she knew his presence was crossing a line. It was just supposed to be the two of us that night, but the notion of the two of us was already starting to erode.

I was drunk by the time we arrived at the venue. The Screaming Seals were only one band in a set of many and I spent the minutes leading up to their performance grappling with my age, so clearly on the wrong side of thirty in the midst of the cool punk girls around me. My hair, I realized, was stupid, my dress ill-fitting. By the time Max's band came on, I was falling-down drunk from attempts to regain my self-esteem. I spent their short set trying to make eye contact with him that I never caught.

He appeared in the crowd after his set and I walked toward

him, waiting for him to exclaim "You're here!" and embrace me, touched by my devotion. It was a shock when he wrapped his arms around another girl. When they extricated themselves from the hug, I realized that I had met her before at a house party Max had thrown. Her name was Rebecca or Rachel and she had been friends with Max in college before he dropped out during his junior year because, as he said, "college was an inauthentic experience."

"They're just friends," I told Meghan, not realizing that Meghan had absconded to a dark corner to make out with her boyfriend.

"Hey!" I said as I approached Max.

It took his eyes a minute to focus, like he couldn't quite remember who I was.

"Oh, hey, Hannah," he said finally.

I tried to wrap my arms around him the way that Rebecca or Rachel had, but his body felt limp.

"You were so good!" I exclaimed.

"Thank you," he said with a grin.

I could already feel myself worming my way back into his heart. There was a plan all laid out in my head that included the two of us descending into a drunken stupor and inviting him back to my apartment. He would love me or at least like me when he saw me naked. We could eat breakfast together in the morning. I would spend the day hungover but happy because, momentarily, Max was within my grip.

Only Max didn't want to descend into a drunken stupor. He resisted my suggestions to go to the bar and, worse, Rebecca or Rachel or whatever wouldn't leave the two of us alone.

"So, Hannah, what do you do?" she said.

That was how I found myself talking about work at a punk show, the least punk thing imaginable.

"I do comms for a nonprofit," I said, and then had to say it again because the venue was too loud for conversation.

"Cool," she said.

Meghan tapped me on the shoulder before I could return the question.

"We're ready to go," she told me.

I didn't care what the two of them wanted to do. Meghan's boyfriend wasn't even supposed to come along and I was just about to tell her to leave me there, saying that I would get an Uber with Max, but before I could speak, Max said, "We're about to take off too."

I spent the car ride back to my apartment lamenting the word "we."

"What did he mean by that?" I said.

"He probably is giving her a ride home," Meghan consoled me.

"Yes, but what did he mean by that?" I asked again.

We never learned the exact time of Anna Leigh's death—her body was too far gone for that—but forensic analysis suggested that as I unwrapped a frozen pizza that had been in my freezer for so long that I couldn't remember when I bought it, Anna Leigh's mangled body was being dumped into the ravine. Already, vermin had begun to burrow their way into her skin as I bit into my pizza and burned the roof of my mouth. This was not to suggest that being murdered and being shunned by a boy that I wasn't even in a real relationship with were equivalent, but to say that it was a bad time for a lot of us.

3

#FindAnnaLeigh was trending when I arrived in the office two days later.

The nonprofit was located in a decrepit multipurpose building that was supposed to indicate that we were "part of the community," according to my boss, but was rapidly emptying due to the building's decay. The weather was uncharacteristically cold for the beginning of November, and the first snowflakes of the year peppered my hair as I made the walk from my car. Ordinarily, the first snow made me happy, but I struggled to find coziness within the chill that morning.

"You look tired," Carole said.

Carole had been sitting next to me since I started the job. At the time, I assumed she was close to retirement and had since learned she was a mere fifty-three years old and would be working for the corporation for what felt like another hundred years. Carole liked to hold her age over me because it was the only thing she had. Like me, she had no power, no money. The only privileges she was given were snide little comments like "You'll change your mind about that in ten years" and derisive snorts whenever I tried to pitch new ideas in meetings.

"I'm fine," I told her.

I wasn't fine. Since the punk show, I'd looked at every picture Max had ever posted on social media. I tried to stalk Rebecca/ Rachel, whose actual name turned out to be Reese, but all her accounts were on private, which felt like a personal attack. I cycled through pep talks, telling myself that I was too good for him, that I didn't even really like him to begin with, that this was an opportunity to find someone better, before reassuring myself that surely he and Reese were just friends and he would text at any moment. Any moment! I decided to start a new exercise program and spent an hour looking at indoor bikes that I couldn't afford and had no room for before closing the browser tabs. I devoted myself to clean eating, only to order greasy Chinese food for dinner that I'd eaten for every meal since. It wasn't even about Max, not wholly, but rather resentment that I was seemingly unable to have a casual relationship, my heart like a hook that latched onto whatever was nearest.

I settled in with my first cup of coffee in front of my computer. Coffee made work more tolerable and I carefully parsed out each beverage as tiny treats that carried me through the day. Too much and my hands became jittery and ineffectual, and too little and I slumped over my desk by noon, deprived of energy like a marathon runner who didn't take in enough carbs.

Technically we weren't supposed to look at social media at work. Technically we weren't supposed to do a lot of things. We weren't supposed to park too close to the building to save those spaces for visitors. We weren't supposed to online shop or eat lunch at our desks. We weren't supposed to use our cell phones or wear athleisure in the office, even the stuff that was designed to look corporate. It was hard to care about technicalities. If Carole could wear her flowy hippy skirts and ugly crochet scarves at her desk, I could wear yoga pants and look at Twitter.

Anna Leigh appeared before me, her face on the screen and her name in the trending topics. On the surface, there were few commonalities between us. She was almost a decade younger than me, married, and a recent law school graduate. She was conventionally beautiful in a way that I could only ever aspire to be, with big blue eyes, blond hair, and a tiny frame. When I met women like Anna Leigh in real life I resented them for their good looks and success. As someone who was missing, she became the everywoman—me, or Meghan, or any other woman who dared to exist in the world—and I felt the pain of her absence acutely.

I shared the post.

"If you know anything at all please come forward," I wrote. "She was last seen in the Atlanta area, but it's possible that she's crossed state lines."

I spent the morning falling into a hole of Anna Leigh. I studied her Instagram, her dormant Twitter, her LinkedIn account. I MacGyvered my way around paywalls in order to read articles about her disappearance. By lunchtime, I was intimately familiar with her life in a way that I didn't even know my own friends.

Anna Leigh was last spotted at the law firm in Georgia where she served as an intern. I assumed, though never confirmed, that the firm was the kind of place with free snacks in the break room and not the kind of place where a person expected to be kidnapped and murdered. Later, we would learn that it was that same firm where William Thompson worked, but William Thompson wasn't yet a name that we knew.

Anna Leigh, in the tradition of female members of her family, got married a month after graduating from college and started law school two months after that. It was expected that she would have a successful career until she had children and then she was to stay home and take care of her family while her husband supported them financially. The difficulty was that Anna Leigh's husband, Tripp, was a poor student in law school and had to settle for lower quality internships until he had the credentials to start at his father's firm, which specialized in personal injury law and was frequently accused of "ambulance chasing."

People described Anna Leigh as disarming. Men often made the mistake of thinking that she was cute and harmless, and she knew how to take advantage of that impulse. Anna Leigh, despite her family's wishes for her, was determined to become a judge. These large aspirations were made acceptable by her disappearance.

"Anna Leigh has a bright future," her parents said on the news. "We need to bring her home."

They spoke in a Georgia drawl that was foreign to my Midwestern cadence. Anna Leigh's mother wore chunky jewelry and too much makeup, which was ineffectual at covering the large bags under her eyes that had formed from crying. Her father looked like a man who processed his emotions through shooting deer in a forest and didn't know what to do with himself now that he was the deer begging for the return of his child.

"We know she's still alive," he said. "We just know it."

They might have discovered that she was missing sooner if Tripp hadn't come home late from a night out with the boys. Most of his college friends were still single and lived in the area and they hadn't fully let go of the notions of their youth. Tripp was drunk when he arrived at home the night that Anna Leigh went missing. He was so drunk that he stripped off his clothes in the living room and fell asleep on the couch in his boxers. When he woke in the morning, he yelled "Fuck" because he was late for work. He assumed that Anna Leigh had already left. She was never late for work.

It wasn't until he got home that evening that Tripp realized that something was amiss. Anna Leigh was in charge of dinner in their house. If she didn't have time to cook, she told Tripp to pick something up or they went out to eat. This was so ingrained in their routine that Tripp didn't notice that it was happening. Dinner, it seemed, manifested itself in the same way that mail appeared in their mailbox each day. There was someone who made these things happen, but the process was invisible to him and that was how he liked it.

His stomach grumbled. Where was Anna Leigh? He hoped that she was amenable to takeout. He wanted chicken fingers dipped in honey mustard. No matter how old he got, he could never get away from those childhood cravings.

He sent her a text.

Where r u?

He sent her another when she didn't respond.
I'm starting to get worried, he wrote.

Tripp called Anna Leigh's best friend. The two of them had hooked up during a drunken night in college, something that Anna Leigh didn't know and would never find out. Since then, he'd kept a careful distance from her.

"Have you seen Anna Leigh?" he asked.

"No, but when you see her can you tell her to respond to my texts? It's important," the best friend replied. She later regretted her flippancy. She was mad at a dead girl and didn't even know it.

"That's just it," Tripp said. "She's not here."

She convinced Tripp to call the police. She'd seen a lot of stuff about the increase in human trafficking on Facebook and she was worried that something terrible had happened to Anna Leigh.

"Maybe she was getting gas and someone grabbed her. I've heard that's what happens," she said.

The police found Anna Leigh's car at the law office where she had arrived the previous day and seemingly never left. According to another intern, she had behaved normally during the day and headed to the elevators at six thirty, saying that she "couldn't wait to sit on the couch and keep watching *Friends.*" Somewhere between getting on the elevator and going to her car, Anna Leigh had been deterred from her plan. Maybe she had gotten a text from a friend and had taken an Uber to a second location. Maybe someone had picked her up. There were so many innocuous possibilities that it didn't even seem worth considering her death.

I was drinking my second cup of coffee and researching Tripp when I first stumbled across the forum. Tripp's sparse social media participation was rapidly being overtaken by the hordes online who were eager to pin Anna Leigh's disappearance on him. In response, he locked down all his accounts, but not before the forum was able to grab screenshots of his recent posts. I went to the forum hoping to find evidence of Tripp's misdeeds. What I found instead was fellowship.

Before I joined the forum, I would've said that I consumed true crime as much as any other ordinary American woman, which is to say quite a bit. We were obsessed with our own impending deaths, imagining danger in even the tamest of scenarios. Do enough research and nowhere is safe, not the Target parking lot, not your apartment complex, not the friendly neighborhood running trail. I wouldn't, however, have described myself as a true-crime junkie. I didn't listen to the podcasts or go to conventions. I drew a hard line in the sand between myself and those women. I was, I told myself, merely a concerned citizen.

In its nascent stages, the forum was united in its mission. First and foremost, the goal was to find Anna Leigh. This was linked to the second mission of persecuting Tripp for whatever harm he'd obviously caused her.

"Most violence toward women is committed by the men closest to them," wrote one user.

"It has to be Tripp," another person agreed. "It's always the boyfriend."

We analyzed his photos. *Look at the way he's holding that dead fish,* we said. *It's hooked right in the eye.* Or how his hand is wrapped possessively around Anna Leigh's waist, like he owns her. It wasn't the posture of two people in love, that was for sure. Or what about that other picture, the one of him and several hot girls who weren't Anna Leigh. Maybe he was cheating on her. Maybe he needed to make her disappear.

Unfortunately for us, Tripp had an alibi. There was CCTV footage of him leaving work, footage of him entering the bar with his friends, and footage of him stumbling toward his car hours later. The bar had a record of all the drinks charged to his tab, including a round of shots consumed minutes after Anna Leigh's disappearance. There were also dozens of people who could account for his actions throughout the evening, including two games of pool, one cigar smoked, and a fight that was narrowly avoided.

"I still don't trust Tripp," I posted on the forum, a post that was endorsed by a wave of approving emojis and gifs. "There's more than one way to kill a person besides with your own hands."

"Men," someone replied, "are never to be trusted."

I dedicated all of the energy that had previously gone into thinking about Max into finding Anna Leigh. *See?* I wanted to tell him. *I'm not thinking about you at all.* I had other hobbies besides obsessing over men who would never feel about me the way that I felt about them. I cared about missing girls, dead girls. I was a good person.

Instead of making graphics promoting the work that the non-profit had done over the year while drinking my third and final cup of coffee for the day, I made graphics raising awareness about Anna Leigh. I felt warm and good as the number of shares climbed into the thousands. Finally! My skills were being used for something important.

As the afternoon deepened, the Anna Leigh backlash began. What about the Black women, the Indigenous women, who went missing with little to no fanfare? Yes, I said. We needed to care about them too, and I quickly reposted pictures of other missing women before watching seven separate videos of people breaking down the timeline of Anna Leigh's disappearance.

I went out for happy hour drinks with Meghan that were bliss-fully free of her boyfriend's presence. As much as I insisted that I was happy for her ("I'm so happy for you!" I told her when they first became official), I longed for a rift to come between them that would re-cement Meghan as my best friend, the person who was always there for me no matter what.

"Have you heard about Anna Leigh?" I asked her.

"Everyone has heard about Anna Leigh," she replied.

"It's awful," I said, sipping my margarita.

"Do you think she's still alive?" Meghan asked.

"I don't want to think any other way."

"It's good," she said, "to keep hope alive."

4

Anna Leigh's body was found in the ravine near her office nine days after she was reported missing. I hated that word, "ravine." It sounded like a word that was invented to describe a place where bodies were found. Her face was decomposed beyond recognition and her long blond hair cut off. They had to identify her by dental records, of which there were plenty, because Anna Leigh never missed an appointment. She'd been strangled and stabbed, the police said, in a manner that indicated that the murder was personal.

I was having a bad day at work for unrelated reasons. I'd learned that a project that I'd spent months working on was getting scrapped at the last minute because funding fell through. No one seemed to care about the ways in which my time had been wasted and only repeated that it was due to "situations out of our control."

What is within your control? I wanted to ask, but I'd been reprimanded for my attitude at a meeting the previous month and kept quiet.

At first, the discovery of Anna Leigh's body felt like yet another failure. All our work, all our posts and pleas for information, had been for naught. For a week and a half, I'd been a passionate advocate for all the missing women in the world and I hadn't managed to change a thing. What a disappointment it all was. Then I logged on to the forum where they took Anna Leigh's death as the opportunity to solve a homicide.

"Do you want to go to lunch?" Carole asked me.

I looked up at her. She wore a flowered caftan.

"I can't," I said. "We have to figure out who killed Anna Leigh."

"Who's Anna Leigh?" she asked.

I squinted at her. Clearly, we were inside of different universes.

"She's a victim of misogyny," I said.

Most of the forum still believed that Tripp was somehow guilty. Someone had managed to run a background check and discovered that he'd gotten a misdemeanor for public intoxication when he was an undergraduate in addition to being a member of a fraternity that had numerous infractions over the years, including claims of women being roofied at their parties. None of those things pointed to murder, but they did indicate some sort of moral corruption that could lead to it.

I spent the rest of the day alternating between refreshing the forum and wandering into the break room under the guise of refilling my water bottle in hopes that there would be someone new that I could tell about Anna Leigh's death.

"I was really involved in trying to find her," I told a coworker. "I made a post that had over ten thousand shares."

"Wow," he said.

When Carole returned from lunch, I walked her through the whole case, starting with Anna Leigh's disappearance, Tripp's alibi, and the information that the police had released about the body.

"It's so dark how everyone is obsessed with killers these days," she said, but listened intently.

"I'm not obsessed with killers," I told her. "I'm obsessed with justice."

As much as I insisted that was true, I already wasn't sure of my place on the dividing line.

I was making a post on Instagram in honor of Anna Leigh's life when I saw Max's post. Max didn't post personal things online, or that's what he told me after I posted a picture of us together and he said that he preferred that I take it down.

"I don't like the surveillance state," he said.

Most of his posts were advertising shows at which his band was playing that got three or so likes at best. The surveillance state was fine, apparently, if it meant they were surveilling the shows that his band played at. It surprised me to see an actual picture, one of Max with his arm around Reese, the girl that he'd been with the last time I saw him.

"My best girl," the caption said.

The post had been liked by forty people.

It was then that the true sadness hit me, an emotion so intertwined with anger that I didn't know how to separate the two. I wanted there to be something that I could do to help Anna Leigh's grieving friends and family, to bring justice to their case, to make myself the person that Max liked enough to post on his Instagram. I felt impotent in ways that were both large and small, unable to change the world or my life.

In some ways, it was easier to face Anna Leigh's corpse than it was to grapple with my own personal failings. My tiny income and even smaller apartment. My novel draft that refused to grow no matter how long I kept the document open. The boys that fucked me and left me like I was nothing at all. I didn't know how to make meaning out of my life, so I found meaning within the body of a dead girl.

I started by raiding the bag of chocolates that I kept stashed in my desk for emergencies that arose at increasingly frequent intervals. Had a bad meeting? Chocolate. Too many emails in the inbox? Chocolate. Trying to heal from a broken heart? Chocolate. Need to solve a murder many states away? Chocolate.

As the candy melted over my tongue. I vowed to find Anna Leigh's killer. I wanted it for her, for her loved ones, but more than that, I needed it for me, to know that I was capable of accomplishing something.

5

One of the forum members found Kimberly's body. She was in the ravine, looking for clues as to the identity of Anna Leigh's killer, something that the police might have missed, when she stumbled across the corpse.

"I didn't even know it was a body at first until I saw her painted fingernails," she wrote.

No one was looking for Kimberly because she was never reported missing. Kimberly had an on-again, off-again boyfriend who was in the "off" position during the time of her disappearance. He didn't know she was gone until the police showed up at his door.

Kimberly worked at a gas station, which meant that lots of people knew her and none of them noticed her absence. She was never beautiful, not even when she was young, which lent her a particular type of sweetness. She called everyone "honey" and remembered which brand of cigarettes they liked best. When the neighborhood children came in, she gave them lollipops that she paid for out of her own pocket.

The gas station was down the street from newly erected condos designed for young professionals. Everything inside was minimalist, rooted in glass and granite. The gas station had been on the street long before the condos and would likely be standing long after, its fluorescent lights a beacon. Though she'd worked at the gas station for over a decade, Kimberly couldn't afford to live in its vicinity and drove an hour to work each day, leaving little time for any kind of life.

William Thompson, a successful lawyer, lived in one of the condos. He walked to the gas station when he needed junk food as a pick-me-up, as he liked to keep only healthy food in his apartment. The police picked up footage of William on the security cameras days before Kimberly's disappearance, but there was nothing to differentiate him from the other men that stopped to pick up a bag of Peanut M&M's. They all wore the same brands, got their hair cut the same way, and made polite conversation the way that their mothers taught them to. Surely, a true killer would never stop to say thank you.

On the day that Kimberly was found, I was seated in my boss's office nervously twirling my hair in my fingers.

"I need to speak with you," she said when I arrived that morning. I thought guiltily of the hours that I'd spent on the forum and wondered if she was able to track my internet usage.

She'd been my boss for only six months. The nonprofit had hired her from another nonprofit. They called her a "fixer," someone who was willing to tinker with everything until it was working the way that it was supposed to. I was grateful to be working underneath a woman, as all of my previous supervisors had been men. I thought that maybe she would understand the additional pressures that women face in the workplace, pressures that weren't relieved by working in the nonprofit sector.

"I'm sure you're aware that Karli is leaving the country and we're looking for someone to fill the associate director position," my boss began.

A glimmer of hope. I had my eye on a one-bedroom apartment that allowed dogs, and a promotion might put it within reach.

"I thought I should inform you that we're going with an outside hire," my boss continued.

I stared at her. She had a corporate background, which was evident by her dress. Carole told me once that she heard she came from money and started working at nonprofits as a type of altruism. Her earrings sparkled beneath the fluorescent office lights.

"Okay," I said numbly. "Thank you for letting me know."

I stood up and paused.

"Please let me know if any other opportunities for advancement become available."

She smiled at me.

"Of course, Hannah," she said.

The self-loathing started to set in before I even arrived back at my desk. I couldn't believe that I had thanked my boss for denying me a promotion and, worse, that upon reflection I could think of nothing better to say, no witty comebacks or delightful gotchas, only an endless pit of begging for table scraps.

Kimberly's predicament was a reminder that there were worse places to be, like dead at the bottom of a ravine.

I looked at her face. It'd been difficult to find a picture of her, as her Facebook profile picture was a stock photo of kittens.

Finally, someone managed to contact a woman who was friends with her and she sent along an old picture to help us with our investigation. Even in that photo, wearing a pink dress and her face made-up, Kimberly still didn't look beautiful. Her lips were lined with wrinkles from years of smoking and the heavy liner made her eyes look small and beady.

Kimberly, to her credit, had stopped smoking five years prior, having finally reached an age where her fear of mortality outweighed the joy of going out back to smoke during her breaks. It made me sad to think about. If only someone had told her to smoke and smoke and smoke in order to squeeze out as many small, euphoric moments within her life as possible before she was murdered.

Though Kimberly had always shown up to work on time and had never missed a shift—except for the two days when she had food poisoning so bad that she was unable to leave the toilet—the general manager of the gas station assumed that she was a no-show and called her cell phone to tell her that she was fired. What the general manager hadn't realized was that Kimberly's phone was dead inside her purse, which she had left inside of her car, which was parked near the ravine. The car was later labeled as abandoned and towed to a lot. Through all of it, Kimberly continued to rot and rot until the forum user came across her body.

Kimberly's name didn't trend and the media coverage was scant, describing her as "the woman found near Anna Leigh." Oh, to be remembered that way, a body found near the presence of another. No one seemed to think their deaths were related. I knew from years of idly watching *Criminal Minds* as a teenager that most repeat killers had a type. Ted Bundy, for instance, was infamous for preferring women with long brown hair, though he strayed from this during his more manic murders. It seemed unlikely that someone would go from murdering Anna Leigh, who was young and beautiful, to murdering Kimberly, who was old and poor. Women died all the time. Who was to say that there weren't two separate killers who decided to throw bodies into the same ravine? Weirder things had happened.

"Did you see the news?" I asked Carole.

She looked up from her computer screen, took a sip of her herbal tea that smelled of grass and dread, and looked at me quizzically.

"They found another body where Anna Leigh was found."

"Oh my gosh. Those poor women."

I noticed how I didn't need to specify that the body was a woman. Bodies were almost always read that way.

"Do they know who did it?" she asked.

"No, they're still trying to figure out if they're connected."

The members of the forum got to work immediately. We never talked about our day jobs, or lack thereof. I got the impression that many people were stay-at-home mothers investigating murder when their children's heads were turned away.

I made an infographic that said "#FindTheRavineKiller" over Anna Leigh's and Kimberly's faces and posted it on Instagram.

"If you cared about Anna Leigh, you need to care about Kimberly too," I wrote in the comments. "Women are dying, and the police are doing nothing."

Within minutes, the post had been shared hundreds of times.

Another user pulled up a list of sex offenders in the vicinity of the ravine and combed through it for possible suspects. There was no evidence that either Anna Leigh or Kimberly had been sexually assaulted, but the murder of women, especially someone as beautiful as Anna Leigh, always felt linked to sex.

Someone else said that she would contact her acquaintance

who worked at a nearby police department in Georgia to see if there was any information he could give.

I almost forgot about the conversation with my boss. The work I was doing was gratifying, if entirely unrelated to my salaried role. I knew that she would call it "time theft," a term she'd used in meetings before, and I didn't care. Did my boss know what it was like to live life always feeling guilty about the smallest indulgences? To feel so unappreciated that I'd begun to forget that I was good at anything at all? On her desk there was a framed picture of her, her husband, and their two children at the beach. I couldn't remember the last time that I'd seen the ocean. Investigating murders was nothing like the beach and the ravine not a sea and yet, I found a certain freedom within its mysterious depths.

6

Before long, I was back on the dating apps and talking to a new guy who was promising in his mediocrity. He wasn't especially attractive, but he was gainfully employed, and sometimes that was enough. I was waiting for the new guy—who I had listed in my contacts as "Dog Boy" because he had an image of his dog as his dating app profile picture—to tell me what he liked to read and I kept picking up my phone, sighing loudly, and setting it down again.

"Don't you have work to do?" Carole asked.

"I am doing work," I replied, and opened my document for the first time that day.

I quickly flipped over to Twitter, where I posted "The eight-hour workday should be ABOLISHED" before returning to the job in front of me. I was just getting into the groove of things when Carole interrupted me, a distraction I resented, though I was constantly interrupting myself.

"Hey," Carole said.

"What? I'm working," I replied, gesturing to the computer in front of me.

"No, it's not that. They found another body in that ravine you're always talking about."

"Oh my god," I said.

I was sad, of course I was. Did that even need to be said? Every new body was another woman lost. Three bodies, however, was a magic number because three transformed the murders from random acts of aggression into those of a potential serial killer. Discovering an active serial killer was like discovering a monster in the closet—something that generated mass fear and paranoia despite the rarity of their existence.

Like Anna Leigh, there was something familiar about the face on the screen. This time, it wasn't because of some ethereal connection that I deemed destined by the universe and the stars, but because I actually recognized her.

"I know her," I said.

"You know her?" Carole asked.

"I mean, I don't know her," I clarified. "But I've seen videos of her online."

Jill was a personal trainer. She had once weighed 350 pounds and, through a strict regimen of diet and exercise, she had whittled her way down to 120 pounds. Jill was semi-famous on the internet for her weight loss. She posted videos that included pictures of what she looked like before and after, with the implicit promise that such a transformation could occur for the viewer too.

"I tried every diet there was," she said. "Then one day I'd had enough and knew things had to change." She said this like there was some secret to her success, a switch that flipped in her brain that she could turn on for the viewer too if only they watched enough of her content.

Before she got skinny, Jill worked as a dental technician. She posted pictures of herself wearing scrubs and smiling in the dentist's office. Her face didn't show her as a person who was suffering, but we were supposed to intuit those feelings from her size.

"I have a smile on my face, but I'm suffering on the inside," she wrote.

After she lost the weight, Jill became a personal trainer at her local gym. Her clients posted photos of their workout stats, thanking her for pushing them until their muscles burned.

It was Jill's followers who first raised the alarm about her absence. They were owed a new workout video, one that promised to help them sculpt the perfect abs, and she was late in posting.

"When is the new video dropping?" her fans demanded.

Within a couple of days, this reached a fever pitch and they started calling her names, "fat slut" and "dumb bitch," hoping they could threaten her into posting.

None of those threats worked because Jill was already dead. When her body was found, the comments went from angry to apologetic.

"I know you'll never see this, but I'm sorry and I miss you."

"You were such an inspiration. You helped me get into shape after my son was born."

"I hope you got to eat pizza occasionally while you were still alive."

"She was so beautiful," Carole remarked to me. "Such a shame."

Carole, in the nature of certain older women, made endless comments about other people's bodies and critiqued her own food consumption to the point that it was difficult to eat around her.

"I'm so bad!" she said whenever cake was brought in for a birthday.

"I don't need this," she said when our boss arrived with surprise donuts.

"I can't believe you can eat that and be as thin as you are," she remarked to a long-since-departed intern.

"Hannah, it looks like you ate well over the holidays," she told me when we returned to the office after Christmas one year.

I wanted to be body positive, to love myself in the skin that I was in, but loving yourself wasn't like flipping a switch. I grew up watching MTV, ogling girls in low-rise jeans that could never cover my own hips. When I slept with a man and he stopped contacting me, I always had to wonder, If I were thinner, prettier, better, would he love me? Jill had obtained the fantasy, the one I still harbored despite my posts claiming that "any body is a beach body." As it turned out, the fantasy wasn't enough to save her from unhappiness or death.

After her body was found, one of Jill's fans leaked copies of her journal online. It was unclear how she had gotten ahold of it and forum members argued that the journal was private, that it should be read only in the name of investigation and not for the purpose of satisfying our curiosity. In the journal, Jill chronicled how much she weighed, what she ate each day, and what she was feeling. The less Jill ate, the more feelings she had, which was a logical correlation to me. Hunger inspired all sorts of emotions inside of a person, and those emotions almost never included self-love. She wrote things like "I meant to only eat a small handful of almonds, but I kept going back for more. I feel like an endless pit that will never be full. I am hungry for so much." It was painful to read such confessions after her death, especially considering the outpouring of love delivered by her fans on all her social media pages.

Energy bubbled on the forum. Certainly, we mourned Jill's

death as we mourned the deaths of all murdered women, but her murder provided us with more clues. Two bodies found in one place could be a coincidence; three was a pattern.

A forum user managed to obtain a list of Jill's personal training clients, which we systematically combed through, looking for clues as to the identity of the killer. We also looked through her social media pages for comments that were particularly threatening, a task that proved to be difficult because any woman with a forward-facing presence was met with hostility.

I agreed to take on part of Jill's client list. I even got Carole to help with a few, though she ended up accidentally posting the names on her Facebook instead of searching for them and I had to help her delete the posts.

The name William Thompson was on my list. Later, I would look back and blame myself for not figuring it out sooner. In my defense, there was nothing about William that screamed "serial killer." His online presence was limited. He had an Instagram account where he mainly posted pictures of scenic places that he'd visited. There were a couple of shirtless post-run shots and I admired his attractive physique. He didn't have a Facebook page or a Twitter account that I could find. There was a link to the law office where he worked, and though the name niggled at the back of my brain, I didn't put together that it was the same law office where Anna Leigh had been an intern. The truth was that I couldn't imagine a man like that wanting to murder anyone. His life looked good, peaceful, and if movies had taught me anything, it was that serial killers always had some underlying trauma. What kind of trauma could this rich, attractive white man have experienced?

It was disappointing in retrospect that I hadn't looked at him and gotten an eerie feeling. I always thought of myself as a person who was capable of sensing things about other people. I bragged to friends that I always knew when couples broke up just from the vibes I got from their online posts. I'd predicted pregnancies and eating disorders, and yet, I was unable to see what was right in front of me.

"No luck on my end," I posted on the forum.

"This is kind of fun," Carole said after a day of investigation.

I smiled at her. Being on the forum was like being in a secret club, and I had just initiated a new member.

My mood dampened a little when I got a text from Meghan calling for a rain check on our happy hour drink plans. She didn't say why, but I knew it was because of her boyfriend. It was always because of her boyfriend. For so long, the two of us had pined over men together and she had gone and gotten herself a man without me. Sometimes the deepest betrayals were things that women did to one another.

My mood further dampened when I posted a new graphic to social media, one featuring all three of the murdered women. It was almost like an art installation, watching the faces pile up on the graphic. On a whim, I checked Max's Instagram. I didn't think about him as much as I once had, only when I was sad, lonely, bored, or eating cheese. I got an error message saying that the page wasn't available. I frowned and switched over to the account that I ran for the nonprofit and discovered that his page was still active and the most recent photo showed his hand intertwined with Reese's and the caption "Love." Oh, I realized. He'd blocked me.

I sent a cry out into the universe for Dog Boy to message me back. I would never have to think about Max again if I found someone new or someone better. The universe, or more accurately Dog Boy, failed to heed my cries.

Abandoned by my best friend, my former lover, and my potential future lover, I was left alone with no one but the murdered women to keep me company.

I went home and watched five hours of Jill's workout videos. I moved along with her until I got tired and then I boiled water for pasta and heated up a jar of spaghetti sauce on the stove. Jill bounced up and down, her tiny legs straining against a black exercise band.

"You don't need much equipment to get in shape," she said. "I started out not knowing anything. It's more about moving your body in a way that works for you."

I didn't yet know how she died, how the killer wrapped a rope around her neck until she was no longer breathing. She'd strained against him, but no amount of exercise was enough to overpower a man like that.

"Don't worry if you can't do everything," Jill continued. "You'll get it someday."

7

Carole didn't want me to go on a date with Dog Boy, who'd finally texted me back. He apologized for the slowness of his communication, saying that he'd been really busy at work lately.

"It's not safe," she said.

I'd lost three pounds since starting a new fitness routine based entirely off Jill's videos. I watched her make salads and made my own less healthy versions. I bounced around my apartment until my neighbor banged the wall in irritation at the noise. It was the best that I'd felt since Max ghosted me, and I wanted someone to appreciate it. Dog Boy's communication was sporadic at best, but when I asked if he wanted to meet in person, he agreed almost immediately.

"It'll be fine," I reassured Carole. "I've gone on dates with lots of men that I met on the internet."

I didn't yet know about Emma, the fourth victim. Unlike me, Emma initially refused to go on dating apps. Dating apps, she told her friends, were inauthentic. She wanted to meet someone organically. One by one, her friends disappeared into coupledom and she remained single. She developed a lot of hobbies, joined an ultimate Frisbee team, took painting lessons, and became a regular at the gym. She devoted herself to being a good friend even as her own friends neglected her in favor of their romantic partners.

One night, at a party, she admitted that she was lonely. It was hard still being single with all her friends married or in long-term relationships. Every year of her life, she felt more and more alone.

"Why don't you sign up for a dating app? That's how we met," one of her friends said, gesturing to her boyfriend.

All of her friends joined in, pushing and pressuring her to make an account until finally, Emma downloaded the recommended app and set up her profile. She used an older picture of herself, one that she regularly used in her profile on social media sites. She had since gained ten or so pounds and a couple of gray hairs and she told herself that it was only dishonest if someone really fell in love with her and in that case, they would love her body as it was.

Her friends, who had all been in relationships for years, were eager to scroll and examine her choices. Emma, though, refused to click on anyone unless he really seemed like someone that she'd want to get to know, and even then, she wouldn't engage with anyone whose picture was too hot because it made them seem fake.

Finally, there was a ding to signal that she had matched with someone, and all her friends screamed with elation.

"Oh, he's cute," one said.

"Message him!" another insisted.

"Doesn't it look desperate if I message him too quickly?" Emma asked. She didn't know the rules to online dating.

"You're looking for love. Everyone looks desperate. Message him."

Emma didn't know what to say. How was she supposed to seduce someone when she was whittled down to text on a screen?

Hi, she wrote. The greeting felt stupid, juvenile.

Hey, he replied. **How are you tonight?**

You're actually the first person that I've talked to on one of these.

That's surprising. You're so sexy.

Emma giggled even though she didn't find it funny. She had always been uncomfortable with compliments, particularly those coming from strangers. She didn't like when men on the street made comments about her appearance and nothing about the digital space made this less uncomfortable. To the disappointment of her friends, she blocked him.

"No good relationship starts like that," she said.

A few conversations in and she found a guy who she actually liked. He was handsome, a lawyer, and his listed height was six foot one. She continued to message him even after she went home, and before she went to bed, they switched over to texting. It couldn't be that easy, could it? All that time she had spent being alone and the answer all along had been to download a dating app.

They decided to meet after they texted for two weeks. Emma told all her friends that she was going on a date with a man she'd never met before. She set up a joke safe word, "narwhal," in case she needed to be rescued.

"If I don't text you by ten p.m., something is wrong," she said.

They met at a bar. Emma didn't know if food was implied in the date, so she made sure to eat beforehand. She was nervous that she wouldn't be able to recognize him, or worse, that he wouldn't be able to recognize her. It was a relief that they spotted each other right away and he looked almost like his picture, the way that a new shirt looked almost the way it looked on the model when she put it on her ordinary body. He wasn't as tall as he said he was, his face not as handsome, and this was a disappointment even though he was handsomer than anyone else that she had previously dated.

It was awkward for the first few minutes. It was strange to meet someone for the first time with the expectation of getting to know them romantically. All of Emma's previous relationships had sprung from friendships, and in that case, it was always the physical aspect that was most uncomfortable. Dating apps reversed that dynamic. She met the man because she could envision herself having sex with him, but she didn't know if there was anything beyond that.

Things got easier after she had a couple of drinks. They had both spent time in France and they discussed their favorite places. He suggested that they order food and she didn't want to offend him by saying that she had already eaten, so she agreed. Emma's entrée was objectively better than his and she offered to share a portion with him. At the end of the night, he kissed her on the lips and then Emma sat in her car for half an hour trying to decide if she was sober enough to drive.

It would be believable if I said that was the man that killed her. Every story about a man and a woman has the potential of ending in death no matter how innocuous the beginning, but Emma never saw him again. She sent him a follow-up text the next day, saying that she would like to go out for a second time, and it was as though he had disappeared from the earth. Emma felt strangely bereft at the loss of this man that she'd only met once. She couldn't understand why he wouldn't want to see her again, not after they'd had such a great time together on their date. It was embarrassing, especially since she'd already told her friends that she was going to see him again.

That was why she didn't tell her friends about the second man that she met on the app.

While I went on a date with Dog Boy, a man who would never escape the moniker I gave him in my phone contacts, Emma went on a date with William Thompson, a handsome, smart, rich lawyer who liked all the same things that she did. No one knew about the date. Not her siblings, her coworkers, or her friends.

Dog Boy and I met up at a brewery. I didn't care for beer, but I pretended to for his sake because he said he "loved beer more than almost anything in the world" and I wanted him, or someone, to love me more than almost anything in the world too.

William and Emma went to an Italian restaurant. She ordered squid ink pasta and he got seafood linguine. He gave her one of his mussels after she told him that mussels were her favorite. Unlike other men Emma had dated, he liked to read, and they spent a good portion of the meal discussing the latest work by Sally Rooney. She might've texted a friend to tell them about how much she liked the man in front of her if only she wasn't having such a good time.

Dog Boy and I talked about work. He was employed at a tech startup where he confessed that he was "overpaid to do very little."

"They'll probably go under soon," he said. He seemed unconcerned.

He was almost cute in the way that many of the boys I dated

were. There was nothing fundamentally wrong with him, but his awkwardness took away from some of his potential attractiveness. I figured it was an asset in the startup world, where social ineptitude was often mistaken for genius.

"What do you do?" he asked.

"I work at a nonprofit," I said, and proceeded to complain about my boss.

William and Emma's server would later say that they didn't look like a couple on a first date, but rather two people deep in the throes of love.

"There was no sign that he was going to hurt her," she said.

William paid the bill and the two of them left together. The server couldn't remember whether or not they were holding hands.

Dog Boy invited me back to his apartment under the premise of watching a television show he liked. His dog greeted me with enthusiasm and the whole thing was worth it if only for those moments I spent with my hands in her fur.

I was surprised when he kissed me because he seemed like the type of man who was uncomfortable with making the first move. He wasn't a good kisser; his mouth too slobbery and eager. It made me think of Max, who for all his flaws was quite good at all things related to sex.

"Should we go to my bedroom?" he asked, and I nodded.

We had sex with the lights off. I got the impression that he was self-conscious about his body. Foreplay was brief, his fingers fumbling around inside my underwear before he pulled them off completely.

We fucked missionary style until he came and rolled off me. He kissed me on the cheek, leaving behind spit. I didn't approach anything close to an orgasm. I hoped Max could sense that I was having sex with someone new.

When we finished, I lay in his bed while he checked emails on his phone. When he started scrolling Twitter, I got out of bed and put my clothes on.

"I'm going to go home," I announced.

"Okay," he replied, glancing up from his phone. "I had a nice time tonight."

"Yeah," I said.

I took an Uber back to the bar where my car was waiting for me and drove home. It was late by the time I arrived back at my apartment, and I greedily gulped down water before putting my body to bed.

"Thank god, you're safe," Carole said when I arrived at work the next morning. "I was worried about you."

I rolled my exhausted eyes.

"Nothing to worry about," I replied.

No one knew what happened between William and Emma after they left the restaurant except that at some point in the evening, Emma was strangled to death and her body dumped in the same ravine where Anna Leigh, Kimberly, and Jill were found. Emma's corpse was discovered faster than the others, her face still easily identified by her best friend, who wept as she confirmed that it was Emma.

Some people blamed the first man for what happened. If he hadn't ghosted her, Emma might still be alive today.

"I wasn't in the right headspace to be dating," the man wrote on Twitter. "I was depressed and I regret my actions."

A few hours later he added a second tweet that said he didn't even think what he did should count as ghosting.

"It was one date. That shouldn't be enough to crush a person. I'm sorry for what happened, but I don't think that it's my responsibility."

William was arrested several hours after the discovery of Emma's body. There were only so many murdered women that a person could know before it became more than a coincidence. Carole put the news on the television in the conference room and we sat and watched William's perp walk.

"This reminds me of the O.J. Simpson car chase," Carole said.

"Except he's not running," I replied.

It wasn't until I saw William's face that I realized that I'd seen him before.

"He was one of Jill's clients," I said. My stomach rumbled the way that it always did when I drank too much coffee. "I looked into him after Jill's death. I thought he was innocent."

Carole gave me a pitying look.

"I'm sure you did your best, honey," she said. There was a pause. "Though you could've saved that girl's life if you figured out it was him."

That was the thing about Carole. She always reminded me why I didn't like her initially.

William was at work at the same glittering glass building where Anna Leigh was last spotted when they arrested him.

"You're right. He doesn't look like a murderer," Carole conceded.

William wore an expensive suit and his hair looked like it was styled before the police cuffed his hands behind his back. I lamented it when William disappeared into the cop car. I wanted the walk to take longer so that I could get to know every inch of his murderous core. I tried to go to his Instagram page, the search tab already filling in the blanks of his handle from the last time I looked him up, but found it had been deleted.

The name William Thompson was trending on Twitter.

"Jill's workout plan was really working," someone posted.

"Of course it was a white man," said someone else.

My boss peeked her head into the conference room. She smiled.

"Are the two of you being productive?" she asked. She was wearing a pencil skirt and I hated how good it looked on her. My own dress was frumpy in comparison.

I smiled back.

"Of course we are. Just collaborating, you know, like you always talk about."

"Great," she said, glancing toward the screen that Carole had thankfully already turned off.

"Well, that's that," Carole said and returned to her desk.

My phone buzzed and Dog Boy appeared on the screen.

We hadn't talked since our date several days earlier. The less that I responded, the more messages he sent. It made me feel powerful. I hated that only men I wasn't especially attracted to could make me feel that way.

"When do you want to hang out next?" he asked.

I ignored the message, planning to respond to it later, and then forgot about it. I never understood how ghosting could be unintentional until I did it to him. I wasn't the type of person to forget things like that. I always remembered to eat, always obsessed over every message I sent, romantic or platonic. It turned out that ghosting was easy. Dog Boy was already gone from my brain.

I was thinking about William, even then. The cool look on his face as he walked from his building like he was walking down a red carpet instead of to a cop car. I wished his hands had been free because I had wanted to see his fingers, to understand the tools that could be so hurtful.

If only I had known that someday his hands would be on my

own body, that the perp walk was a beginning rather than an end, then maybe I would've spent the rest of the day focusing on my work instead of reading articles about William until it was time to go home. Or maybe I would've started saying my goodbyes.

8

I tried to move on with my life.

With the killer caught, the forum died down and slowly I returned to my regular internet usage. I was empty without the urgency. I went to work. I tried a new group class at the gym. I got a sourdough starter from a friend and made two loaves before I forgot about it in the fridge. I started knitting a blanket and gave up after I made too many mistakes to possibly fix. I took a cooking class with a friend and spent a week thinking that I should quit my job to become a chef and changed my mind after getting food poisoning from undercooked fish. I completed three days of a thirty-day clean-eating challenge. I lost five pounds and gained it back again. I sent Meghan text messages inviting her to happy hour and she responded, **Maybe next week!** so many times in a row that I gave up.

Moving on, unfortunately, had never been my forte. Max still lingered in my brain in times of loneliness, which were many and frequent. Though I knew better, I wanted to see the Instagram posts that he'd blocked me from seeing on my personal account, a masochistic gesture. During our lunch break, Carole helped me create a fake account. We picked out a picture to use on my profile of a pretty punk girl, someone who looked like they might be friends with Max.

"That one," Carole said.

She was bored too. The nonprofit had recently filled the associate director position, the job that was supposed to be mine, with a man who looked and acted like a rat. He made a habit of standing over our shoulders and making sure that we stayed on task.

"I'm an adult, for Pete's sake," I heard Carole mumble one day after he walked away.

The fake Instagram account was about more than Max. There was pleasure in our defiance, in the creation of a punk girl who could challenge societal expectations in ways that we never could.

I wanted to find Max heartbroken. His band broken up, his relationship with Reese dissolved. Instead, the Screaming Seals were booking an increasing number of gigs and Reese was officially his "girlfriend," a word Max treated as poison when we were sleeping together. He'd posted pictures of them at the park, his arm around her shoulders. The two of them on a holiday weekend, out to dinner, trying out a new bar. Every picture stung anew and I couldn't pull myself away from the phone screen.

I didn't notice that the new associate director was standing behind me in the break room until he spoke.

"Hannah, let's get back to work," he said.

"Sure thing." I smiled at him and seethed over the comment in my head for the rest of the workday.

I hated that Max still had the power to hurt me. I hated the new associate director for taking my job. I hated William for killing those women and I hated him for getting caught and leaving me without purpose. I wasn't allowed to comment on Max's pictures, nor was I allowed to talk back to the associate director, who was technically my superior, though I'd been at the nonprofit for years longer than he had, and so I wrote to William.

The letter started as an abstract thing, a composition inside my head that I revised repeatedly throughout the day.

You're a monster. I hope you know that, I thought as I prepared slides for an upcoming presentation.

You deserve whatever it is that you have coming, I composed as I wandered the aisles of the grocery store.

You are the scourge of the earth and even though I don't believe in the death penalty, I hope that you die, I told him as I boiled water for boxed macaroni and cheese.

When my food was ready, I sat down at the table with a spiral-bound notebook to get the words that ruminated through my head on paper. I was always buying notebooks and never using them. It seemed like I was waiting for the perfect purpose to present itself to me before I soiled any of the pages. William, it turned out, was the purpose.

It impacted me greatly when Anna Leigh died. Do you know what it's like to walk through the world knowing that you're never truly safe? I bet you met each other at work. She was so beautiful. I assume that you lusted after her and she rejected your advances. It's always dangerous for a woman to say no.

You're a man who has everything. You're rich, you're educated, you have a full head of hair. I guess the conundrum

is where you go from there. Some men like you decide to climb
Mount Everest or run a marathon. Jill was your personal
trainer, so presumably you had some sort of physical
aspiration. Other people volunteer or get a job. You decided to
kill women.

I live my life with a quiet rage inside of me and the worst
thing that I do is drink too much. There must be something
that you get out of killing. Is it sexual arousal or something
else? Maybe it's revenge on someone who hurt you, an ex-
girlfriend or your mother.

Guess what? Everyone hurts, William. Only monsters
become murderers.

It's unfair that the worst people on this earth get the most
attention. I try my best and that trying only serves to make
me more invisible. More than anything, I'm afraid of ending
up like Kimberly. How rotted would my corpse become before
someone realized I was missing? Your name was trending for
hours after your arrest and it sickened me. I hope everyone
remembers the names of your victims as much as they
remember you.

I have been in Emma's position. I didn't die, of course, but I
know what it's like to put your hopes and dreams into a date
with someone. It all could've gone differently. You could've
gone on a date with her and then another. You could've fallen
in love, gotten married, had children. Moved out of your condo
and bought a nice house somewhere. Was killing her better
than all of that?

Sometimes I feel like we're split between people who are
promised a life that they'll never be able to achieve and people
who are living the promised life and don't want it. Then again,
it's possible that this is what you wanted all along. You're

famous now. Everyone, forever, will know the name William
Thompson. Who do you want to play you in your movie?
Someone handsome, no doubt. You just better hope that you
live to see the ending.

    I want you to listen when I tell you that I'll never be able to
go on a date again without thinking of you. Every moment I
will wonder whether he wants to love me or murder me. What
kind of relationship can come from that?

    If there is any karma in this world, you will suffer the way
that you've made others suffer.

I wrote until my hand cramped up and my bowl of macaroni and cheese was empty. It was the way that I'd always longed to write. I liked to think of myself as an aspiring novelist who was restricted by the forty-hour workweek and the lack of inspiration around me. William provided inspiration where before there was none. He allowed me to reverse my normally myopic gaze onto things outside myself, and that was what enabled the words to finally flow.

I didn't think I would send the letter, not really. I figured I would stuff it in a drawer, forget about it, find it again when I moved apartments, and laugh at my younger self who was so stupid as to write a letter to an accused serial killer. But then, at work the next day, I got into researching where and how to send a letter to someone in jail and I thought, *Why not? What was the very worst that could happen?*

I sent the letter the same way that I sent Max strings of unanswered text messages long after it was clear that he was done with me. I didn't send it for the recipient. I sent it for me because I wanted to. Because there was something that I needed to get off my chest, even if I never heard back.

Sending the letter felt good, like kissing a stranger that I knew I would never see again at a bar. I thought it was closure to the whole William Thompson thing. I even logged out of the forum on my work computer and phone. But as I said before, I was never good at moving on.

9

It was raining the day that the response came, and I wasn't thinking about William. Men had a way of doing that. It was like they knew when I was finally focused on myself, eating right and exercising, and they squirmed their way back into my life.

The cold of winter had broken, bringing with it showers that mixed with the remaining snow and covered the streets in a brown slush. I'd forgotten to bring an umbrella with me to work and struggled to find a parking spot close to my apartment building, arriving home soaking wet. I had planned to eat a salad for dinner and even already had all the necessary ingredients in my fridge, but the rain created a misery inside of me that called for pizza delivery.

I was in such a hurry to get into dry clothes that I didn't check the mail until the delivery driver buzzed my apartment to let me know that my pizza had arrived. The box was warm and smelled good and I might not have checked my mail at all if I hadn't spotted a letter through the glass slot.

Most mail, as a rule, was disappointing. It was so rare to receive anything other than spam from credit card companies or
other nonprofits trying to get me to donate my meager salary
to them that when I saw a real-looking envelope I stopped to
retrieve it.

"William," I said out loud to no one when I saw the return
address.

Though I wanted to rip the envelope open right then and
there in the foyer, I made myself wait. I was always doing that,
denying myself immediate pleasure for the sake of setting a
scene. I liked to watch cooking competition shows—a kind of
company in the loneliness of my studio apartment—and there
was a term they used, "mise en place," that described the act of
lining up ingredients before starting a recipe. To prepare myself
to read a letter from an accused serial killer, I put on my biggest, coziest sweatshirt, set a piece of pizza on a plate, and
poured a Diet Coke over ice. It was the same thing I did before
starting a binge watch of a new season of one of my favorite
shows.

William's handwriting was small and neat, the type of handwriting that belonged to a killer. Of course, I would've said that
no matter what his writing looked like. I read people as I wanted
them to be.

I took a picture of the envelope and the letter with my phone,
the way that two people might pose for a photo together. I had a
desire for proof before I even knew what I was proving.

I thought that the letter would be the rantings of a psychopath, perhaps a manifesto of his guilt. I was already picking out
my outfit for the inevitable docuseries about William's crimes.
What I got instead was almost more disturbing: he wanted to
know about me.

Dear Hannah,

Thank you for your thoughtful letter. I can't blame you for
how you feel. Women are most certainly treated abhorrently
in our society. I'm sorry for the ways in which I have failed to
be an ally. I don't know you, but I'm sure that you deserve
better.

I bit my tongue when I read the end of that paragraph. A stupid thing that happened because suddenly I no longer knew how to chew, a basic human function that I'd been doing for nearly the entirety of my life. It was painful that an accused serial killer wanted better for me than most of the people I knew.

I can tell from your letter that you already know all
about me. Considering that I'm not especially interesting
at the best of times, I want to hear more about you. What
are your hobbies? Your passions? Your likes and dislikes?
What is your favorite thing to eat, your favorite candle
scent? Which Taylor Swift song have you listened to the most?
    Something that you might not know from the media is
that I always have a maple bourbon candle in my apartment
and my favorite Taylor Swift song is "exile" with Bon Iver. I
pretend that I like the song because Bon Iver is on it. Really, I
like the song because I like Taylor. It's tricky being a man,
isn't it? Liking things is always a confession.

I stopped reading to get another piece of pizza. My heart was pounding like I was in spin class. I chastised myself for drinking caffeine so close to bedtime. I was always defying suggestions that helped people sleep at night.

You seem like a person who reads. I would love a good book recommendation. I used to be really into self-help stuff like How to Fix Your Life in Ten Easy Steps. Now that my life is beyond repair, I'm finding new enjoyment in fiction. They don't have a good selection here. A lot of trash, a lot of classics, and almost nothing in between. I recently read The Scarlet Letter, a book that I last read in high school. I thought it was so stupid then. I knew nothing about being marked.

I understand if you don't want to write me back. You seem like someone whose priorities are in the right place. I don't expect anyone to feel bad for me for being lonely. Loneliness is the least of what I deserve. If you have time though, I would truly love to hear from you.

Sincerely,
William

After finishing the letter, the air in my apartment was the kind of silent that became noisy again. I put on music, Taylor Swift, not because of William's mention of her, but because that was what I listened to when I got ready for work in the morning and it was easy to press Play. My apartment walls seemed closer together than usual, like they were inching ever nearer until they would suffocate me completely. I reminded myself to continue scrolling listings for new rental units when I got to work in the morning.

I stood up to get a third piece of pizza and ate it while standing at the counter, staring at the letter in my hand. I lamented my sloppiness as grease smeared across the page.

William hadn't confessed his guilt, but neither had he protested his innocence. Instead, he lingered in a place of vague self-deprecation that I recognized as a similar impulse within myself. It was hard, even for those of us who hadn't been accused of killing anyone, to love ourselves. Oftentimes, I found it easier to accept the bad things that happened to me than the good, if only because I struggled to find myself worthy of anything rewarding.

My neighbor, an eternally crabby man, banged on the door.

"Turn down the music," he said.

I scoffed but did what he asked. I assumed that living by myself implied a certain kind of freedom until I found out it didn't, not really, at least not while I shared walls with neighbors who went to bed unreasonably early and had a preternatural aversion to all of my music tastes.

I turned off the music and let the silence enwrap me. My tongue still hurt from where I'd bitten it earlier. I pulled out my notebook and took a seat at the table.

If William were an ordinary man like Max, I would've waited to write him back. It was bad to be too eager, to admit that I was alone in my apartment with nothing to do and too much anxiety. No matter how long I waited to correspond with a man, it seemed that they were able to sense my eagerness within my sparse texts. I could only ever pretend at being withholding. With William, I didn't have to worry about any of that. We were corresponding through letters, which, like the deaths of the women that he mutilated and dumped, were impossible to pinpoint to an exact time. He was in jail, which meant that he was limited in the modes through which he could converse and the people he could contact. Most importantly, William was an accused killer. What was the worst thing that could happen if I was too overzealous in my communication? It wasn't like he could kill me. He was already behind bars.

Dear William, I wrote. There was the tiniest pause of hesitation where I stopped to wonder if I should say "dear." I thought of the way that Max would've recoiled if I ever admitted that he was dear to me. I kept writing.

I don't know that you have any right to ask me about myself. In fact, I could probably report you to the police for that kind of questioning. If you really lamented the things you've done, you would abstain from contacting women entirely. I wouldn't be surprised if this type of questioning was a trick. The bar is so low for men that all they have to do is show the barest respect for a woman's interests and suddenly they're regarded as a feminist icon. Listening to Taylor isn't enough to erase all your sins, though it does give you a leg up over the last guy I dated who called her a "talentless hack."

I will give you this much, though not because you deserve it. My favorite Taylor Swift song is "Cruel Summer," but my favorite album is 1989. I didn't listen to the whole thing until years after it came out. I used to pretend that I didn't like pop music. I can't remember why, like getting in a fight with someone and then forgetting what caused the original argument. I thought I was too cool for pop music or I wanted people to think that I was cool. I'm not sure anyone ever thought that though. I find that the older I get, the less I care about things like that. I used to be mortified to leave the house in anything other than a perfect outfit and now it's a struggle to put on real shoes. It's painful to think of all the things that I didn't let myself love when I wanted to love them.

You're the only man I've ever known to have a favorite candle scent. Every other man begins and ends their olfactory experience with Axe body spray. The last guy I dated didn't even wear deodorant. I told him that he didn't smell and it was a lie. I rotate my candle collection with the seasons. I can't carry a Christmas tree myself, but I can buy a balsam fir candle and it's almost the same thing. I spend more money on candles than I should. I can't help myself. I live in a studio apartment and it's difficult to keep the smells of the kitchen separate from those of the rest of the space. It's hard to deny yourself small luxuries when you're denied everything big.

I paused what I was writing and took a chocolate from the candy bowl that I kept on the counter. I couldn't write about my hobbies or passions because as I searched through my life, the only hobby I could think of was William himself.

Asking about other people's hobbies is something that doesn't even work on a dating app. Everyone always lies and says that they like to hike. Hiking is fine, I guess. What I really like, though, is sitting in front of the television and watching too many episodes of a TV show in a row or that feeling when you eat a really good meal. I like going to bars, drinking too much, and sleeping in too late. I'm not supposed to admit these things, but I can admit them to you because even the worst of my habits are nothing compared to yours.

I thought about recommending something to read, but I always found recommendations to be mortifying. It was like looking at my reflection in a car window, a mirror image that was warped in ways that I could never fully place my finger on. The question felt like a test, the way that boys in college used to ask what bands I listened to and I only ever felt confident naming Neutral Milk Hotel as something that would garner their approval. I appreciated that William liked to read though. It gave him a certain moral credit in the midst of all his unforgivable misdeeds. I too had read *The Scarlet Letter* in high school and remembered how the boy who sat behind me jokingly called her a slut.

I didn't know how to sign off. "Sincerely" or "Best" both seemed wrong. Finally, I settled on *"—Hannah."* It was better to have nothing attached to my name.

I ripped the letter out of my notebook and put it in an envelope. I liked the chemical taste of the glue as I ran my tongue over the lip and sealed the paper inside.

Before getting ready for bed, I pulled the forum up on my laptop. There were few developments as the trial was still a ways off and William was in jail. There were the usual arguments over whether he was actually guilty, new pieces of distantly relevant information, but nothing particularly noteworthy. I knew that if I posted "Guess who I got a letter from today?" I would generate a flurry of responses. Everyone would suddenly want to talk to me, regard me as an expert.

I held back. It was nice keeping William's letter to myself, a secret just for me. There was joy in knowing things that other people didn't, experiencing a closeness that could be admired only from a distance.

Before I went to sleep, I touched myself beneath the covers. It wasn't unusual for me to masturbate before bed. What was unusual was how much I enjoyed it. Normally, I found self-gratification to be subpar to that provided by other people. That night, I had an orgasm like an exploding galaxy. The kind of pleasure that seemed like it might be able to create new life.

10

I incorporated William's letters into my life the same way a person might make room for a new hobby, except I wasn't learning how to cha-cha or how to identify birds. Instead, I was getting to know a serial killer.

I checked my mailbox when I left for work in the morning and looked forward to arriving home so that I could check it again at night. On the weekends, I made excuses to go downstairs to see if anything had arrived. For the first time in my life, my laundry was always clean, because I had to walk past the mailboxes on the way to the washing machines. I used to consider what it was like to live without the constant pressures of a cell phone, an existence that I'd experienced briefly in my childhood, and my obsession with my mailbox taught me that people had always been confined, just in different ways.

Can I tell you a secret? His second letter began. Yes, I wanted nothing more than to know the things ensconced in the deepest, darkest parts of him.

I never wanted to be a lawyer. A disappointment. Secrets were supposed to be about love or murder, not career aspirations.

All of the men in the Thompson family are lawyers. My father, my uncles, and their father before them. From a young age, my brother Bentley was eager to join that lineage. I was determined to be different. Growing up, if I wanted to make my father mad, I would threaten to not attend law school, to become an actor or journalist or some other career that he despised. In the end, I chose to become a lawyer because it seemed like the practical choice. I thought that maybe I would be able to do some good in the world. I was wrong. I wish I'd been brave enough to be my own person.

I suppose you can say that I am desperate for human contact, as you suggested in your last letter. I didn't like hanging out with lawyers when I was one of them and I like it even less now that I'm a defendant. In some ways, everything is about me and in others, it's like I'm not even in the room.

When my parents come to visit me, my mother cries the entire time and complains to the officers about the conditions in the jail like I'm supposed to be contained in some sort of luxury prison. My father is convinced that I can somehow find my way out of this with the right work ethic. I have a hard time talking to them. The thing that you understand that they never will is that I deserve this. I have earned every spore of mold on the bread, the ill-fitting clothes, the cough that I developed the first night they brought me here that's never gone away.

You're right that I shouldn't contact you. Not because this contact is some threat to your life, but rather because it is an unearned distraction from the life that I have created for myself. You mentioned the difficulty you have in denying yourself small luxuries and that's what this contact is to me, a small luxury. For a long time, I lived a life of excess that I didn't deserve and I kept waiting for the universe to take it from me. There's something comforting about karma even if I'm the one that's the recipient of its ire. For what it's worth, I think you should buy yourself the candles without guilt.

It sounds like people take you for granted, Hannah. Just know that will never be true of me. I know we don't really know each other yet, but I treasure everything you have to say.

Sincerely,
William

I spent an entire morning at work writing him back. I told him about how I'd been thinking about going to graduate school for years, but I worried that I was too old. *I think I missed my chance to create a new life for myself,* I wrote. *Besides, I don't even know what I really want.* I wrote about Carole's outfits, how I wished my office would revert to a four-day workweek. *Who could I be if I had more time?* I almost forgot that I was confiding in an accused serial killer and not an ordinary man on a dating app. Almost, but not quite.

I hope the jury puts you away forever, I ended my letter.

Sincerely,
Hannah

He started his third letter by declaring *I've never told anyone this before*, and then launching into a depiction of his childhood.

Even though my mother stayed at home with us, my brother and I were raised by a series of nannies. It was understood that my mother's job was to make sure that the house looked good, that we were dressed the right way, attended the right schools. Everything else, the grimy parts of childhood, was left to the nannies.

My brother and I have a complicated relationship. We are polar opposites in a multitude of senses, not the least of which are our political beliefs. In other ways though, we're very close. We used to fight a lot when we were children. On more than one occasion, we hurt each other in ways that required hospital visits. A few black eyes, a broken arm, that sort of thing. I don't think either of us ever intended for it to go that far, but it was easy for things to get out of hand.

I've always been the black sheep. My brother did everything that my parents expected of him. He got married young, to a woman like our mother. They met while he was in law school and she was still an undergraduate. They have two children whom I love and don't know how to relate to. I thought I would understand once I had my own children, something that has become an impossibility. I suppose Bentley's children will take up the Thompson family legacy and become lawyers when they're old enough.

My father presents himself as being one way in public and another in private. I've heard people describe him as kind on more than one occasion, which is an adjective that I struggle to connect to him. He was tough on Bentley and me, the kind of father who thinks if children aren't spanked, then they'll become spoiled. Arguably, we were spoiled despite the spanking. Money doesn't inoculate people from destroying their children.

*We were expected to excel in everything and when we
didn't, we were punished. It was a disappointment when I
didn't make the varsity football team in high school when
Bentley was the starting quarterback. They didn't listen
when I told them that I didn't want to play football to begin
with. It's what everyone in our family does, my father said.
Sometimes when people are under too much pressure, they
start to crack.*

I realized by that point that he wasn't simply going to hand
over a confession. He expressed remorse without admitting to a
particular crime, referenced hurting his brother badly enough
that he needed medical care, but only as an accident. Our correspondence was more like a television show than a movie, every
letter building upon the last.

I described my relationship with my own parents.

*My parents love a version of me that doesn't exist.
I've never confided in them, told them about the boys
that I liked or my hopes and dreams for the future.
They think that I could be great if only I believed in myself.
They don't understand that believing in myself isn't enough
to get a better job or a mortgage. They want to know why I'm
not married but recognize that it's insensitive to ask.*

It all sounded so trite compared to William's childhood. My
parents never spanked; they didn't believe in spanking children.
They merely had expectations of me that were out of line with
who I was, in part because I kept the lesser parts of myself secret
from them. However, I wasn't wholly convinced that this lack of
violence was the difference between William and me, why he

turned out to be a serial killer and I was a person who sometimes skipped going to the gym when I told myself that I would go. Such correlations were too easy, too simple, and William was anything but that.

"What's up with you?" Meghan asked when we finally got together for happy hour. "You look different. I can't tell what it is."

She peered at my face as though a closer examination would reveal a haircut or whiter teeth.

"I'm writing William Thompson," I told her in a hushed tone.

"Who is William Thompson?" she asked, and it felt like she'd asked me what was air. It hadn't occurred to me that William wasn't in the forefront of everyone's brain the way that he was in mine. Much of my communication was with other members of the forum, who were as equally invested in William and the outcome of the trial as I was. It was as though Meghan and I existed in two different worlds.

Meghan and I used to be best friends, I told William. *And then she got a boyfriend and forgot about me.*

"He's the man accused of murdering Anna Leigh. You know, the serial killer."

Meghan made a face of interested disgust.

"Oh my god, you're writing him?" she said.

If there's any relief in being locked up, it's that people reveal their true selves to me in all sorts of ways, William said in his response.

"Yes. I mean, I've only written him a couple of times. It's not like we're pen pals or anything. I didn't expect him to write back. I really didn't. I guess he's lonely in jail."

Is the food as bad as people say? I asked him.

It's worse, he replied.

"That's so fucked up," Meghan said. "It's kind of cool though, right? You're communicating with a serial killer. It's like you're talking to Ted Bundy."

"Ted Bundy killed at least thirty women," I said quickly, trying to put some distance between William and Ted.

I have to admit, you're nothing like I thought you would be, I wrote.

Likewise, he said.

"Does it matter?" Meghan asked. "How many women does a man have to kill before he becomes irredeemable?"

"I think it's irredeemable to kill anyone. I'm not writing him to redeem him. If anything, I'm searching for the truth. You know, to get justice for the victims," I said.

"Just don't become one of those women. You know, like what's her face that showed up at Bundy's trial." She made the face again when she said the words "those women," like they were marked.

"Carole Ann Boone? I'm not her. I'm just writing him. Carole Ann Boone had sex with Ted while he was locked up and had his baby. I don't think I could have sex in a jail and if I did, I would definitely make him use a condom," I said.

I thought about William's perp walk. The way his suit hugged his figure. In a different life, where he wasn't a murderer and I wasn't several states away, I would be attracted to William.

The server brought another round of drinks to the table, interrupting our conversation. I licked the salt off the rim of the glass before eagerly sucking down my second margarita.

Meghan avoided my gaze when she spoke next.

"I've been meaning to tell you," she said. There was a pit in my stomach before she even finished her statement. "I'm engaged."

It was then that I noticed the sparkling ring on her finger. I should've been suspicious when she invited me out for drinks. It had been weeks since I last saw her, our ritual happy hour long since dissolved. It wasn't that she "missed me," as she wrote in the text; it was that she was engaged and thought I would be weird about it.

"Congratulations," I said, faking a smile.

"I wanted to tell you before I posted about it online."

"Yeah, of course."

I sucked up too much liquid in my straw and began to cough.

"Do you have a date set?" I asked when my throat cleared.

"We're thinking December."

"A winter wedding."

"Yes."

"I'm so happy for you."

I wish I wasn't jealous when good things happen to other people. I can't help myself. Why can't those things happen for me? Sometimes I wonder if I am actually self-sabotaging the way that my parents claim.

"Thanks," Meghan said, and then hesitated like she was going to say something else, but remained silent.

We each paid our separate bills.

"It was so good to see you," she said.

"Yeah, you too."

Meghan turned to me before she left.

"Don't fall in love with a serial killer or anything," she joked.

I laughed. It sounded fake.

"Hahahaha. I won't."

I went home and drunkenly composed a letter to William. My

handwriting was so sloppy that I worried he wouldn't be able to read my words.

She's supposed to be my best friend and yet, it feels like she only hangs out with me out of pity.

I wondered if Meghan understood what her engagement reduced me to: a person with only a serial killer to reach out to for comfort.

11

I knew I liked a man when I started to feel like I might die if he didn't contact me. With Max, that manifested in eating cheese until I was constipated and sending him long strings of unanswered text messages about any relevant topic in hopes that he might reply. When I went too long without a letter from William, as often happened due to the slowness of the jail mailing system, I scrolled the forum relentlessly, looking for any new pieces of information. The other forum users didn't know that I was corresponding with William and I knew that the moderators would likely block me if I told them, though not before quizzing me about every word he'd written. There was a type of pleasure in keeping the secret, like having an affair and then coming home to my spouse at the end of each day and pretending that all was well.

When a new letter arrived, I swore I could feel the dopamine hit my brain like the way I felt after my first few sips of coffee in the morning.

I bought a protective case to keep William's letters in and kept the case inside my purse so that they were available to me at all times. I reread my favorite parts in my downtime at work or when I struggled to focus on whatever television show I was watching in the evening. I told myself that I was looking for clues, something that I'd missed on my first read-through. Finally, I was conducting analysis the way that my high school English teacher had wanted me to.

I judged my brother when he got married, William wrote in one letter. *I thought he was too young and I worried that his wife was wrong for him. I'm envious of their relationship now. He has someone who will always be there for him no matter what. I can't remember why I was so frightened at the prospect of a committed relationship. I think I was afraid of getting hurt or, worse, hurting someone else. I would leap at the chance to be with someone now.*

This might sound stupid, but I miss my couch, he wrote in another. *You know that feeling when you're really tired at the end of a long day and you're finally at home on the couch, and it's such a relief to be there? I'll admit that sometimes I'm grateful to be left alone in my cell after a long session with my lawyers even though I'm nearly always alone now. The loneliness is a penance that I have to pay, but I wish that they would at least allow me the pleasure of a cushion. Of all the things that I took for granted, I didn't realize that furniture was one of them.*

You're very funny, Hannah, he wrote in a third. *I confess that I like to imagine what you look like. I hope that's not weird to say. Maybe you could send me a picture of yourself sometime, if you're comfortable, so that I know who I'm talking to.*

I knew I was behind in work, though I didn't realize how behind until my boss pulled me aside one day.

"Hannah, this is a disaster," she said.

"I'm sorry. Time got away from me," I apologized. I looked down at my hands. I wasn't used to failing like that.

One of my biggest tasks of the year was helping plan the spring gala held every April, which was meant to encourage our deep-pocketed donors to keep us funded for another year. Something that I hadn't realized before getting involved with nonprofit work was that fundraising was expensive. I always thought that fundraising meant sending out a couple of mailers or emails each year and that was the end of it, which revealed my middle-class ignorance about how charity worked. Fundraising for rich people meant throwing giant parties and at the end of them, the guests wrote checks so that the nonprofit could continue to scrape by.

It was my first year planning the event on my own and I'd assured my boss that I could handle it. As it turned out, planning an event on my own was neither as gratifying nor as simple as I thought it would be.

It was stupid of me to ever think that I could change the world, I wrote William.

"We don't have the caterer arranged or a photographer. What were you thinking?"

The March calendar stared at me accusatorily from my desk. A frightening number of days had already been checked off. I didn't know how to explain that time didn't feel anything like those boxes.

"I've been busy working on other things. I—"

"Working on what? Hannah, what have you been doing?"

I tried to picture the last few months of my life and the only thing that appeared in my brain was an image of William's face.

"I'm sorry," I said again.

My boss assigned the associate director to oversee my efforts. Carole raised her eyebrows in my direction when he pulled up a chair and sat down behind me. I mentally told her to shut up. William's words floated through my head: *Take it from me, Hannah. It's not worth staying where you're not appreciated.*

I spent the rest of the week making endless phone calls to caterers, finally securing an Ethiopian restaurant that was able to provide what we needed, albeit significantly over budget. I thought that I would be able to make everything balance in the end by finding an inexpensive photographer, only to learn that there was no such thing as an inexpensive photographer who could produce the quality and quantity of images that we wanted.

"This is why we do things earlier," the associate director said when I hung up the phone in frustration.

With his eyes on me, I could no longer spend my days scrolling the forum or scribbling letters to William in my notebook, and I craved it the way that I used to crave looking at my phone. I went home and wrote tomes complaining about my job, my coworkers, and my apartment to William. I almost felt bad for sending such trivial concerns to him when he no longer had any of that, but then I reminded myself that he was a serial killer. He would take what I could give him.

Despite my lackluster efforts, the spring gala happened as planned.

I got ready by myself in my apartment, putting on the dress that I had bought on sale from a fast-fashion website. It'd been a while since I'd dressed in anything other than work clothes or the loose-fitting athleisure I wore at home, and it felt good to look nice. I took some pictures of myself to post on social media and then, after a moment of consideration, I ordered some physical prints to send to William.

I knew it was ill-advised to send photos of myself to a serial killer, but imprudence had never stopped me from sending pictures of myself to men before. It seemed that I barely needed to know a guy before he was comfortable requesting naked photos over text. I always refused at first, as I understood that such pictures could end up getting spread online, but after a few requests, I always found myself caving. There was pleasure in knowing that another person found me attractive enough to want to see me naked when a world of porn existed at their fingertips. In return, men liked to send pictures of their penises, which I didn't particularly care for and mostly used for fodder for jokes with Meghan. Or at least I had when Meghan and I were more regularly in touch. Without Meghan to send them to, the disembodied dicks seemed more tragic than anything else.

Sending William pictures in jail was almost safer than the nudes that I sent those other men. For instance, I wasn't naked and the pictures were printed, which meant they had limited spread. Besides, I liked knowing that he had a face to my name; it seemed only fair after I had watched his perp walk so many times that I had memorized his stride.

Any confidence I had going into the gala was broken when I walked inside and found myself surrounded by opulence. The whole thing was like prom for rich people, and, like my actual prom, it was a disappointing experience.

I listlessly picked at a plate of food, making small talk with the guests that my boss directed to me.

"Oh my gosh, it's the best place to work," I lied. "There isn't a better cause to give your money to."

Rich people donate money because they think it gives them license to do anything they want, William wrote.

When my boss got on the microphone to thank everyone for their generous donations, she omitted my name from the long list of thank-yous she gave. I knew the exclusion was purposeful.

At one point in the evening, a married man of at least fifty approached me and asked if I was single. I didn't know who he was but knew that if he was at the event, then it meant he was wealthy.

"I'm not married," I said with a polite smile on my face.

"What? I can't believe someone hasn't snapped you up," he replied. His eyes flickered down toward my chest.

"Oh, you know. Dating is hard these days," I told him before excusing myself.

I clapped along with the rest of the crowd when my boss announced that the fundraising totals had surpassed the amount raised the year before. My fuckups, it turned out, hadn't even mattered. When my boss called me into her office on the Monday following the event, I expected to be congratulated for a successful gala. Instead, her face was grim.

"Hannah, what are your goals here?" she asked. Her office was cold. No matter how many layers I put on, I could never achieve warmth in the workplace.

I stammered out something about helping people. I wasn't accustomed to getting in trouble. I was the sort of person who always did everything they were told.

"Listen," she continued. "I don't know what's going on in your personal life, but this isn't like you. You're normally someone that I can count on. Lately, though, it seems like you're somewhere else. I'm sorry, Hannah, but I'm going to have to put you on probation."

"Probation," a word used for people after they committed a crime. My body tingled like how my mouth felt when the dentist was injecting Novocain. A burst of pain followed by numbness.

"I'm sorry," I said. "It won't happen again. I'm just going through a lot right now." I didn't elaborate. I knew whatever she imagined would be more satisfying than the truth. It wasn't fair of me to ask her to extricate trauma from my vague statements, but it seemed like the easiest way out of her office.

"We're rooting for you, Hannah," my boss said as I left, like she was Tyra Banks and I was a beautiful model.

It's all such bullshit, I wrote William that night. *Is it a relief to be outside of this system? To know that no matter what happens, you can never go back to who you used to be?*

I picked up the prints I'd ordered from the convenience store after work. Though I'd taken the shots only days earlier, it was like looking at a different person whose lips pouted sexily. The woman in the pictures didn't care that she was on probation at work, didn't mind that she was increasingly isolated from her friends and family. She gazed at the camera confidently, as if to say, *What would you do if you got your hands on me?*

12

There was a drought in letters from William after I sent him the pictures of myself. I stared at my reflection in the mirror in the mornings and wondered what was so awful about my face that even an incarcerated serial killer didn't want to talk to me. I looked at the digital versions of the pictures I'd sent him again and again, trying to detect what it was that had turned him off of me.

I attended my monthly dinner with my parents with a gaping wound on my face from where I had picked at a zit until it turned into a sore.

"What happened?" my mother asked, glancing at my forehead as I got into the car.

"I bumped into a door," I lied, embarrassed by my own skin-picking.

I'd made reservations at one of my favorite restaurants that I couldn't afford to eat at when I was the one paying. It existed in a strange realm of spaces that I'd only been to with potential love interests and my parents.

"How's work going?" my dad asked.

He was on the verge of retirement. So much of his life was dedicated to his job that I wasn't sure how I was going to conceptualize him without it.

My parents were good parents, but they don't understand what it's like to be a person right now, I told William.

"It's good. We had our most successful gala fundraiser in history," I said, omitting the fact that I'd been put on probation because I'd spent too much time at work obsessing over an accused serial killer.

They never insulted me. Instead, they crushed me with the size of their expectations. When I was a child, they thought I was a genius. If I got lower than an A on anything, they asked me what was wrong and said that I wasn't performing up to my potential. They wouldn't listen when I explained that sometimes I could put all my effort into something and still only get a B. They always told me that I would do great things and what am I doing? Working in communications at a nonprofit that doesn't appreciate me. Nothing I say can make them see the reality of my life.

"That's great. Any chance of a raise?" my dad asked.

I took a sip of the expensive cocktail that I had ordered. I wished it were bigger.

"Maybe next year!" I said in my most cheerful voice.

They think things still work the way that they did when they were in their thirties. They ask me about raises, promotions, and how many vacation days I get a year as though I can afford to take a vacation. My dad continually asks if I've paid off my student loans as though that will ever be a possibility. If only they understood all the things that are out of my reach.

"What about the novel you're writing? Any progress on that?" my dad continued to press.

"Well, the creative process is complicated," I started to say and was almost relieved when my mom interrupted me to ask whether I was dating anyone, her favorite line of inquiry.

"I would tell you if I was dating someone," I lied. I could feel William's letters in my purse, which hung over the back of my chair. I wondered what my mom would do if I told her that I spent most of my time obsessing over an accused serial killer. How as we sat there in the restaurant, a part of me was still fixated on why he hadn't written me back.

"I'm sorry for asking. In the past you haven't always been transparent," my mom said.

I rolled my eyes.

"I'm not going to tell you about every single person that I go on a date with. I promise that I'll tell you if I get in a serious relationship with anyone."

Our squabble further devolved as my mother pointed out how secretive I could be and how she wanted to know more about my life, which had been a point of contention between us for years. She wasn't wrong; I did keep secrets from them. I found it mortifying to show my entire self to them and so I kept it all hidden: the boys who I dated, the music I listened to, the food I ate, my performance at work. I couldn't explain to my mother, who thought I was smart and beautiful, all the ways in which I debased myself on a regular basis.

"Let's change the subject," I said finally, and my father started talking about his retirement plans.

I ate too much and then ordered dessert because I didn't want to miss out on an opportunity to indulge. The ice cream made my stomach hurt in a way that ice cream often did, something I conveniently forgot before ordering. Rather than soothe my emotions, the three cocktails I drank made everything feel heightened. The zit on my forehead suddenly a mountain.

"You seem cranky," my mother said when we walked back to the car.

"I'm not," I said crankily. "Just tired."

There won't be a letter, I told myself in the car. To hope for a letter would be to set myself up for disappointment and I already felt so thoroughly crushed. *What if,* a tiny voice said, *there's a letter?* No. There would be no more letters. Besides, what did it matter? He was a serial killer. Not someone worthy of love.

I stomped into the foyer of my building, preemptively angry about the emptiness of my mailbox. I tried to convince myself it was a trick of the light when I saw the edge of an envelope through the window. It took me several tries to input the correct combination to unlock the mailbox. My fingers understood my drunkenness in a way that my brain never would. When I finally got it open, I ripped into the envelope, tearing the paper in the process.

Sorry for the delay in writing, William said. It took me a few days to articulate what I needed to say.

I forgave him immediately, though I'd been suffering in his absence and the self-inflicted wound on my forehead pulsed as a reminder.

You're really very beautiful, Hannah. I don't know how I've found myself in this position of being locked in a jail cell

*with a beautiful girl writing to me. If there's any brightness
in the dark, it's you. I hope you know that you deserve
someone better than me.*

"Beautiful." My worm brain glommed on to the word and immediately I went back and looked at the pictures that I'd sent him, pictures that hours ago I'd derided as ugly, and now, suddenly, I glowed.

I didn't want to think of myself as susceptible to flattery, as I considered myself to be self-aware, but it was possible that flattery influenced my decisions more than I liked to admit. The first time I met Max, at a party hosted by a friend of Meghan's that she'd dragged me to, there was no part of me that considered him a potential love interest. For one, I didn't find him especially attractive, and two, he was a thirty-year-old man who still had a punk band. Late in the evening, we wound up sitting outside together drunkenly smoking cigarettes.

"You're intimidating, you know that?" he said to me.

I laughed. I was anything but.

"I'm serious," he insisted. "You're beautiful, you're smart, you're funny."

I didn't hesitate to give him my number when he asked, though I still had no intention of going out with him. He sent me texts for a couple of weeks, inviting me to this and that, until I finally agreed to meet up with him. Somewhere along the way, sex became implied within our conversation.

What an insult it was to discover that I liked him after all and that he was the one to insist that he didn't want anything further from me. He'd called me intimidating, said I was beautiful, that he had to see me again. Such compliments were the only reason that I liked him to begin with and somehow I was the one left destroyed.

I could see the pattern repeating itself when I read William's letter.

Beautiful, it said.

The situation with William was different from the situation with Max because William was something worse than a thirty-year-old with a punk band. William was a serial killer. And yet, my heart soared when I saw those words.

If there was any chance of turning back, it died that night.

"Don't become one of those women," Meghan had said the last time we spoke. It was like she could smell it on me. Like "that woman" was a perfume that I sprayed on in the morning.

The letter I sent that night was the line in the sand. A before and after that I could point to between the time where I pretended that I still detested William as a killer and the acknowledgment of my love.

What I didn't realize is that becoming one of those women wasn't like getting your hair dyed or nails painted and instead more like a tattoo, something that stains the skin irrevocably for everyone to see.

I wish you could've been at dinner with me tonight, I wrote.

I think about you all the time. I can't explain it, I continued.

I don't condone what you did, but everyone deserves a second chance, I said after foraging through my fridge for the remnant of a bottle of pinot grigio.

Why are you there for me more than anyone else in my life?

I was so lonely before I met you and we haven't even met. I pondered as I finished my glass.

Is it weird to say that I wish we could hug?

Can you touch a woman without ending her life? I asked before crossing the line out and replacing it with the words *Love, Hannah.*

13

Once the floodgates opened, all we had were feelings.

You think I'm beautiful? You must know that everyone is talking about how handsome you are, I wrote to William while I was at work.

You're indescribably beautiful, he replied. *I hung your picture on my wall. I look at it at night before I go to sleep.*

I think about you more than I should, I confessed.

I talk about you like you're someone that I've met in person, he said.

I showed Carole the letters. I couldn't stop myself. I needed someone else to see how much William liked me. I giggled as I did it. A fake laugh meant to make the situation sound trivial, unimportant, like it wasn't the only thing.

"You sent him your picture?" she said. Her forehead creased, an unattractive look.

"It wasn't like it was a naked picture."

"Doesn't it frighten you?"

"What?"

"That he knows what you look like."

"Why should it frighten me?"

"Because he's a killer."

"He's in jail," I replied, like jails had ever done anything to keep communities safe.

"Please be careful," she said.

It bothered me how worried she was. I didn't like the way in which it dampened my joy.

I still read the forum the way that celebrities read social media in search of their own names. Whenever I saw the words "William Thompson" my brain interjected "the man who thinks I'm beautiful" behind it, no matter what kind of atrocities followed. I still cared about Anna Leigh, Kimberly, Jill, and Emma, but in the way that I also cared about historical atrocities. Yes, their deaths mattered. Yes, I could barely remember their names when William told me things like *Your words are the best part of my day.*

There were still some people on the forum who argued for William's innocence or at least insisted that he hadn't acted alone. It bothered me that of all the things that William and I had discussed, his guilt was never one of them. It was always something that was implied, a starting premise that was so obvious that it didn't need addressing. Part of me wanted him to tell me that he was innocent so that I could love him without shame. Another part of me wanted him to trust me enough to tell me about every wrong he'd ever committed, secrets that could bind us together from the rest of the world.

As it stood, I knew equally as much as every other person who had been obsessively scrolling the forum for months. I hated feeling so ordinary.

———

I was looking at the forum when my boss approached me at my desk and asked if she could speak to me in her office. I wasn't certain how long she'd been standing behind me. Had she seen the pictures of William? Watched me as I giggled over a comment that one of the forum members made and typed out a response?

"Hannah, please sit down," my boss said when I arrived in her office. She wore pearl earrings and I wondered if they were real.

I didn't anticipate what was about to happen—as a middle-class white woman, the system typically ensured that I was successful in my pursuits. When my boss said, "We have to let you go," I thought I misheard her.

"What?" I said.

"I'm so sorry, Hannah."

I couldn't take her apology as sincere, even if it sounded like it was. Someone who was actually sorry wouldn't fire me. Someone who was actually sorry would give me another chance and then another one. They would recognize my absentmindedness, my procrastination, as a cry for help instead of a symptom of who I was.

She gave a list of reasons why they were letting me go: frequent tardiness, neglecting my duties, doing personal tasks while at work, distracting my coworkers, insubordination. I struggled to register what she said. I thought I might vomit and regretted eating a donut from the break room for breakfast.

When she finished speaking, I stayed seated in my chair.

"Hannah? Are you okay?"

I nodded numbly. I didn't want to stay inside of her office but I also didn't want to leave. I knew what happened when people were fired, how people whispered about them. A couple of years prior, someone was fired for sexual harassment and everyone knew about it. The harassment itself wasn't what got him fired; rather, it was that he tried to retaliate after the woman he harassed reported him to HR. He wrote her an email warning her to never do it again. "Learn to take a compliment," he said. It was that email, more than the constant texts and phone calls, the cornering in small rooms demanding that she go on a date with him, that got him fired. Surely, I was less bad than him. I hadn't hurt anyone. I had merely been negligent, distracted.

I imagined Carole talking about me once I was gone, if she wasn't talking about me already.

"Hannah's obsessed with this serial killer," she would say, her voice lowering to a whisper. She would say "She sent him a picture" like it was the ultimate crime.

The comments, though manifested entirely by my imagination, were hurtful. I wished I could wither away and disappear.

I left my boss's office with a cardboard box in hand. I had recently watched the entirety of the show *Vampire Diaries* while working on a knitting project. Aside from bloodlust and immortality, what differentiated the vampires from the humans was that they had the ability to turn their emotions off. That was what I pretended to do as I carried my box back to my desk and loaded any personal items inside. I didn't take much. A couple of coffee mugs, some pens, and Post-it notes that probably technically were company property, but I didn't care. I didn't take the time to sort through the desk drawers or riffle through the filing cabinet. I didn't say goodbye to any of my coworkers, not even Carole, whom I had been sitting next to for years. The concept of "work friends" suddenly seemed meaningless. I was made of stone, impenetrable.

On my way to the car, the box slipped out of my hands and the coffee mugs broke. It seemed symbolic in the way that all tiny tragedies seem symbolic when a larger bad thing is occurring. I left the box outside of the building.

"Let them clean it up," I muttered.

I cried in the car, big gulping sobs that were so heavy that I couldn't drive.

"I need to go home," I said out loud to myself after a few minutes. "Things will feel better at home."

I managed to stop crying long enough to make it out of the parking lot, but the tears came back each time I was stopped at a light, which made it difficult to drive. Somehow, I made it back to my building, and a new flood of tears arrived as I realized that without a job, I wouldn't be able to pay rent much longer.

"What am I going to do?" I wailed.

I contemplated the life in front of me. I would have to move home to my parents' house, admit to them all the ways in which I had failed. My résumé was short outside of my job at the nonprofit and surely, no one would want to hire me without references from the job that I'd held for almost a decade. Worse, I was sure that I would never get a date again once I was jobless and living in my childhood home. Life, it seemed, was over. All I had in front of me was misery.

Thankfully, there was a letter waiting from William like he knew that I needed him. There were kindnesses that should've been attributed to the efficiency of the postal service that I granted to William himself.

My face still hurt from weeping when I sat down on the couch to open the letter. One of the greater injustices of having a body was how much it physically hurt to be sad. I could cry one day and wake up the next morning with my face still swollen from tears.

I read William's words and suddenly, I was floating.

This might be wrong of me to say, but I can't hold it in any longer. I'm tired of being alone in this world and though I know that we cannot physically be together and for that I'm sorry, I want you to be my girlfriend. That is, if you'll have me.

It had been years since anyone had used the word "girlfriend" in reference to me. It was so taboo that I thought of it almost as a slur. I was attractive enough for men to want to sleep with me, even for months on end, but it was different for a man to express the desire for monogamy. To indicate that there was something about me that made him feel less alone.

Possibly, if the letter had come at a different time, when I hadn't just been fired and the future didn't feel like a giant black hole waiting to swallow me up, I would've spent more time considering the situation rather than reacting with elation. William, after all, came wrapped in red flags the way that the murdered women were wrapped in tarps before they were disposed of in the ravine. As it was, I couldn't make myself care. Boyfriends who were serial killers were still boyfriends. In some ways, William was better and more attentive than the men that my friends dated. He was smart, well-read, considerate. He listened to Taylor Swift and liked a house that smelled good. Most importantly, he wanted me, just me.

I wrote him back right away.

Yes, I'll be your girlfriend, I said. I hesitated before writing the next line. Like all jokes, it was also serious and I wasn't sure if that translated over paper. I decided to put it down anyway. It needed saying, like asking a man to be sure to put down the toilet seat after taking a piss.

But you have to promise not to kill me, I wrote.

14

I sat down the morning after getting fired with the intention of updating my LinkedIn. It had been years since I last looked for a job and I wasn't sure where people found them, but I was an expert at editing social media profiles and so that seemed like a good place to start.

I got distracted by the forum as I always did. It turned out that I was the same person whether I was employed or not. Jobs weren't as linked to our identities as we made them out to be.

It was there that I saw the post asking "Is anyone else going to the trial to investigate? Would love to meet up."

Up until that point, going to the trial hadn't occurred to me as an option. It was like asking if I wanted to climb inside of a wardrobe and find my way to Narnia. William wasn't wholly real to me and the prospect of seeing him felt as though I were being offered Turkish delight—a dessert I'd never had—and considering whether it was worth giving up my entire life to eat it.

I abandoned my half-finished LinkedIn profile and started

researching how long it would take to drive to Georgia. After that, I checked my account balance and grimaced. I had enough money to get there, but not enough to stay for very long. Luckily, I only had a month left on my apartment lease. If I filed for unemployment and got a new credit card, I might be able to make it work.

I called my mom and told her, "I'm going on a road trip."

"A road trip?" she asked.

I understood her confusion. I never told her when I was going anywhere. I was an adult. But I needed her to know I was leaving in case, for some reason, I never came back. The way that Anna Leigh's, Kimberly's, and Emma's families all had a final phone call to say goodbye and didn't even know it. Or maybe I wanted her to dig deeper, to ask what I was really doing, to know, implicitly, that I was up to no good.

"Yes, to Georgia."

"The state?"

"I don't think it's possible to drive to the country."

"Why?"

"I need to get away for a bit."

"And work is giving you time off?"

"Yeah," I said. It was technically true.

I hadn't told my parents that I'd been fired. I knew they would be angry on my behalf, which somehow made it worse. Surely, their brilliant daughter hadn't messed up so much as to warrant being let go. Surely, there was something that I could do to rectify things.

"I'm so glad you're finally taking a vacation, honey," my mom said.

"Me too, Mom," I replied. "I really need a break."

As much as I was grateful that she didn't ask any further

questions, it wounded me that she hadn't seen through my easily provided lies. A mother should have been able to sense when her daughter was traveling across the country to see the serial killer that she was in a committed relationship with.

I started packing immediately, tearing pictures down from the walls and stuffing my clothes into the tote bags that I had somehow accrued en masse over the years that I lived in the apartment. I worried that if I stopped, left too many shirts on hangers or books on the shelf, then the plan would fall apart.

Dismantling the life I'd built in the studio apartment caused a small sadness within me. In the years that I'd lived there, I'd weathered endless maintenance problems that took too long to fix. A brief infestation of fleas when a neighbor took in a formerly feral cat. Hours of tears and hangovers and heartbreak. Still, the apartment was the first place that really belonged to me and only me. For all its faults, it was who I was.

This romanticism was disrupted by the realization that almost everything I owned was garbage. I'd never had enough money to invest in nice furniture or good clothes. The furniture that wasn't acquired secondhand was all things I'd put together myself, which resulted in a multitude of crying sessions as I did my best to decipher poorly written directions. There was a direct correlation between the price I paid for an item and how well the particle board holes lined up where they were supposed to.

I notified the rental company that I wouldn't be renewing my lease and rented a storage unit for my things until I was ready to return to my life. I was too embarrassed to ask my friends for help moving, so I drove the smaller stuff one carload at a time to the unit and asked my neighbor for help carrying my larger furniture down the stairs, leaving it all on the curb.

I got together with Meghan before I left. She was in the midst of wedding planning, which seemingly took all of her free time. She acted like agreeing to go out for drinks was a gift that she'd bestowed upon me rather than something we used to do with regularity because it was fun.

Meghan looked skinny. When we were both single, she made fun of girls who went on extreme diets before their wedding day.

"If he doesn't love you the way that you are, then why are you getting married?" she'd said and swore she wouldn't diet before her own wedding. "If that ever happens," she'd added.

The Meghan in front of me ordered a skinny margarita and told me that I could order an appetizer, but she wouldn't be eating any of it.

"How's wedding planning going?" I asked, and then regretted it as she described all of the venues she and her fiancé had toured, the cakes they had tasted, and the photographers they'd interviewed.

"I just think the idea of a winter wedding is so romantic. People really need love at that time of year, you know?" she said before finally asking how I was.

"I left the nonprofit," I said.

Her face moved through an emotional range from sad to happy and then a pretend kind of neutral.

"Finally," she said. "I know that you haven't been happy there for a long time. Do you have a new job yet?"

"No, I'm going on a trip. Taking time for me."

"That's amazing, Hannah. Where are you going? We're trying to plan our honeymoon and it's a nightmare."

"Georgia."

"Like, the state?" She looked at me quizzically.

"Yeah."

"Oh my god, oh my god," she said. "You're going to see him, aren't you?"

I smiled. I couldn't help it.

"Who's 'him'?" I asked, though we both knew.

"That serial killer that you're always talking about. William Thompson. That's his name."

I looked at her coyly.

"Maybe," I said.

"What the fuck? Why?"

"He's not like people think," I said.

Wasn't he? I didn't know if that was true or not. I hoped the trial, if nothing else, would help me determine who William really was.

"Do you love him or something?"

She stared at me like there was a disgusting bug on my face. I couldn't bring myself to answer. To say "no" seemed like a lie and saying "yes" was unforgivable. And the word "boyfriend," as much as I coveted it, would come across as comical in that context.

"You don't," she continued before I could speak. "You don't know what love is. Why can't you just find someone normal? I work with this guy who's really nice. I can introduce you to him."

"I don't want someone who's 'nice,'" I replied. *Nice*—what a milquetoast nothing thing to be, compared to someone that was potentially a killer.

"You know that I just want you to be happy, right?"

Our eyes locked and then we both looked away.

"Yeah. I know," I replied finally.

We finished our drinks in near silence. She asked about my parents and I asked about hers. She made vague references to things that we could do together when I got back from my trip. We paid our separate bills and she hugged me tight before we walked to our cars.

"Be careful, Hannah," she said.

"I will," I promised.

I thought it was true. Even then, I couldn't imagine a universe where William would be allowed to touch me.

15

I ran into Max Yulipsky and Reese at the grocery store when I was buying snacks for the trip. My apartment was nearly empty. The emptiness made me feel antsy. I knew I was on the edge of something. I just didn't know how tall the cliff was.

Max and Reese didn't see me at first and I watched the two of them laugh in the pretzel section before putting peanut-butter-filled pretzels in their cart. They were so clearly in love that I couldn't pretend that it was any other way.

In another lifetime, I told myself, *that could've been me.* That was a lie, of course. It was never going to be me. There was nothing that I could've done to make Max love me. It wouldn't have mattered if I were thinner or smarter or more mysterious. He didn't love me because he didn't love me.

Max looked in my direction and froze. We made eye contact. I thought about turning around and walking the other way. *No,* I decided. I didn't want to make decisions based around his comfort.

I walked toward him, forgetting about the rice cakes that I was considering putting in my cart.

"Hey, Max. Hey, Reese."

"Hey, Hannah."

"It's been a while," I said, like it was just a coincidence that we hadn't seen each other.

"It has."

"You've been good though?"

"Yeah," Max said and looked at Reese. "Really good. You?"

I knew I shouldn't say it. I tried to keep it in, but it came out of my mouth like bile.

"I'm good. I met someone."

Max looked relieved. It wasn't the feeling I wanted him to have.

"Yeah," I continued. "He's a lawyer. Very handsome and wealthy. Nice hair. All of that."

In my head I made a list of all the things I left out of the description. *Accused serial killer, in jail, might get the death penalty, lives in Georgia.*

"I'm so happy for you," Max said. Reese gave a subtle tug on his arm. I recognized the move. The girlfriend pull, the one that said *We need to leave now.*

"It was good to run into you," I said.

Later, I would regret all the things that I didn't say. *Why wasn't I good enough?* I should've asked. What was it about Reese that was worthy of love that wasn't true about me? Was it the sex? My body? Was there some deficiency that was obvious to everyone except for me?

"You too, Hannah," he replied.

The two of them walked off. I grabbed the same peanut-butter-filled pretzels off the shelf that they had, suddenly struck with a craving for that particular flavor.

"I need to get out of this city," I said under my breath.

Minneapolis was large, but eventually every city grew too small.

The last thing I did before leaving my apartment building for the final time was send a letter to William.

I've never put much stock in the idea that everything happens for a reason. I've never believed in fate or soulmates, but right now I feel like all of this is happening for a reason. I think I will look back and see this as a pivotal time in my life that changes everything.

I was meant to lose my job when I did because it means that I can come see you. I guess the "seeing" is literal in this sense. I know that we will be unable to touch, unable to speak. It'll be nice, if nothing else, to be in the same room together.

I don't know what the future holds, but I know that I need to do this. For me, for you, for us.

I got a breakfast sandwich on my way out of town and a large coffee. There was no one to wave goodbye.

My fingers gripped the steering wheel, my body tightly wound like I was about to climb a mountain instead of drive for nearly seventeen hours. I took a deep breath and tried to lean into the fear. I always resented how cautiously I lived my life. Becoming an English major shouldn't be the bravest thing that anyone has ever done.

The tension started to leave my shoulders a couple hours outside the city. I put the car on cruise control and blasted my favorite songs from my youth. The Spice Girls, I thought, wanted me to do this. Britney would applaud my choices. The May air was warm without being too humid and I tried to open a window to let my hair fly back with the wind like a carefree character from a movie, but the long strands wound their way around my face and made it hard to see. I rolled the window back up and appreciated the peacefulness. My fingers unclenched. I sang along to songs that my vocal cords had no business trying to match.

After eleven hours of driving, I stopped at a hotel in Kentucky. Too overwhelmed to attempt to find a restaurant, I compiled dinner from a series of vending machine snacks. When I lay down in an attempt to sleep, my heart pounded with the intensity of a bass drum. It was like being inside of an Edgar Allan Poe story, but the only heart beneath the floorboards was my own.

The second day of the trip was a blur of sleepiness. I passed several road signs that warned of the dangers of driving while tired and didn't listen. I tried singing along to the same songs I had played the previous day to lighten the mood and discovered that they no longer worked. Although I had never been a podcast listener, I put on an episode of a true-crime podcast dedicated to discussing the murders of Anna Leigh, Kimberly, Jill, and Emma, and, by extension, to discussing William. I laughed out loud while the podcast hosts talked, because there was so much they didn't know. I wanted to interrupt them, tell them all the things I'd learned on the forum, all the things that William had written to me.

I wonder sometimes if anyone has ever really known me, William wrote in one of his letters.

I found a cheap hotel in Atlanta. I charged the room to the new credit card that I'd gotten for the trip. They had an outdoor pool that was plagued by suspicious-looking algae, but at least they provided continental breakfast every morning.

I sat down on the bed. The mattress squeaked a little as I shifted my weight. The room was reflective of the inexpensive price. There were water stains on the ceiling and the bathroom was dated. I shuddered to think of the things that might have occurred in the bathtub or on top of the comforter. There was a novelty to the shittiness of it, like the whole thing was a kind of roleplay instead of my life.

I looked up the distance to the courthouse on my phone and picked out what outfit I wanted to wear to the first day of the trial, settling on a red dress with a black blazer that had a rip in the armpit that I hoped would remain hidden. The feeling inside my chest was recognizable, the same as the day before the first day of high school or when I moved into my college dorm. On both of those occasions, I told myself that it was a chance to start over, become someone new, only to find that I was exactly the same person that I'd always been.

I'll be wearing a red dress, I'd written William several days prior. I hoped that he would get it in time.

I alternated between telling myself that I was at the trial in order to investigate William and that I was there in my role as his girlfriend. In truth, those were the same activities for me. I didn't want to be with him in spite of his misdeeds; I wanted to be with him because of them.

At that time, I wasn't worried he would kill me. I worried only that he wouldn't find me beautiful when he finally saw me in person. Like I, Hannah, would be disappointing to him, an accused serial killer. In retrospect, it was possible that the order of my fears was misguided.

PART TWO

16

Undisclosed Location

His face is so familiar to me that I'm not sure how to take this level of violence seriously.

"You're awake," he says.

I'm almost happy to see him. I've spent the past few hours drifting in and out of consciousness, a side effect of whatever he used to drug me. At some point, I urinated on myself and was too out of it to be embarrassed. At least with him here, I won't be alone when I die. What a comfort that will be when he wraps the rope around my neck and tightens it until I'm no longer breathing. In the window across from me the sun is setting, the only clue as to how much time has passed.

I pull at the restraints. Movies have given me the unrealistic expectation that at any moment the ropes will suddenly loosen and I'll be free. The protagonist always has some secret skill that comes in handy during their deepest moment of need. Nothing I've done in my life has prepared me for this. Gentle flow yoga classes seem silly and ineffectual in retrospect.

"It wasn't a great nap," I reply.

"I didn't want to do this," he says.

He doesn't need to clarify what "this" is. We both know that he means death.

"I think you do. You've done it before."

"Yes, but that was different. I didn't know them the way that I know you."

He talks about "knowing" like the victim knowing the perpetrator has ever prevented any kind of harm. Historically, knowing a man is only ever a detriment to a woman's safety.

"You could let me go."

"I can't."

"I won't tell anyone."

"I don't believe you."

He's probably right not to believe me. I've never been a good secret keeper. The whole fun of obtaining secrets is figuring out whom to tell them to. To be fair, almost every secret that someone has told me has been inconsequential. In high school, it was all about who liked whom, information that was protected like a bank vault. I can't remember why this mattered.

He's holding a briefcase in his left hand. Illogically, I wonder if he's going to have me sign an NDA. Everything makes more sense when he sets the briefcase on a chair and pulls out a rolled-up piece of cloth, which he unrolls to reveal a set of knives typically used to fillet fish and a coil of rope. I can no longer pretend that this is anything other than a crime scene.

I think of the picture of Anna Leigh's face rotted beyond recognition. I can't stop myself from caring what I'll look like as a corpse. Please let me be beautiful in death.

"You could at least make it quick," I say. "Something painless; pills, maybe."

He looks at me.

"I don't think that's what you want, Hannah. I think you want to suffer."

"No one wants to suffer."

"Then why have you brought yourself so much suffering? Everything that's happened has been your choice. You chose to keep investigating even after the trial. If this isn't what you want, then I don't know what is."

Dotty once said something similar to me.

"It's kind of sexy, isn't it? How dangerous William is," she said with a wink. "Of course, I believe he's innocent. We all do."

I look at the man before me. I'm not turned on, not exactly, though my body tingles all over. I'm not sure if this is a side effect of the adrenaline or the drugs he fed into my system. Whatever it is, I feel electric.

"Is that your psychoanalysis of me?" I say. "Please, tell me more. What else did you learn in Psychology 101?"

He comes closer to me, knife in hand. I tremble involuntarily.

"I know that an ordinary relationship will never be enough for you, Hannah. You don't want to be with someone that loves you and you love in return. You're in love with longing. You want someone that always withholds a part of himself from you. The type of man that never reveals himself completely. Fortunately for you, I'm that type of man exactly. Unfortunately for you, it means that I need to kill you."

I resent the way that he's read me fully. Uttered things that I've only thought about myself. I want to tell him that he's wrong. I could live the American dream if only I was given a chance. Two kids, a dog, and a white picket fence. I don't need to let murdered women lurk in the recesses of my brain. I don't need a man to be a killer to be in love.

He's not wrong though. There are ways in which the world has destroyed me and there are ways in which I have welcomed that destruction. As much as I want to deny it, there is a kind of pleasure that comes from being tied up with a knife against my throat.

17

I met Dotty in the security line for the courthouse.

I didn't sleep the night before the trial. I couldn't stop envisioning the moment when William and I would see each other for the first time, our eyes meeting across the rows of spectators. He would mouth something sweet like *I love you* and I would understand his lips implicitly, though it would be impossible for us to hear each other at such a distance.

I worried that he wouldn't find me beautiful in person.

I got out of bed at four in the morning and stared at my face in the bright, unforgiving light of the hotel bathroom, wishing that I'd gotten one of those facials where they stripped the skin down to its base, and had my teeth whitened and my hair dyed. I'd stupidly thought that my gray hairs were cute and that my slightly crooked bottom teeth gave me character. What an idiot I was. William didn't want a crunchy girl who wore cotton dresses with pockets, or so I assumed. He wanted someone like Anna Leigh, a woman capable of taming every hair into its proper place. A woman worthy of being murdered.

"Don't you look nice" was the first thing that Dotty said to me. She held out her hand for a shake.

She could've said anything after that and I still would've wanted to be friends with her.

Dotty lived in the suburbs of Nashville and had seen William's picture on the evening news and was immediately smitten. She'd since separated from her husband and was at risk of losing custody of her two kids because of all the time that she spent fixated on William.

"It's just not right," her husband said. "Exposing them to someone like that."

She showed me a picture of her husband once. He wore a polo shirt embossed with the logo of his favorite college football team, a beer belly making an appearance through the fabric. It was clear that his hair was starting to thin and that he hadn't yet accepted this thinning and thus kept it longer than was flattering on top.

"He used to be so hot," Dotty said. "I don't know what happened."

Dotty's evaluation of her husband was the same opinion that I had of Dotty herself. She had a fake tan and was thin in a way that made me think that she worked for it. She wore a flowy shirt and strappy sandals and donned a complete face of makeup.

Under different circumstances, I might've been threatened by Dotty's obsession with William, but that first day in front of the courthouse I could only be grateful.

She told me later that she knew I was in love with William because of my earrings.

"No one wears something that sparkles like that for someone they don't care about impressing," she said.

I, in turn, knew that she was in love with William because the second thing she said to me was "You're here for him, aren't you?" Our eyes met in understanding and I nodded.

Surrounding the line were protestors holding signs condemning William for his actions.

GIVE HIM THE DEATH PENALTY, said one sign.

JUSTICE FOR ANNA LEIGH, said another.

JILL'S WORKOUT PLAN, said a third, with fake blood smeared across the black text.

"A lot of ruckus out here," Dotty said.

"Yeah," I replied, scanning the crowd.

I knew from their posts that there were members of the forum amongst them. I took solace in the fact that no one had seen a picture of my face or knew my real name. They didn't yet know the ways in which I'd betrayed them.

My body buzzed with energy. I imagined that I could've held a lightbulb in my hand and lit it with the anticipation that leaked from my pores.

"I hope we get in," I said, trying to peer at the line ahead of us.

I was grateful for the security precautions even as I resented them. There were people who wanted to kill William. Families in mourning, women enraged, men seeking a way to atone for their own sins. Aside from the very real crimes he'd likely committed, William was a scapegoat for all kinds of things.

"We'll kill someone for a seat if we have to," Dotty said and winked at me.

When we finally reached security, I nervously placed my bag on the scanner. I watched as William's letters slid away from me on the conveyor belt. I wondered if the security guards could see the words written through the X-ray screen. In addition to the packet of letters, I'd also brought my notebook so that I could write to William while watching the trial. There was something romantic about writing to someone who was in the same room as me, yet not allowed to speak.

Inside the courtroom, Dotty and I managed to find two seats toward the back. I scanned the room around us. The whole thing felt like an inverse wedding ceremony. The family and friends of the victims gathered together toward the front. I recognized from Jill's social media accounts Jill's mother and sister, who were seated near Tripp and Anna Leigh's parents. In another part of the courtroom was a cluster of journalists who scribbled away on notepads.

William's family sat behind the defense's table.

From all of his descriptions, I expected William's parents to appear obviously cruel. Instead, his father was the kind of handsome that lasted deep into middle age. His mother had sharp features and wore big jewelry that was visible from all the way in the back of the courtroom. William's brother, Bentley, was a taller version of William himself. Next to him was a petite woman who I presumed was his wife. For understandable reasons, their two kids were nowhere to be found.

Despite being at a murder trial for his son, people were deferential toward William's father. Men came up to him and shook his hand and he greeted each visitor genially. If he was nervous, he didn't show it.

I, on the other hand, was a wreck. While Dotty chatted away about her kids (Jaxon and Avery), her ongoing beef with her hairdresser ("I can't go somewhere new; she's the only one that can get the coloring right"), and finally William ("There's just something about him"), I grew increasingly anxious, certain that my rib cage would crack open, exposing the heart beneath, if I had to wait much longer for his arrival.

Dotty was talking about her son's baseball league ("You would think those kids were getting paid, the way some people act") when a murmur spread across the crowd. William had arrived.

The previous year I'd attended a friend's wedding and found myself getting misty-eyed when she rounded the corner and entered the courtyard where the ceremony was taking place. It wasn't that she looked so beautiful, though she did, but rather the enormity of emotion that brought tears to my eyes. It didn't matter that I didn't really know or trust her fiancé—all that mattered was the idea of love.

William's entrance was like that, a bride entering their own wedding. I hoped that my carefully applied eyeliner didn't smear as tears welled up in my eyes. Finally, my boyfriend and I in the same space together. The moment that I'd been waiting for, that pulsed within me as I drove across the country and that I lay awake fantasizing about the night before.

The suit he wore was of a cut similar to that of the one he'd been wearing when he was arrested, but was a slightly different color. He looked thin and I recalled a comment he'd made about the poor quality of the food in jail.

I stared at him desperately.

Look at me, I thought.

Please, please. Look at me.

There were too many people, too many journalists, mourning family and friends, all vying for his attention, for me to become visible through the crowds. My disappointment was palpable. A Gusher squeezed until all the filling spilled out.

Suddenly, my dress was all wrong. My bright red lipstick a smear across my face rather than a perfect pout. It was wrong, all wrong. Nothing like the moment that I'd imagined in my head.

Had I made a mistake? It wasn't too late to get in the car and drive home. I wouldn't even have to break up with William. All I had to do was stop responding. My hand was on my purse. I was ready to go right then and there. Meghan was right. It'd been a stupid idea to drive to Georgia to attend the trial of a man that I'd never met, one who was accused of perpetrating enormous acts of violence against women.

Then, right before he sat down, William turned and his eyes met mine. I detected a tiny smile, a knowing blink. He didn't mouth any words because he didn't need to. I already knew everything that he had to say.

The eye contact lasted for only a second and yet, it was every-thing.

There he was. My boyfriend. My love. The man who may or may not have been guilty of serial murder. For better or for worse, I was there with him. For his sake and mine, I was going to help uncover the truth.

18

In order to prove his guilt, the prosecutors needed to establish William's connection to the women, ties to the scene of the crime, and motive. The first part was easy. William worked in the same office as Anna Leigh, frequented the gas station where Kimberly was employed, took personal training from Jill, and had gone on a date with Emma the very night of her murder. The other two components were trickier. Though all of their bodies were found in the same place, it was unlikely that the women were actually killed there. Instead, there was a second, as of yet undiscovered location where the murders had occurred, making it difficult to collect physical evidence beyond what was on the women themselves. Proving motive was perhaps the most difficult task of them all.

The main prosecutors were an older bearded man and a white woman whom I pegged as being around my age. Once or twice my parents had suggested that I go to law school because law was the acceptable career path for people with a penchant for reading and writing. I resisted because all the people I knew in college who wanted to go to law school had been assholes and because being seen as respectable in other people's eyes didn't seem like a good enough reason to go deep into debt for a career I didn't even want. I regretted that decision on days when my bank account balance was particularly low, but by that point I thought myself too old to go back to school.

I considered the prosecutor who stood at the front of the courtroom. She wore a tight gray dress beneath a black blazer. I couldn't attest to her legal chops, but she looked every bit the kind of lawyer who would ruthlessly imprison someone for life.

Perhaps a third, secret reason that I hadn't wanted to go to law school was that I worried I wouldn't be able to cut it. The prosecutor looked like a woman who didn't give in to her indulgences. She probably never drank too much, ate too much, slept too much. She'd probably never been fired from her job. She'd almost certainly never fallen in love with a serial killer.

"Looks like a bitch," Dotty commented.

I thought I was the kind of person who called out misogyny in other women. I was wrong. I remained silent as the prosecutors began their opening statement.

In my notebook I wrote *Dear William* at the top of a blank page. *I saw you today for the first time. Even though we can't speak or touch, I cherish getting to spend this time with you.* I couldn't focus on what I was writing while the prosecutor was talking. It was strange going from having spent months of my life suppressing my desire to talk about William to suddenly being in a space where everyone else wanted to talk about him too.

I turned to a new page where I wrote *Evidence* and divided the page into two columns: one that said *Guilty,* and the other, *Innocent.*

Meghan's voice entered my consciousness.

Are you making a pro/con list for William's guilt? she asked.

Shut up, I told her, getting mad at the fictional version of my best friend. *This isn't less reliable than a jury of peers.*

The female prosecutor paced the courtroom, her heels clicking against the floor.

"We're going to show that William Thompson is guilty without a shadow of a doubt," she said. "This is a man with the means to kill, a man with a violent past, and a man with a motive."

I looked at the back of William's head, which told me nothing. I wrote *violent past?* in my notebook and underlined it. Was there something more than fights between brothers as he'd confessed in his letters? Hurting siblings was considered acceptable in a way that hurting people outside the family wasn't.

The male prosecutor walked through the condition that the bodies were in when they were found, showing the painstaking care that the killer had taken to conceal his identity.

"Only a very intelligent man could've done such a thing, and I'm here to tell you that William Thompson is an intelligent man," he said.

"In addition to being intelligent," he continued, "the killer would need access to a second location, somewhere private that would allow him time to murder his victims, and William, with his successful law career, has the funds to acquire such a space. He would also need to be strong enough to lift a body on his own, as was William, who played football in high school and more recently received personal training."

What the prosecutor failed to mention was that William hadn't been particularly good at football, lacking both the size and so-called football IQ required to excel at the game. It was the first of many occasions when I had to stifle my desire to raise my hand to correct the prosecution's case with my personal knowledge of William.

He then dove into William's violent past, which consisted of two separate suspensions for fighting, one in middle school and one in high school. In the second instance, he said, the kid that William fought had to go to the emergency room and get stitches. I wondered if such an incident could possibly be connected, if the harm boys wrought on one another in their youths could turn into the deaths of women later on.

When the male prosecutor finished, the female prosecutor closed their opening statement by describing all the reasons why William might've been motivated to kill the four women.

"Maybe William—like many people—underwent trauma," she said. "We know he was a football player. He could have CTE—his brain suffering so many hits on the field that it altered his chemistry."

She went through the victims one by one, speculating as to the events that might've brought about their death.

"It's possible," she told that jury, "that William approached Anna Leigh in a sexual manner and when she refused his advances, he strangled her by the copy machine while her husband waited at home.

"Perhaps Kimberly was sold out of William's favorite chocolate bar or refused to provide change for a hundred-dollar bill and in retaliation he killed her, wrapped her in a tarp, and dragged her the two blocks to where his car was parked at his condo," she continued.

"It's easy to imagine that a man like William was threatened by Jill's physique and athletic skills. What if she pushed him too far in one of their sessions, humiliated him physically in some way, and to punish her, he wrapped his hands around her neck until she was no longer breathing?

"And Emma, that's simple," she concluded. "Men are always killing women during dates. She doesn't look like her picture in the dating app? Dead. She tries to leave the date early? Dead. She doesn't want to have sex? Dead. She does everything right? Dead. It's impossible to know why some women die and some women live, though certain demographics of women are at higher risk than others. As a white, middle-class, cisgender woman, Emma had everything going for her and she still died after going on a date with the wrong man. What a shame."

Rattled off in a row like that, the evidence against William seemed incontrovertible. I looked down at my list where I'd added *intelligent*, *rich*, and *has motive* to the guilty column. There was nothing on the list of reasons that he might be innocent.

I knew that my boyfriend might be a serial killer, but it was different hearing someone else say it. In the front row, Jill's sister was weeping while her mother rubbed her back. I doodled at the top of the notebook page, running the pen over the paper until it made a hole.

Beside me, Dotty picked at her cuticles. I couldn't tell whether she was bored or nervous.

It was a relief when the defense took over. Court trials weren't intended to be a sporting match, but I couldn't help but think about them as being a part of my team, which at that point consisted only of me, Dotty, the lawyers, and William himself. It was a David and Goliath situation where David had been accused of killing a bunch of women.

Both of William's lawyers were older white men who bore a passing resemblance to his father and had Southern accents so strong that they sounded fake. If nothing else, William had the advantage of being well-connected in the legal world. In any other circumstance, their assuming demeanor would've rubbed me the wrong way. It was clear that they were men who were used to getting what they wanted, no matter whom they had to step on to do it. As it was, I was happy that we were on the same side.

"The prosecution would have you believe that this is a slam-dunk case," one began. "In fact, it is anything but. Outside of mere coincidence, there is nothing to tie William Thompson to these four women. No DNA evidence, no fingerprints, nothing in his car or his apartment."

I swore that I heard Dotty growl in approval beside me.

"William Thompson is a good man. He's a lawyer, a taxpayer, a member of his community who has been taken down by proximity to tragedy. How would you feel if someone you knew was killed and while you were still mourning their death, you were accused of causing it?"

I wrote *good man?* in the "innocent" column across from where I'd written *violent past?* I looked at the back of William's head, which remained unspeaking.

"Do you think he did it?" I asked Dotty at the end of the first day.

She looked at me.

"There are some things that only God needs to know," she replied.

As I would learn over the coming weeks, we all had our ways of coping with loving someone that the world told us we weren't supposed to love. Some of us were just more honest with ourselves than others.

19

While the prosecution began to interview witnesses and forensic experts, I had a list of my own of people that I wanted to talk to, namely the other members of the Thompson family. The prosecution was interested in the happenings surrounding the deaths of the women, but I wanted to know who William was at his core.

I watched the back of William's head, which by default meant that I watched the family members who sat behind him. On the third day of the trial, I saw William's mother head to the bathroom during one of our breaks and I scurried after her.

William's parents, Mark and Cindy, had been high school sweethearts. Mark was on the football team and Cindy was a cheerleader. Mark's father was a lawyer and Cindy's father the CEO of a bank. Both of their mothers stayed at home. Depending on who was listening, it was either the perfect love story or a type of slow asphyxiation.

They went to college together with the knowledge that they were going to get married upon graduation. Cindy got pregnant on their wedding night and they bought a house in their home-town with the understanding that they'd eventually move into the Thompson family estate when Mark's father passed.

In his letters, William described how Mark liked to think of himself as a man who pulled himself up by his bootstraps, even though he was born already wearing boots.

> My father thinks we live in a meritocracy only because it has never been suggested to him that he is without merit.

He was friends with the mayor, half the city council, and multiple state legislators. Every morning, Mark got breakfast with other lawyers in town at a breakfast spot that hadn't changed their prices in thirty years. On the weekends, he golfed at the local club that his grandfather helped found, and there were multiple billboards around town that featured pictures of his face.

> The only reason that my father hasn't run for office himself is because he likes the strings that he pulls to be invisible. No one can critique you if they can't see what you're doing.

Cindy didn't fit the mold that was made for her quite as nicely, though from the outside, no one would've seen it. She didn't like being a mother or staying at home and coped by hiring a brigade of nannies and joining the board of every charitable organization that would have her.

> People think that my mother is a good person because she volunteers for numerous charities. As a nonprofit employee, I'm sure you know that there's a difference between being on the board and getting your hands dirty. My mother likes

to go to lunches and galas and have her picture taken. She is an expert at holding auctions and theme parties and getting tax breaks for my father.

Though their lives were perhaps more complicated than they were made out to be from the outside, the one thing that Mark and Cindy Thompson were certain of was that neither of their children would grow up to be serial killers and thus, they were frustrated by recent developments that caused a deviation in their already paved path.

I have to admit that there is some schadenfreude in destroying the perfect image that my parents try to project of themselves. The mayor refuses to be seen with my father in public and some of my mother's charities have asked that she step down from her role—while continuing to still give anonymously, of course.

After I followed Cindy into the bathroom, I wasn't sure what to do next. I lost sight of her before she disappeared into one of the stalls, and though her red heels were recognizable, I decided against peering beneath the doors to figure out her location. I waited at the wall of sinks for Cindy to emerge, ignoring my own full bladder.

That was when I met Lauren.

"Do you have a tampon?" she asked.

I could see her face in the mirror, young and pretty. I guessed that she was one of Anna Leigh's friends. I rummaged around in my purse and handed her a tampon after wiping some lint off the packaging.

"Thanks," she said.

Cindy emerged from the stall. Lauren and I watched as she washed her hands before reapplying her lipstick.

"That's William Thompson's mother," Lauren whispered after Cindy left the bathroom.

"I know," I replied.

Like had found like, we realized. Lauren wasn't at the trial for Anna Leigh at all, but rather for William, who was the second murderer that she'd fallen in love with. The first was a forty-five-year-old white man, Kris Cooper, who was accused of setting his house on fire and killing his wife and son in the process. Cooper insisted that he had not set the fire and would never hurt his family.

"You don't know what it's like to be accused of causing the biggest tragedy of your life," he told the media.

Lauren learned about Kris Cooper from a true-crime podcast when she was a sophomore in high school. She'd made being a fan of true-crime podcasts one of the key components of her personality, which she figured was better than the girls who made "being a member of the soccer team" or "liking horses" their primary persona. The podcast made a convincing case for Cooper's innocence, and Lauren, who had been told repeatedly that she could do anything, became determined to set him free. In the end, Cooper lost his appeal, and when Lauren's parents found the sexually explicit letters that he'd been writing their underage daughter, they forbade her from ever talking to him again. It was difficult to forbid someone from writing letters, and Lauren would hide stamps around her bedroom in order to continue contact. It was Cooper who eventually lost interest in her when he found someone younger, still fresh, who was eager to love him.

Lauren shrugged when she talked about it.

"I was young," she said. "I didn't know what true love was."

Now nineteen, Lauren had long, dark hair and a skinny frame that I was envious of. She wasn't beautiful in the conventional sense. Instead, she was something worse, a unique sort of beauty that was appreciated in adults and lost within the cruelty of high school.

"Aren't there boys your own age that you're interested in?" I asked her.

Lauren laughed.

"Boys my age are boring," she said. "All they want to do is play video games."

I didn't know how to break it to her that boys didn't get better after that either. I suspected that if she was choosing to spend her summer break watching the trial of a serial killer, then maybe she already knew.

There was security in our little group. Sitting there between Dotty and Lauren, I experienced a kinship that I hadn't felt since high school when all of my friends would gather in the theater classroom before the first bell rang. How I'd taken those days for granted and then longed for them in retrospect. It was silly that as an adult, a person needed to become obsessed with a serial killer in order to make new friends.

I hadn't told them that William was my boyfriend. It seemed like something that I'd made up, even though I carried the letters in my purse as proof. Dotty and Lauren thought that we were the same. Three women in an unrequited relationship with an accused serial killer. I didn't want to break that uniting bond to explain that, no, actually, I was in a requited relationship with him, especially considering that I hadn't received a letter from William since I'd arrived in Georgia.

While the prosecutors called up witnesses, I wrote letters to

William and took notes on anything the witnesses said that stood out as being particularly important.

Dear William, Your hair is looking especially good today. Do they allow you to use hair products in jail or is that all natural?

- Guilty: police found William's business card tucked inside of one of Anna Leigh's purses.

Dear William, I made friends with a few other people at the trial. You've probably seen me sitting with them. You have seen me, right?

- Innocent: Anna Leigh had business cards from a number of people in the same purse. She was actively working on building a network.

Dear William, You're getting my letters, right? It's been a while since I've heard from you. It's so strange being in Georgia on my own. I've never really been on my own before, not like this. I've always had my parents nearby or Meghan.

- Guilty: video footage of William in Kimberly's gas station days before she died.

Dear William, I found a good donut place near the courthouse. I wish I could bring you one. Personally, I love a good cake donut. If I threw one at you, would you catch it?

- Innocent: hundreds of people went to that same gas station in that time span.

Dear William, I sat by the hotel pool after the trial today. It was almost like being on vacation except for the relentless sound of leaf blowers in the distance.

- *Guilty: Jill made a note of a personal training appointment with William on her calendar two days before she disappeared.*

Dear William, You got so close to me today that I almost reached out and touched you. I'm not sure that you noticed me.

- *Innocent: there was no sign of William at the gym on the day that Jill actually died.*

Dear William, I tried the taco truck that parks outside the courthouse today. The pork taco was a 10/10.

- *Guilty: William was the last person that Emma was ever seen with.*

Dear William, I hope to hear from you soon. I miss your words.

- *Innocent: no other woman that William met from a dating app was ever murdered, though one did die in an unrelated car accident.*

If some of the testimony was difficult to watch—and much of it was—I focused my attention on the Thompson family.

When the forensic experts showed pictures of the corpses, bruised and rotting, I watched Mark wrap his arms around

Cindy's shoulders. When they described the torture that the women had undergone before they were ultimately killed, I noted how Mark whispered something into William's brother's ear.

As the jury tried to determine whether William was guilty, I looked for signs that Mark and Cindy were as conniving as William made them out to be in his letters. Surely, if I watched them for long enough, I would see the places where their masks started to peel away from the skin to reveal the monsters behind them.

20

I retreated to my hotel at the conclusion of the trial each day. Before going to my room, I checked with the staff at the front desk to see if any mail had come for me. I still hadn't received a letter from William since arriving in Georgia a week and a half prior and I worried he hadn't gotten my new address or, worse, he'd seen me and decided that he didn't want to be my boyfriend anymore.

"Are you waiting for something important?" the woman at the front desk asked.

"A letter from a friend," I said.

"A love letter?" She raised her eyebrows.

"Something like that," I replied.

In the days since, she'd figured out that I was waiting for a letter from William Thompson when I mentioned that I was in town to watch a trial and told her not to be alarmed when the return address was a jail. I acted embarrassed when she put it together, but I think I wanted her to know.

"I'm obsessed with him," she confided in me when she found out that I was in town attending his trial. "I love all types of true crime. You always hear about serial killers in the past, but it's wild to have one today, right in my backyard. You know, my friend's cousin went to high school with Kimberly."

"Wow, what a coincidence," I replied.

I held back from bragging about how much closer I was to William than her. It was easy for proximity to danger to turn into a competition, the way that people liked to get into fights over whose childhood was worse and more traumatic.

"I'll be on the lookout for any letters," she assured me.

I resented that she would get to touch the envelope before I did. Things like that became important when physicality in a relationship was manifested through paper.

After checking in with the desk, I went to my room, which already felt like it had only ever been mine. Living in a hotel wasn't the fantasy I imagined as a child. I'd purchased a loaf of bread, a jar of peanut butter, and a pack of plastic knives with the intention of making sandwiches for dinner in order to save money, but my hunger, which was both physical and not, usually got the best of me and I'd developed a habit of stopping at fast-food drive-thrus during my trips back, a type of cheap indulgence that I never typically allowed myself in my ordinary life.

I ate my food in bed, watching marathons of home renovation shows. I tried to do Jill's workout videos when I had the energy, which was almost never. The trial was a physical and emotional leech. Sometimes I wrote letters to William, but more often than not I went to bed early, falling asleep on piles of crumbs from my dinner, for lack of anything better to do.

A week and a half into the trial, I still hadn't connected with the Thompson family the way that I'd wanted to. The atmosphere of the courthouse made it difficult to start a conversation. Dotty, Lauren, and I weren't the only clique that had formed. The friends and families of the victims had formed their own kind of community, one that was rooted in grief. Anna Leigh's friends connected with Emma's friends, and Jill's sister led them through gentle flow yoga sessions in a spare room of the courthouse to help release the negative energy that built up in their shoulders. They traveled to the bathroom, the water fountain, and the food trucks parked outside in little pods. I knew that the pods were meant for protection rather than exclusion, but still, I felt excluded like they were the cool girls in high school and I was the loser.

I wanted to explain that originally I was on their side. *I'm one of the people who helped figure out that it was William*, I wanted to say. Only that wasn't totally true, as I'd seen William's picture and dismissed him as someone who couldn't possibly be guilty. They avoided me like they could sense William's presence on me even though I'd never touched his person. Being one of "those women" had a scent to it, apparently.

I know that I'm not here to make friends, but I wish they were friendlier, I wrote William. A selfish statement considering that William was hated globally.

Since I couldn't approach the Thompson family inside of the courthouse, I decided that I needed to find a way to talk to them outside. That was when I started minorly stalking the Thompson family.

Instead of going back to my hotel room after the trial, I followed Mark and Cindy Thompson. Their estate was an hour outside of the city and to ease the burden of travel, they'd gotten a long-term rental close to the courthouse that was big enough to also accommodate William's brother Bentley and his wife. I suspected they would find it unsettling if they knew how easy it was for me to track their location.

The first night that I tracked them, I followed them back to their rental and sat in my car across the street waiting for something to happen. A delivery driver arrived at one point with bags of food and my stomach grumbled as a reminder that I too needed to eat. Eventually, I drove home out of boredom and composed a dinner out of vending machine snacks.

I returned the next night with a laptop full of downloaded movies that I ended up not watching because Mark, Cindy, Bentley, and his wife left the rental and drove to a restaurant ten minutes away.

The restaurant was a steak house that was far out of my price range even in the best of times.

"Do you have a reservation?" the host asked when I walked in. There was disdain in the question. If she had to ask, she already knew I didn't belong.

"No," I admitted.

She sighed.

"How many?"

"Just me."

"You can take a seat at the bar if you'd like, otherwise the wait is going to be over an hour."

I took the offer of a seat at the bar, disappointed that it faced away from the rest of the room. My chair was squished between a couple enjoying an appetizer and two friends out for drinks. My heart panged thinking about Meghan.

The lack of prices on the drink menu frightened me, so I ordered the cheapest thing on the dinner menu that I could find, which was a house salad. My neck hurt from straining to look behind me. I finally spotted the Thompson family seated in a corner. Mark and Bentley each had an amber-colored cocktail, while Cindy sipped something out of a martini glass.

I could tell, even from a distance, that Mark and Bentley dominated the conversation. They were those kind of men, the ones who liked to take hold of every room that they were in. Occasionally, Cindy and her daughter-in-law chimed in with a comment or a laugh, but largely they were quiet. I strained my ears trying to hear what they were saying, which proved impossible over the din of the restaurant.

My house salad was small, unsatisfying, and cost sixteen dollars. I hated thinking about how many items I could've purchased at Taco Bell for the same price. I kept waiting for something to happen and nothing did. The two men ordered more drinks. It was a large amount of liquor for a Tuesday, but I wasn't a teetotaler; drinking a few cocktails didn't imply a family that was evil to the core.

I finished my greens in a mere five minutes. The couple next to me had ordered steaks and I watched red juice dribble out of the meat as the woman cut into it. I didn't normally like steak, but now that it was being withheld, it was all that I wanted. I had the bartender give me another menu and I desperately scanned it, willing an affordable cut of meat to appear. Finding none, I begrudgingly paid for my salad and went to use the bathroom before leaving.

It was one of those nice restrooms with big swinging doors that offered total privacy and cleaning products strong enough to overpower any smells that attempted to permeate the air. I emerged from the stall to find William's brother's wife, Virginia, washing her hands in one of the sinks. We made eye contact in the mirror, a glimmer of recognition on her face before she quickly looked away. She opened her mouth as though she was going to say something and then closed it again. She dried her hands on a paper towel and left the bathroom without a word.

I was in a bad mood when I left the restaurant. All of that time and money spent for nothing. I hadn't illuminated the dark depths of the Thompson family and I was no closer to discovering the truth of what had happened with William and the murdered women. Instead, I'd watched them eat dinner at a distance and consumed some limp greens that failed to fill my stomach.

In my hungry, vulnerable state, I couldn't stop thinking about why William hadn't written me back since I'd arrived in Georgia. Had he ever really cared or had it all been a ruse to get me to attend the trial where I spent eight hours a day staring at the emotionless back of his head? In a real relationship, I thought, I wouldn't have to follow his family at all. Instead, he would introduce me to them himself and I would get to witness their psychoses for myself.

If William had been Max or any of the other men I'd dated, the kind who had a cell phone readily available in the palm of his hand, that was the point at which I would've started sending anxious, needy text messages, the kind that inevitably turned men off of me and that I could never stop myself from sending. As it was, all I could do was write him a crabby letter, and I planned the words in my head as I walked back to my room.

You asked me to be your girlfriend and then you respond with radio silence. I understand that I have low expectations, but they're not that low. I'm still a person, you know. I'm not like those women that you killed that won't talk back to you. That's the nice thing about a corpse, isn't it? They can never critique your actions, not like the living that are left behind.

Do you even want me here or was this all a game to you? Maybe it was stupid of me to think that you were being serious when you said you wanted a relationship. Haha. Gullible little Hannah, always looking for love. I guess you tricked me.

You say all these things about your family, but I've spent the last two days watching them and I have to say, they seem perfectly normal to me, enviable even. I think there's something broken inside of you that makes you hurt people this way. Stop trying to blame the world around you and take responsibility for your actions.

The door to my room beeped as I swiped my key card and then closed behind me with a bang. All of the words that I'd repeated to myself on the drive home vanished as I saw what was waiting for me on the bed: a packet of envelopes with a note from the front desk employee that said, "I wanted to make sure you got these."

William had finally written me back.

21

When I was seeing Max, he used to text me late at night and ask, **You up?** A phrase, when translated, that meant "Are you willing to debase yourself enough to leave your apartment at this late hour and fuck me?" I always wanted to leave him hanging, but every sexual encounter carried with it the possibility of being the one that would make him love me, and there wasn't enough willpower within my bones to give that up, so I went every time he asked.

William couldn't text me. Whatever contraband may or may not have existed in the jail where he was being held, a cell phone wasn't part of it. And yet, he still managed to interfere with my sleep. I didn't know how to love a man without giving up at least one of my basic needs.

I spread the letters out in front of me on the bed, arranging them in the order that they had been written. It was like having a husband away at war who'd finally returned to the base.

Dearest Hannah . . . The mere sight of my boyfriend's handwriting sent a shiver down my spine.

You once described depression to me as a feeling of isolation even when surrounded by a crowd. That's how it felt to walk into that courtroom today. There was so much hatred in the air that I could taste it. And then I saw you, Hannah. You're even prettier in person than you are in photographs. I know that you gave up a lot in order to be here for me and I cannot express how much I appreciate it. Just knowing that you're there helps me get through the day.

My bad mood dissipated with every word. It was silly of me to be mad at William for his poor communication when he had so little control over any facet of his life. In truth, he was more reliable than most people that I'd dated. At the very least, I got to see a glimpse of him five days out of every week.

I continued reading as William described how despite the hatred, it was nice to get out of jail and put on real clothes. *I don't feel like myself without my clothes,* he said. *I'm glad that I get to look nice for you. They do their best to denigrate you in every way possible in jail, and one of those ways is by taking away everything that ever made you feel good about yourself.*

William didn't say much about the actual testimony, which was a disappointment, though I knew that his lawyers had advised him to say as little as possible. There was no such thing as private correspondence when a person was accused of serial murder and I didn't want the prosecution to be able to use the words he'd written me against him. Admittedly, I liked the idea of testifying and spent much of my time during the trial imagining what I'd say if they called me up as a witness.

Sometimes I imagined scenarios where I pleaded his innocence.

"Please," I would say on the stand. "This man asked me to be his girlfriend. How could someone like that be a killer?"

Other times, I contributed to his guilt.

"This man asked me to be his girlfriend. How could he be anything other than a serial murderer?"

Though cameras weren't allowed in the courtroom, in my fantasies, each of these statements was followed by the clicking of dozens of old-fashioned cameras, the people desperate to capture the face of William Thompson's girlfriend.

In reality, I knew that I couldn't take the stand because no matter what I said it would be a betrayal to somebody.

There were two points about the trial that William repeatedly circled back to in between anecdotes about the food he was provided for lunch and summaries of the books that he was reading.

The first was in reference to the comment that the prosecution had made about his so-called violent past.

The prosecutors love to talk about my "violent past." Does the phrase imply violence inflicted by the person or violence inflicted upon the person by those surrounding him? I don't want to suggest that I've had more harm done to me than most people, as certainly there are a number of ways, namely financial, in which I am more privileged than the average person, but I do think that I experienced things in my youth that no child should be asked to experience.

I don't think that any of us arrive at adulthood fully intact. At least now I don't have to pretend that I'm not broken.

In another letter, he wrote, I like to think that if people knew me, really knew me, then they would have more empathy for my situation, but I worry that it would only make them condemn me further. I struggle to pinpoint what exactly I deserve.

The second and perhaps related topic that he ruminated on was his family's physical proximity in the courtroom.

I wish that I could invite you to sit closer to me, he said. *The lawyers are friends with my father, as seemingly everyone is friends with my father, and thus, he's granted access to me that nobody ever asked if I wanted. I'd rather have you there instead.*

> *This trial has hurt them. They remind me of that constantly. My father is obsessed with the Thompson family name. "It's all we have," he likes to say, as though he doesn't also have a plethora of material possessions. I can tell that he hasn't stopped to consider the ways in which his own actions have brought us here. Sometimes I get so angry at him that I start to shake. In those cases, I think about you, Hannah. You're my only light in the darkest of worlds.*

I alternated between being frustrated by the vagueness of William's statements and delighted by his love for me. Something, or a multitude of somethings, had happened in William's childhood; that much was clear. I wished he would tell me what it was so that I could reassure him that I would love him regardless or, alternatively, decide that it was enough, that I couldn't love him at all.

I struggled to reconcile the Thompson family as they were depicted in William's letters with the family that I'd spied on as they ate dinner earlier in the evening. People weren't always who they portrayed themselves as being in public. As a woman, I knew that well enough. It was one of the reasons why people struggled to believe the claims of women who accused their charming abusers. Surely, they said, if that person was a monster, then we would know.

I thought of the way that people treated Mark Thompson in the courtroom, almost like he was the family member of one of the victims rather than the father of an accused killer. If he was a monster, it didn't show on the skin.

As per my custom, I wrote William back immediately. I made no mention of following his family to their rental, or to the steak house, or about the mediocre salad that I'd eaten. I only said, *Being in the same room as you is the greatest gift. I'm glad that I can be there to support you.*

22

The first suspicious behavior I witnessed from Mark Thompson came over the weekend following the second week of the trial.

I woke up early on Saturday and drove to their rental apartment, happy that Mark and Cindy's car was still parked out front. Trial weekends were lonely as Dotty drove home to be with her kids and Lauren went out to bars that were too young for me. Even if it didn't reveal anything, sitting outside the Thompson apartment gave me something to do.

I saw Bentley first. He came running down the block, dressed in workout clothes, and I almost didn't see him in time to duck. Bentley was good-looking, something that Dotty liked to remind me of on a daily basis.

"It's too bad that he's married," she said. "I would jump him in a heartbeat."

You're married too, I didn't remind her.

Bentley stood outside, fiddling with his watch, before going in.

Mark came out half an hour later and got in the car. I ground my teeth as I followed behind him. I was an unconfident driver and I didn't relish the prospect of following him all around the city. Luckily, Mark stopped at a gas station a short while later, parked at a space in front of the doors, and went inside. It took me a second to realize that it wasn't a random gas station, but rather the gas station where Kimberly had worked before she was murdered.

Mark stayed inside for a few minutes. He came out with a Styrofoam cup and a packet of Nutter Butters and got back in the car. He started the engine and sat there looking at his phone. I couldn't see what he was doing. I briefly saw his mouth move like he was talking to someone.

Eventually, Mark pulled out of the spot and I did my best to tail him. Mark was a fast driver, weaving in and out of lanes, and I lost track of him on the highway. It didn't matter. My gut told me where he was going. I entered in my GPS the address of the gym where Jill had worked. I wasn't surprised to see his car in the parking lot when I pulled up. He wasn't in the car, which meant that he'd already gone inside. I didn't follow him. My clothes, though comfy, didn't pass as workout gear.

Mark was gone a whole hour, during which time I made notes about his activities in my notebook.

Mark Thompson appears to be visiting the places where the women were last seen. I don't think that it's the first time that he's done this. It almost looks like a ritual to him.

Mark continued his murder tour after he completed his workout with a trip to the restaurant where Emma and William had eaten. I surreptitiously followed him inside. This time, it was Mark who sat at the bar and I was seated at a table close behind him.

I was pleased to see that the restaurant had affordable lunch specials. I ordered a pasta dish that came with a salad and bread-sticks. The meal could only be described as nourishing. Both Mark and I looked at our phones while we ate—the difference was that I also watched him as he scrolled. I couldn't believe that no one around me seemed to realize what was happening. This was Mark Thompson, father of William Thompson, who was ac-cused of killing a woman immediately after eating in this very restaurant, and yet, he was being served like any other man.

I ate quickly to ensure that I finished before he did. There was only one last place to visit and that was William's former of-fice building. Because it was Saturday, the large parking lot was nearly empty, the building abandoned. Mark didn't attempt to go inside. He stood in the parking lot, gazing up at the glittering glass tower while I watched him from my car. He didn't notice me, or if he did, there was nothing to signal it.

Afterward, I hoped that he would do something more, some-thing I could use to figure out what his intention was, but he merely drove back to the rental, where he stayed for as long as I sat outside in my car.

"Do you think that there's something suspicious about Mark Thompson?" I asked Dotty and Lauren when the trial resumed on Monday.

"I think that all rich men are suspicious," Lauren replied.

"It's suspicious that his son is on trial right now, if that's what you're asking," Dotty said. "Otherwise, he appears perfectly nor-mal to me."

I told them what I'd done over the weekend, how I'd followed him from site to site of where the women had disappeared.

"What are you suggesting? Do you think that he killed them?" Dotty asked.

"I don't know what I'm suggesting," I replied. "There's something off about him though."

I decided to do my own murder tour, one without Mark.

I drove to Kimberly's gas station on the way to the trial to get a coffee. An older man stood outside the door, eating a chocolate donut that I presumed he had bought inside.

"Excuse me," I said. "I'm so sorry to bother you. I was wondering if you come to this gas station a lot."

"You're not trying to get me in trouble or anything, are you?" he asked in a joking tone that if he were younger might've been interpreted as flirtatious.

"No, nothing like that. I was wondering if you knew a woman named Kimberly that used to work here."

"Oh, you're one of them," he said.

"One of who?"

"The women that come around asking about Kimberly. They've slowed down recently, but for a while there were a bunch of them. I'll tell you what I told all of them. Yeah, I knew her. She was real nice and I'm sorry that she's dead. No, I never saw that guy they say killed her, or at least I don't think. There's a lot of people that come in here that look like him. I can't tell them apart from one another." He laughed. "They all just look like white guys to me."

I slipped my phone back in my pocket that had an already prepped photograph of Mark Thompson and one of William. It embarrassed me that the man had pegged me as being one of "those women" just as Meghan had. I wanted to explain that I wasn't one of many as the man had implied, but William Thompson's girlfriend. I understood, suddenly, why the Manson girls were so willing to carve swastikas on their foreheads as a symbol of their love. Each of them wanted to be recognized as a devoted follower, someone special, even if it meant being hated forever.

I went inside and selected the largest Styrofoam cup they offered and filled it with coffee. After a moment of hesitation, I got a chocolate donut from the case as well. There was nothing artisanal about my purchases and there was something satisfying about that. Sometimes all the body wanted was garbage.

The new person behind the till was a pretty young Black woman. Ordinarily, I didn't endorse the idea of keeping a gun for protection since more often than not, weapons were fired upon the people who owned them, but I hoped that they gave her a gun or, at the very least, a can of Mace to help protect herself from any future killers.

I had planned on asking the cashier on duty about Mark but changed my mind after my conversation with the man. I didn't want the woman to look at me the way that he had, like I was some sort of lunatic. I paid and left without saying a word.

The man was still standing outside when I went through the door.

"Hey," he said.

"Yeah?"

"Be careful out there."

I smiled.

"Thanks."

"You never know who's trying to hurt you," he continued.

I didn't like the tone shift in his voice. During our first conversation, the man had seemed harmless—friendly, even—but now there was something ominous there.

"Okay," I said and scurried off to my car. I hoped he didn't think that I was hurrying in an attempt to get away from him, even though that was exactly what I was doing. I'd forgotten, momentarily, that members of the Thompson family weren't the only dangerous people in the world.

I arrived at the courthouse with chocolate smeared across my face from the donut and the taste of bad coffee still in my mouth.

"What happened to you?" Dotty asked.

"You have something on your face," Lauren said.

I was frustrated. My visit to the gas station had turned up nothing other than a reminder that Kimberly had perhaps never been safe.

I glanced at the Thompson family at the front of the room. Bentley leaned over to his father and murmured something in his ear. Mark laughed. I knew that there were members of the forum who would crucify them for that behavior. According to them, the Thompson family was supposed to remain forever in mourning for the lives that their son had allegedly ended.

"I think I need to talk to Mark Thompson," I told them.

23

The opportunity to get closer to the Thompson family came through an unexpected route during the third week of the trial.

Following Mark to the gym where Jill worked gave me the idea to get my own membership. It was, I thought, a way to kill two birds with one stone. It would allow me to further investigate what had happened to Jill, what Mark's involvement was, and I would be able to get a workout at the same time. Unfortunately, I couldn't afford an actual membership, so I settled for a week-long trial membership.

Jill's sister still frequented the gym. The two of them had been close. They lived together for several years during their early twenties, worked out together, and lost weight together. The only thing they hadn't done together was die.

During her testimony, she described the last time that she'd seen her sister alive.

"We got together early for a workout, which we do—did—several times a week. I was happy because I reached a personal record in how much weight I could squat."

"And what happened after that?" the female prosecutor asked.

"I went to the locker room to get ready for work." Her voice, which was timid at the best of times, quavered. "I waved goodbye to Jill. She was already with a client. I didn't—I didn't think it was going to be the last time I ever saw her."

"When did you start to suspect that something was wrong?"

"I texted her a funny video while I was at work of this dog wearing a bunch of different outfits and she never responded. Sometimes it takes her a minute. She doesn't always have access to her phone when she's working with a client, so I didn't think much of it. A couple of hours later, I got a call from the gym saying that Jill missed a training session. It was so unlike her. I tried calling and she didn't pick up."

"When did you call the police?"

That was when Jill's sister started crying. They weren't pretty little tears, but ugly gasps that also manifested in a runny nose.

"I still thought she might be okay. You know, maybe she forgot to write down an appointment or something. It wasn't until the next day when she still wasn't answering her phone that I called them. I can't express how much I regret this. Maybe if I had called earlier, she would still be alive."

Something I learned over the course of the trial was that when someone died, no matter how they were killed, everyone around them was eager to blame themselves as a symptom of their grief. The exception to this was Kimberly, who had no one close enough to save her even if they were given the chance.

"Did you ever hear Jill mention a man named William Thompson?" the prosecutor asked.

"Yes," Jill's sister said with an unquestionable firmness to her tone.

"What did she say about him?"

"She said that he was weirdly competitive, always trying to prove that he was stronger than her. Jill was considering asking if he wanted to switch to a male trainer."

I looked at William's head when she said that. In his letters, William claimed that he'd always been a subpar athlete compared to the expectations that his father had of him. I was under the impression that his father and Bentley were the competitive ones and William was merely along for the ride. I wasn't sure if William's self-perception was wrong or if he was lying. There was also the possibility that Jill's sister was exaggerating in the wake of her sister's death.

"I heard," Dotty whispered into my ear, "that she does Jill's workout videos obsessively."

"Oh," I whispered back, like that was a novel thing and not a practice that I also engaged in.

On their cross examination, the defense asked if there were other men that Jill found frightening.

"Of course," her sister responded. "Jill was famous. She got threats from a lot of people. They got mad when she didn't give them attention or said that she was faking her weight loss. They were just people online though. They didn't know her in person, not like William."

"And did William ever actually threaten your sister?" one of the defense attorneys asked.

"No," Jill's sister admitted. "He never actually threatened her, or at least not that I know of."

I recognized the weirdness of going to the same gym as Jill's sister. However, I figured that it was no stranger than following around members of the Thompson family. I also benefited from being an average-looking white woman; no one looked at me and saw someone with the capacity for violence.

I knew from Instagram that Jill's sister, like Jill herself, liked to work out early in the morning. She made posts of herself wearing workout gear with captions that said things like "Exercise is the only thing holding me together right now. Without it, I might get in bed and never leave."

I was never one of those people who got endorphins from exercise, though I strove to be. I showed up at the gym one morning before the trial, bleary-eyed and wearing leggings with a suspicious amount of pet hair on them for someone who didn't own a pet. It wasn't hard to find Jill's sister. In that space, she was a celebrity.

"How are you doing?" muscled white bros and older Black women alike came up and asked her.

"It's amazing that you're here," they said. "Jill would be proud that you've continued your fitness journey in the wake of this tragedy."

I didn't know what I was doing. I tried my best to avoid staring outright. I picked up a twenty-pound weight and then exchanged it for fifteen. Even living bodies were in a constant process of atrophy. I lifted the weights over my head and then approximated dead lifts before moving to the machines. I studied the instructions on the side and hoped that my movements weren't embarrassingly wrong. The closest I got to Jill's sister was a quick "Hey" at the water fountain, an ordinary kind of nicety. I spent the rest of the day sleepy and famished and used the workout as an excuse to order three tacos from the food truck at lunchtime. I struggled to keep my eyes open while a forensic expert testified that the rope used in all four murders was the same. It was a common type of rope, he said. One available in any home improvement store.

While I didn't run into Mark at the gym, I slowly got closer to

Jill's sister. By the third day, our conversation extended all the way to "Hey, how are you?" It didn't seem like that far of a leap from friendly greetings to actual friend status.

In the trial, another forensic expert described the injuries sustained by the bodies that couldn't be ascribed to the cause of death or the tumble down the ravine.

"It is very likely that these injuries were inflicted before death," he said.

His testimony was followed by that of a psychiatrist who said that anyone who did such things clearly took a type of pleasure in causing pain. These were not murders of necessity or convenience. These were murders of fantasy fulfillment.

By the end of my free week at the gym, my body was sore and my brain tired. Rather than try to further stalk the Thompson family, I spent the evening alone with a cheap pizza that I picked up on my way back to the hotel.

It was on the last day of the free gym membership that Jill's sister recognized me.

She was using the squat rack.

"Are you almost done?" I asked her while she rested between sets as though I knew anything about using a barbell.

She nodded and took a sip from her water bottle.

"Sorry, I know that I've been hogging the rack for a long time. It's been a tough week," she said.

I saw my opening.

"I heard about your sister. I'm sorry."

"Thank you," she said. It was clear from her posture that she considered the conversation finished.

I lurked behind her as she completed her set. She was strong in a way that I'd never been. I wondered what it was like to have that much control over your own body.

"I'm done," she told me as she took another swig of water.

She glanced at me again.

"I've seen you before," she said. "You've been watching the trial. You're one of his supporters, aren't you?" The volume of her voice increased with every word. Other people in the gym were looking at us.

Oh no. Like the man outside the gas station, she'd smelled it on me, the scent.

"No, I—" I said, searching for a defense. I had none. I was worse than a supporter. I was his girlfriend.

"You need to leave," she said.

I saw the gym bros looking at me, two senior citizens on elliptical machines casting shaded glances in my direction.

"Okay," I said. "I'm sorry. I really don't mean to hurt you."

I wanted her to say something else. She didn't.

I left and lamented that I hadn't been able to finish my workout first.

Our confrontation carried over to the courthouse. I saw Jill's sister pointing to me from where she sat with the friends of the other victims. They were hungry for someone to hate, someone who was more accessible than William himself.

"Leave Jill's sister alone," one of Emma's friends hissed at me in line for security after lunch.

"How can you live with yourself?" said another while I washed my hands in the bathroom.

They found my Instagram page, the real one rather than the one that I'd made to spy on Max, and left comments calling me deranged and sexist. Despite having thoroughly researched all of them online, it was a shock to realize that they could do the same thing to me. I'd forgotten that I wasn't invisible, that my actions could impact other people. Begrudgingly, I made my profile private and blocked the girls one by one.

In the end, it was Mark Thompson who approached me.

"I saw those girls being nasty to you and wanted to introduce myself," he said. "My family appreciates your support of my son."

Mark had a firm handshake and a distinctly Southern accent. Strangely, I'd never imagined William as having an accent. It occurred to me that I didn't know what his voice sounded like.

"Nice to meet you. I'm Hannah," I said.

"I can't wait to get to know you better, Hannah."

That was how I became entangled with the rest of the Thompson family.

24

I stopped following the Thompsons around once they knew my face and name and started greeting Mark whenever I could: at the water fountain, outside the bathrooms, in the hallways, as he walked to his car at the end of the day. This was made difficult by the fact that I knew William wouldn't like it if he saw me speaking with his father and thus, I needed to avoid said interactions in places where he could see.

Mark invited us out for happy hour drinks following the prosecution resting their case. I thought it was going to be an intimate affair, just me, Dotty, Lauren, and the immediate Thompson family with the exception of William, since William was obviously in jail. Instead, I walked into the room that Mark had reserved at a local restaurant to find it full of people. Even with a son on trial, the Thompson family was well-connected and people were more than willing to show up to a party, particularly if that party was being held behind closed doors.

Mark as a host was a man within his element. He welcomed

each guest enthusiastically and directed them toward the trays of appetizers and the open bar. Anyone who didn't already know better would never have guessed that his son was on trial for serial murder.

He greeted me with a hug that served as a reminder of how physically isolated I was.

"So glad you could make it," he said.

Cindy was icier. Though she was significantly older than me, she reminded me of the popular girls in high school who could put me in my place with a single glance. She looked at me and I was suddenly conscious of my split ends and the ancient mascara that I'd scraped against my lashes before leaving the hotel room.

"Nice to meet you," she said, her gaze still analyzing the price of everything on my person. "I've seen you around, talking to my husband."

There was a harshness to her tone that made me feel embarrassed, though I wasn't sure what I'd done wrong. I understood how flies felt when people swatted at them as they buzzed innocently about the room.

"Yes, Mr. Thompson has been so kind," I said and shook her hand, taking note of the giant sparkling ring on her finger.

Lauren and I were out of place at the gathering. We were too young, our clothes too shabby, and our accents in contrast with the heavy Southern ones that permeated the space. Dotty, on the other hand, fit right in. The room was filled with her kind of people, wealthy and white. After only a few minutes, she'd amassed a group of women around her who were telling her their favorite places to work out and get their hair done.

I ordered a drink from the bar and hovered near the appetizers, watching Mark. At first, I'd taken his gregarious nature to be the opposite of the cruel man William had described. The more

I watched him, the more that his friendliness seemed a feature of psychopathy. His son was in jail and there he was, telling people to help themselves to food and drink.

"Hi there." An older man sidled up next to me. He looked like everyone else at the party—rich and drunk.

"Hi," I said politely. He was blocking my view of Mark. Under the guise of saying hello, men were always interrupting women while they were doing important things.

"How do you know the Thompsons?" he asked.

"It's a long story. How about you?"

"Oh, we go way back. I've known Mark and Cindy since high school. Shame what's going on. Such nice folks. They don't deserve this."

Neither, I thought, *did the women deserve to die.*

"Say," he continued, "I love your dress."

I touched the cotton fabric with my fingers. I'd purchased the dress several years earlier on a shopping trip with Meghan from the clearance rack at Target. It had never fit me quite right, but I held on to it for its moldability as my weight fluctuated up and down.

"Thank you," I said.

"Are you here with your husband? Boyfriend?" he asked. He glanced at the empty fingers on my left hand.

"I'm here with friends."

The man took a step closer to me and I realized too late that I should've lied, made up a Brad or a Peter who accompanied me everywhere I went.

I was trying to figure out how to exit the conversation when a male voice at my side said, "You're Hannah, right?"

I turned to find Bentley Thompson standing next to me.

"Yes. And you're Bentley," I replied, grateful for the interruption.

The man took one last look at me.

"I see someone over there that I need to talk to. Nice to meet you," he said.

"Nice to meet you too," I echoed, though it hadn't been.

"That's Verne," Bentley said when the man was gone. "He was hitting on you, right? He does that to all the pretty ladies."

I blushed at the word "pretty." I held back my impulse to explain that, no, I wasn't actually pretty. I was just young enough and wearing makeup.

"You really saved me there," I told him instead.

He smiled a handsome smile that made me hyperaware of my ordinariness.

"Glad I could be of service," he said.

Bentley and I hadn't talked much. He was nearly always with his wife, Virginia, and didn't attend the trial as religiously as his parents did. I knew from William's letters that Bentley worked for their father's law firm the way that William himself had been expected to do. Bentley and Virginia had met at a bar when Bentley was in law school and Virginia was an undergraduate with a fake I.D. He said that Virginia had gone to college with the express purpose of finding a husband, something that I wasn't aware that women still did. She knew from a young age that she liked nice things and not working and men who could provide that for her. In return, Bentley liked being the provider.

Virginia is happy to let Bentley make all of the decisions and Bentley is happy to make them, William wrote.

I was intimidated by Virginia. She was model pretty with hair that looked like she'd come straight from the hairdresser each day. Like the rest of the Thompson family, she was friendly at first glance, but her meanness was closer to the surface, probably due to all of the facials that had thinned out her skin. Her presence made me paranoid that she was the type of woman that William was really supposed to be with, the type that he swore he didn't like.

I don't want to marry another version of my mother, he said.

There was no sign of Virginia at the party.

"Where's your wife tonight?" I asked.

"She drove home to see the kids. I would've joined her, but I needed to make my appearance here. Most of these people I've known since I was little. Except for you and your friends, of course."

I watched Dotty and her group of ladies. She told me once that she had been a baton twirler in high school and college, and seeing her with those women was like seeing her in action, directing them with the same finesse with which she'd twirled her baton through the air. The women chose that moment to burst out laughing as though on cue.

Lauren had been cornered by several older men who looked like lawyers. I hoped that she was young enough that they wouldn't try to hit on her the way that Verne had with me, though I didn't feel confident in that assumption. I would've joined her, but I didn't want to sacrifice the time with Bentley.

"Where are you from originally, Hannah?" he asked me.

We moved to a table.

"Minnesota," I told him. "The Twin Cities."

"So far from home," he said and took a sip of his drink.

"Yeah, I guess you could say that I was captivated by this case."

I applauded myself for finding a nice way to say that I was obsessed with his brother.

"My father mentioned."

"Oh."

It was both unnerving and delightful to discover that I was a topic of conversation amongst the Thompsons. If only they knew the full extent of my relationship with William, then maybe they would welcome me as one of their own. I would be able to eat steak dinners at the table with them rather than spy on them from a distance.

"Tell me more about yourself," Bentley said.

I was reserved at first. I didn't want to give too much away. I was the one who was supposed to be investigating the Thompson family, not the other way around, but Bentley was a gifted conversationalist and soon I found myself telling him about the nonprofit and losing my job and deciding to attend the trial on a whim. In turn, Bentley told me about his kids, the quirks of living in a small town where everyone knew one another, and his recently picked up hobby of cycling.

"Do you want to get out of here?" he asked after a while.

I hadn't realized how late it was. Lauren was nowhere to be seen and Dotty was arguing with someone on the phone, probably her husband.

"Sure," I said.

We ended up in a bar that was darker and more intimate than our previous location. It wasn't the type of place that I imagined Virginia going. It was strange being out with Bentley, and not just because he was the brother of the serial killer who I was dating but because we fit into seemingly incompatible archetypes. I had always been too artsy, too crunchy, too liberal, too distrustful of rich, handsome men to spend time with people like Bentley, and even if I'd wanted to spend time with men like that, I doubted they wanted to spend time with me. It wasn't that I thought myself unattractive; rather, I wasn't attractive in the way that people like Bentley thought of the term.

"How did you end up here?" Bentley asked. He was drinking an old-fashioned. "Me, I have to be here. It's my duty as a brother. You, though, you could be anywhere in the world and instead you spend day after day sitting at my brother's trial. What exactly is it that you find so captivating?"

"I couldn't be anywhere in the world," I replied. I was drinking a beer, which I didn't normally drink because it made me feel bloated, but I knew that I needed to slow down. "I can't afford to go anywhere. Not like you. And besides, I want to be here. Obviously, I want to be here for William. It's more than that though. I felt sick of my life. Do you ever feel that way? Like you need to escape your skin and become someone else?"

"All the time," Bentley said, utterly serious.

I laughed.

"What could you need to get away from? Your life is perfect. You have a great job, a beautiful wife, you're good-looking. What else could you want?"

"You think I'm good-looking?" Bentley said, winking at me.

The wink destabilized me. If I didn't know better, I would've said that he was flirting with me, but thankfully I did know better. Men like Bentley weren't attracted to women like me.

"I mean, in, like, an objective sense, yeah," I said.

"Well, thank you," he responded, as though no one had ever called him handsome before.

"My life isn't perfect though," he continued. "For starters, my brother is on trial for murder."

I laughed uncomfortably.

"I guess that was a big omission on my part," I said.

"Things aren't great in my marriage either," Bentley admitted.

"Virginia wants me to cut off contact with William and I just can't do it. I mean, I know what he did was horrific, but he's my brother, you know? I would do anything for him."

I nodded. I was an only child and had always felt like my own family's love was predicated on my success, but I understood making irrational choices for William.

"Can I tell you something funny?" Bentley asked.

"Of course."

"My mom thinks that you're trying to hit on my dad. She calls you 'that girl that is always around.'"

"Oh my god. No." I put my hand over my mouth. That explained the dislike that emanated from Cindy when we met earlier in the evening. She thought that I was attracted to her husband when really it was her son who I was after. I thought of all the times I'd sought Mark out in the courthouse to say hello. The way that I lingered longer than I should have. Cindy's conclusion, although wrong, wasn't entirely illogical.

"Don't worry too much about it. My dad is a talkative guy. This isn't the first time that something like this has happened. She gets jealous of any pretty woman that tries to talk to him."

There it was again, that word, "pretty." William complimented me in his letters, but there was only so much he could say as someone who had only ever seen me at a distance. It was nice to consider that I might be pretty up close too.

"I'm definitely not trying to hit on him. If anything—"

If anything, I was growing increasingly suspicious that Mark Thompson was somehow connected to the murders as evidenced by his little tour.

"If anything, I'm in love with William," I said finally.

Unexpectedly, Bentley laughed.

"I figured as much," he said.

"You did?"

"You're here, aren't you?"

There it was, that recognition. I was once again labeled as one of "those women." Bentley, at least, looked free of judgment. Though the love we had for William was different, presumably we both still loved him. Outside of Dotty and Lauren, he was the first person I could really talk to about my feelings.

"We write each other letters," I confided, and pulled the case I kept them in out of my purse.

Bentley raised his eyebrows at the folded letters in front of him.

"Wow, so you're really serious about all of this?" he said.

I hesitated, unsure of how much I wanted to tell him.

"We're dating," I said finally.

"Dating? Even though you've never met?"

"Yes, dating. It's less weird than it sounds. We were writing each other for months before he asked me to be his girlfriend. It's like meeting someone over the internet, only we met over paper."

"And he's in jail," Bentley said pointedly.

"Well, yes, and he's in jail. But it's not about that. I'm not one of those women that's obsessed with serial killers or true crime or whatever. That's Lauren. I like William. That's all."

Bentley fiddled with his wedding ring.

"What do you and William talk about in these letters?" he asked.

"Oh, you know. Our hopes and dreams," I joked.

I couldn't tell him the truth, which was that we did discuss our hopes and dreams, only that they turned into discussions about the various ways in which our families had fucked us up. How Bentley himself was a source of consternation for William. Though we had just met, I didn't want to hurt Bentley's feelings by suggesting that he had contributed to William's murderous tendencies.

Despite my omissions, Bentley's expression grew serious. He was one of those men who was always joking in a way that verged on flirting until suddenly he wasn't, and the difference was palpable.

"Please be careful, Hannah."

"I'm being careful."

"William is a complicated person. He can be dangerous," Bentley said.

"I think I know that already. I mean, he is on trial for serial murder."

Bentley shook his head.

"It's deeper than that," he said.

"It's fine," I replied, making eye contact with him. "He's in jail; it's not like he can kill me or anything."

I was grateful when Bentley laughed, a lightening of the mood.

"You're right," he said. "It's not like he can kill you or anything."

Bentley looked down at his watch, an expensive-looking thing.

"I should go," he said.

I didn't want him to leave. There was so much more to be said about William and on top of that, there was something exceedingly normal about sitting in a bar with Bentley. It made me feel like the person I was before, the one who had friends and social outings and didn't spend all her time in a hotel room writing letters to a serial killer.

Bentley paid my tab, for which I was grateful.

"It was so nice to meet you, Hannah," he said. "I'm sure we'll get a chance to speak again."

We hugged outside the bar.

Bentley isn't what I expected, I wrote in my notebook back in the hotel room. *I think he knows something that he can't (won't?) tell me. It might be good to spend more time talking to him since Cindy Thompson thinks that I'm hitting on her husband.*

Though Cindy had nothing to worry about from me, I would soon learn that she was right to be suspicious of Mark.

25

The defense's case relied upon three primary suppositions.

The first was that though William had some kind of connection to all four of the women, there was little that linked him to their bodies.

"Ladies and gentlemen, I don't know about you, but we like to rely upon facts in this courtroom, and the fact of the matter is that there is no evidence that William Thompson ever touched any of these women," the lawyers said.

The second was evidence that suggested that a different yet unknown person had been in the presence of the women. These were small things. Blue fibers that were found on both Anna Leigh and Emma's bodies that didn't match any items of clothing that William owned. Hair from the same cat found on Emma and Kimberly when William was allergic. The fact that no rope was found in William's house, car, or office and that his car had never been spotted in the vicinity of the ravine.

"It's easy to make assumptions," the lawyers told the jury.

"Convenient to point a finger at the first person who appears and say, 'Case closed! We're done!' The easy thing to do, however, is not always the moral thing to do. It is our moral obligation to look at every last piece of evidence and ask ourselves, 'Does this point to guilt, or does this point to innocence, or do we not know?' Those times that we don't know, well, is it not a moral imperative to presume innocence?"

The last supposition was based upon William himself, namely that he was a good person. It was difficult to pinpoint the level of goodness inside of someone. Unlike intelligence, there were no tests that claimed to make such a measurement, and if there were, being accused of serial murder almost certainly disqualified William from the label. Nevertheless, the defense attempted to construct a kind of proof on the matter by presenting a series of character witnesses.

I entered the latter half of the trial filled with anticipation about seeing Bentley at the courthouse after our night of bonding. Bentley, however, wasn't at the trial as the defense started to present their case. I looked for him in the security line and scanned the courtroom after I was seated.

"Who are you looking for?" Lauren asked.

"No one," I replied.

Bentley was nowhere to be found.

I tried not to be disappointed. After all, there was no reason for disappointment. Bentley and I were only barely acquaintances and it seemed like my desire for a closer friendship was one-sided.

The first witness was William's nanny from when he was a child, an older Black woman. William had never mentioned her by name, though he frequently referenced the nanny that raised him in lieu of a mother.

"Can you tell us how many children you've cared for over the course of your career?" the defense attorney asked.

"Dozens," said the nanny. She had the soft demeanor of someone who'd spent years caring for children.

"And can you tell us what William was like as a child?"

"He was a sweet little boy. Very bright. Always doing things for other people."

"Can you give us some examples of those things?"

"Oh yes. He knew I liked flowers and one day he went in the backyard and picked a bunch of flowers for me. I don't think that the landscapers were particularly pleased about that."

"Did you ever witness any violence from William?"

"I think that all little boys are violent at times. You know, play fighting, stuff like that."

"What about animals? Did you ever see William interact with any animals?" the lawyer continued.

"Well, his mother never allowed animals in the house. The only time I saw William around animals was when we went to the park. He loved dogs."

The next witness was William's fourth-grade teacher, a woman who requested she be called "Miss B.," as she was by the children. Miss B. was long retired and looked frail.

"Can you describe what William was like as a student in your class?"

"It's been a long time since I had William, but I still remember him. He was always very sensitive. He loved to read. I looked through my old files and found his note that said 'a joy to have in class.' That's how I would describe him as, a joy."

"And how did he get along with the other students in the class?"

"If I remember correctly, William was very popular."

"Any fights? Trouble?"

"No, nothing like that. William was a good boy. Not all of them are good boys. I've certainly had my share of troublemakers, but he wasn't like that. I can't imagine that he—"

The defense attorney cut Miss B. off before she could continue. There was a script that each witness was expected to follow. Together, they were building a depiction of a man out of clay.

We broke for lunch and I grimly examined the smushed peanut butter and jelly sandwich in my purse before getting in line for the taco truck. By that point, the owners of the food truck knew my name and my order and greeted me like a friend. The familiarity almost made me feel like I belonged.

I sat at a picnic table with Dotty and Lauren. Dotty's lunch, per usual, consisted entirely of a bottle of Diet Coke, while Lauren ate a vegetarian burrito. She stopped eating meat as a child because she couldn't bear the thought of animals suffering.

"I have news," I told them after shoving my first taco in my mouth, the juice dribbling down my chin. "I hung out with Bentley the other night after the thing at the restaurant."

"Isn't he married?" Dotty asked. She took a sip out of the plastic bottle.

"It wasn't a date. We were just having drinks. And get this— he warned me to be careful around William, said that William is dangerous."

"Of course he's dangerous," Dotty replied. "That's what makes him sexy."

I was disappointed by the lackadaisical response. I expected an enthusiastic gossip session where the three of us unpacked every word that Bentley had said. Instead, Dotty yawned, covering her mouth with her hand. I longed for Meghan, or at least the person she'd been before she was engaged, who was always willing to gossip with me.

"Mr. Thompson and I are getting coffee today after the trial," Lauren said like it was nothing at all.

I stared at her.

"You and Mark?"

Since Bentley had told me about Cindy's suspicions that I was flirting with her husband, I'd done my best to give him space. I tried to watch him from afar, a distance that revealed only smiles and handshakes. Mark Thompson was a master at emotional opacity.

"I was talking to him at the thing we went to and told him that I was thinking about applying to law school and he said that we should get coffee together so that I can pick his brain."

"You don't think that's weird?" I asked.

"No, it's nice. He's a really good lawyer, you know."

I thought about trailing behind Mark as he visited all the locations where the murdered women had last been seen.

"Listen," I said. "I don't know if it's a good idea for you to get coffee with Mark Thompson. I'm not saying that he has bad intentions, but there's something off about him."

"How is me having coffee with Mr. Thompson different from you having drinks with Bentley?" Lauren asked.

"Because Bentley and I are around the same age and we both understood it was a platonic situation. I don't want you to go thinking that one thing is happening and it turns out to be something else."

Lauren rolled her eyes.

"It's platonic between Mr. Thompson and me too. He's married and, like, forty years older than me. I think that he genuinely wants to help me."

She thought I was being stupid and overly cautious. I knew this because I was nineteen once too and convinced that I was never going to die. Lauren's hubris was especially pronounced considering her obsession with serial killers.

"Please just text one of us and let us know that you're safe afterward. You can't be too cautious."

"Sure," she said in the same tone that I used to use on my mother, and finished her burrito.

After lunch the defense questioned a college professor who had taught William in a creative writing course. He'd since left academia for the private sector, but he remembered William, whom he called "one of my favorite students." He still dressed in the role of professor, with his tweed sports coat that he wore despite the temperature outside. He had white streaks in his hair and a gut that poked out from his button-down shirt, though I imagined at one time he had been young and handsome, the kind of guy whom I lusted after in my own creative writing courses in school.

"What year was William in when he enrolled in your course?" the defense attorney asked.

"I believe he was a sophomore. He wasn't a creative writing major, just taking the course as an elective."

"Can you tell me what William wrote about in your class?"

"His big project for the semester was a short story about a man who worked at a factory that his father owned and kept breaking off bits and pieces of the machine until they could no longer produce any goods. He said it was inspired by 'Bartleby, the Scrivener.'"

"Did William ever write about anything misogynistic?" the defense attorney asked.

"No. If anything, William got along well with the girls in the class. Creative writing tends to be full of girls. It can be tough to be a man in that setting, but William fit right in."

"Was there anything violent in his writing?"

"No, I mean, as someone who grew up working-class, I think that it's a little unrealistic for him to write a story about someone in a factory, but there was no violence between the characters in the story, if that's what you mean."

Later, I would look up the creative writing professor online. He was savvy enough to post regularly on Twitter, but not savvy enough to realize that serving as a character witness for William was enough to sink him. He hadn't yet put his profile on private, but I suspected he would by the end of the day.

"Only monsters defend monsters," someone wrote underneath one of his posts, and it was liked by hundreds.

Not for the first time, I thought about how limited we are in our conception of the word "victim."

26

For safety reasons, I decided to spy on Lauren and Mark Thompson on their coffee date. I didn't trust him, but nothing I had said had convinced Lauren of his untrustworthiness. I reminded her how he'd driven around the city, visiting sites connected with each of the women.

"So what?" she said. "You're the one that followed him while he was doing that."

I didn't know what to say after that.

They met up at a Starbucks close to the courthouse. I made a detour to my car to grab my sunglasses, the only way that I could think of to disguise myself. Following Mark had been significantly easier before he knew who I was. It was ironic that I spent all my time wanting to be seen and when I was finally visible, I longed for anonymity. I figured that if either of them saw me, I could pretend I was there getting a cup of coffee. After all, I hadn't been sleeping well, my dreams filled with visions of murdered women.

It took a couple scans of the Starbucks to find them and I was momentarily worried that I was too late, that something had already happened, but there they were, seated close together at a tiny table, nothing obviously wrong going on.

Mark gesticulated with his hands. Lauren nodded along with what he said, occasionally stopping to jot something down on a notepad. She was right about one thing: they looked more like father and daughter than like two people on a date.

I sat with a book in my hand, the same book that I was always reading and never had the concentration to finish. Though I longed for a latte, something with caramel and chocolate, I couldn't afford anything more than a plain coffee. People liked to suggest that if only young people didn't buy fancy beverages, then maybe they would have money in savings, a suggestion that only made my plain coffee more bitter. I sipped too quickly and lamented the loss of the drink when it was gone. I gazed enviously at the lemon loaf that the man at the table next to me was consuming.

My envy caused me to miss the moment when the shift occurred between Mark and Lauren. His voice, usually loud and boisterous, lowered to a whisper and she had to lean in close to hear what he was saying. It irked me that she was privy to information that I wasn't. All those times that I'd said hello to Mark, made small talk with him in the security line or on the way to the bathroom, and she was the one that he invited out for coffee, while all I got was suspicion from his wife. Yes, it was about youth and beauty, but it was also about potential. Lauren could be invited to pick his brain because she had a future ahead of her. All I had was the trial and William.

Lauren shook her head in response to something that Mark said. Her lips moved and I wished that I could read them. When she finished talking, she glanced in my direction with an expression that indicated that she knew I was watching. The sunglasses weren't enough of a disguise after all.

The two of them stood up. My eyes widened as they hugged, but it was a chaste thing and they pulled apart without anything more happening. They parted, Mark disappearing into the bathroom and Lauren walking in my direction.

"What a coincidence seeing you here," she said.

"I wanted to make sure you were safe."

"What could happen to me here?" she asked and gestured toward the people around us. "I know how to take care of myself."

"Everyone thinks that," I replied.

"Well, he didn't try to hit on me."

"No? It seemed like the two of you were awfully close."

"He mostly just talked about law school. He told me that he would help me apply to his alma mater."

"Did he say anything else?"

Lauren hesitated.

"Yeah. He asked me what else I knew about the murders. Things that maybe were overlooked during the trial."

"I told you that there's something shady going on. Do you think that he has something to do with it?"

"It seemed more like he was investigating. He kept talking about how great William's lawyers are and then, in the same sentence, expressed frustration that he couldn't do the job himself."

I understood the feeling. I was frustrated with how little Lauren had asked him in return. Some people loved serial killers because the violence intrigued them, and others, like Lauren, were obsessed with innocence. They couldn't imagine any man, never mind a handsome one like William, committing the acts that they were accused of doing. She didn't need to have a moral rationalization the way that I did because she believed she was in love with a man who had been falsely accused and that justified her actions. The problem was that she couldn't ask too many questions, otherwise her fragile ethics might start to crack. If Mark was involved with the murders in any way, she didn't want to know.

"I like you, Hannah. I do," Lauren said before she left. "But it's weird to spy on people. Just text me or something next time."

I stopped myself from telling her that she would've been grateful for my presence if anyone had attempted to murder her.

"Sure thing," I said.

She left the coffee shop and I was about to do the same when Mark reappeared and sat back down at the table. He looked at his phone for a couple of minutes, peering at the screen through a pair of reading glasses, when an attractive woman approached and tapped him on the shoulder. He stood up and they hugged.

The woman sat down across from him. She looked closer to my age than to Lauren's, though she was still decades younger than Mark. I was too far away to see if there was a wedding ring on her finger. She wore a shift dress and heels, an outfit better suited to a business professional than someone meeting for a sexual affair, but there was an intimacy to their conversation that indicated familiarity. The woman made me feel unattractive on both a physical and a mental level; she was prettier than I was and my jealousy of that made me feel ugly on the inside too. It seemed ridiculous that Cindy had ever gauged me to be a threat when this was who her husband was meeting with alone.

Like in his conversation with Lauren, Mark did most of the talking. He was the kind of man who dominated a room without noticing because to him that kind of domination seemed normal. At one point, he reached out for her hand and rubbed her fingers between his. It wasn't an open-mouth kiss, but it wasn't nothing.

Something about the way they were interacting made me self-conscious, like watching a sex tape of two people who didn't know they were being filmed. Despite the publicness of their meeting, their low tones and close heads indicated something private.

The woman nodded along in agreement to everything he said, occasionally finding the space to interject single-word answers. She glanced in my direction once in acknowledgment of my stares and I quickly turned and looked in the other direction. I wanted to tell her to run, though I wasn't sure what she'd be running from. Surely, she knew that she was speaking to a man whose son was accused of serial murder.

Their faces were serious. The end of an affair, perhaps? *I can't see you anymore,* I imagined Mark saying. *My son needs me right now.* He would be the sort of man who would break bad news in a public space so that the woman wouldn't cry. *The eyes of the world are upon my family. I don't want to drag you down with us,* he would say convincingly.

When Mark finished his monologue, the two of them stood up and hugged again. They exited together and I watched through the window as they got into separate cars. Whatever was happening, Mark wasn't fucking or killing her. At least not at that particular moment. I had to stop myself from being disappointed. It wasn't fair of me to wish ill upon another woman because it would make for an exciting story to tell Dotty and Lauren. Instead, all I had was Mark talking, and I didn't quite know what to do with that.

27

I spent the rest of the evening doing frantic searches across social media and the forum trying to figure out who the woman was, staying up late into the night and nearly sleeping through my alarm in the morning, only to have her identity revealed upon the start of testimony. Her name was Alexis Hutchington and she was a longtime friend of William and the Thompson family.

The bright lights of the courthouse only emphasized her beauty. Her skin was smooth, devoid of the creases that had already started to plague my own forehead. I wondered if she did Botox. Though her friendship with William probably meant that my suspicions of an affair between her and Mark were misguided, I was still wary of Alexis.

"How would you describe your relationship with William?" the defense attorney asked.

Alexis fiddled with the necklace at her throat. Even at a distance, I could tell that her manicure was perfect.

"We've been friends since we were ten or eleven, somewhere around there," she said.

I experienced an aching jealousy that she'd met versions of William that I'd never know. For better or for worse, the William that I knew would always be a man accused of serial murder, the kind of identity that was impossible to escape.

"How did you and William meet?"

"Our parents are friends. Our dads played golf together. The two of us would always sneak off together during parties."

I imagined the two of them finding hiding places in the kind of mansion that I'd only ever seen on television. Later, as teenagers, they would abscond with liquor, getting drunk before they were legally allowed. My own high school friends were too well-behaved for such behavior. I didn't even know where to get ahold of alcohol if I wanted it. Those poor little rich kids, having to entertain themselves while their parents threw parties.

"Tell us about your friendship as adults."

"We see—saw—each other every couple of weeks. I recently went through a bad breakup and William was very supportive of me during that time."

What did she mean by "supportive"? Had William comforted her while she cried? Brought her ice cream and watched the 2005 version of *Pride & Prejudice* the way that Meghan used to for me? Or was it a different kind of comfort? One where the two of them made love and agreed that if they weren't married by the time that they were forty, they would marry each other. I wished that Bentley was at the trial so that I could question him. Maybe he knew things about their friendship that Alexis was unwilling to admit on the stand.

"Did you ever hear him mention the names of Anna Leigh, Kimberly, Jill, or Emma?" the defense attorney asked.

Alexis swallowed.

"He mentioned Emma before they went on a date together. He was excited. Not any of the other names, no."

"What did he tell you about Emma specifically?"

"He told me that he was excited for the date. William has always been very focused on his career and I think that's made dating difficult for him. He said that Emma was smart. They had great conversations."

"Did you ever get the sense that he was going to harm Emma?"

"No, no. Of course not. I didn't think—I never thought—that William would harm anyone. He's always cared so much about other people."

I looked at the back of William's head as he gazed at his long-time friend.

If William had killed those other women, what had stopped him from killing Alexis? I was no killer, but looking at the woman on the stand, she seemed a perfect kind of victim—beautiful and easy for him to access. Maybe he cared for her too much or not enough for her to die. I couldn't decide whether to be jealous of her because of her closeness with William or relieved that she was still living as proof that William could spend time with a woman without needing her to die.

I comforted myself with the fact that I was the one that William was writing letters to, the one that he'd asked to be his girlfriend. No matter what Alexis knew or had experienced, I had something she didn't and I liked that. I took the packet of letters out of my purse and held them close to me like a woman grabbing her boyfriend's arm in a public space in order to stake her claim.

28

Bentley returned to the trial at the end of the week, without Virginia. I waved at him enthusiastically when I saw him in line for security and was hurt when he gave me a mere hand raise in response. I worried that I had misconstrued the depth of our friendship after the night we'd spent talking. He'd been so protective of me, first rescuing me from having to converse with the older man who had called me pretty and then warning me against getting too close to William, and I took that protectiveness as a sign of intimacy. It was possible that I was wrong. I was always misreading the things that men wanted from me.

The defense moved to questioning witnesses about the things they'd seen in the hours before the women disappeared. Nothing they had to say proved conclusively that William was not a killer; rather, the suggestion was that there were potential killers all around us.

I wrote in my notebook:

- *Jill had a client who repeatedly asked her on dates.*
- *A drug bust went down at the gas station shortly before Kimberly's death.*
- *There are a limited number of cameras with views of the parking lot at the building where Anna Leigh worked. Anyone could've been hiding in the blind spots.*

Look at all the bad men, the defense tried to say.

Things had been tense with Lauren since she'd caught me spying on her and Mark in the coffee shop. She pointedly sat down on the other side of Dotty rather than next to me.

"Honey, Hannah was only trying to protect you," Dotty tried to intervene on my behalf.

"I don't need her to do that. I'm an adult," Lauren insisted.

The statement made me jealous, if only because I struggled to conceptualize myself as an adult even in my early thirties. Whenever any small inconvenience surfaced, I longed for someone older, wiser, and with more money to come fix it for me.

It surprised me how much Lauren's snubbing stung. The three of us had bonded quickly over our love for William and it hadn't occurred to me that the glue was so fragile or how much I depended upon the two of them to get through the days. It made me miss Meghan and I started typing several text messages before deleting them and putting my phone out of reach.

Another packet of letters from William arrived. The front desk employee looked at me when she handed them over like I was going to open them in front of her. It felt like she'd asked me to send her nudes.

I took them back to my room and read them while eating

spoonfuls of peanut butter. Every meal reminded me of my precarious financial state. I'd always struggled with money, but the difference was that I also used to have a paycheck, regardless of how insufficient it was. I was caught in the catch-22 of wanting to splurge on food that comforted my anxiety and having anxiety about spending money on food.

Dearest Hannah, the first letter began.

The only way I've been able to get through these days is by disassociating. Physically, my body is in a courtroom. Mentally, I'm somewhere far away with you. At first, it seemed silly to daydream because I knew they were impossibilities. Then I realized that daydreams are the only thing that they can't take away from me. I think that treating you well would be a type of justice in itself.

You mentioned once that you've never been able to take a real vacation. In truth, I haven't either. I always meant to go places—Japan, Iceland, Brazil—but my job was so demanding that I never found the time. Traveling was something that I was going to do in the future when I made partner or had a family. It never occurred to me that the future might not exist. Now I dream of taking you to the beach. As much as I love visiting cities, the allure of the ocean is that it disappears into nothing. This is both calming and exciting. Anything could be over the horizon or below in the depths.

We would stay in one of those bungalows that is on top of the water. At night, the sound of waves lapping would put us to sleep after our lovemaking (I hope this isn't too forward to say). In the daytime, we would drink those ridiculous beach cocktails and eat any foods that our hearts desired. We would forget what day it was, what time it was.

We would get to know each other, really know each other, in ways that are impossible with letters. I would throw my phone into the sea so that I could devote all my attention to you and you would devote yours to me. I would make sure that you had everything you ever wanted, no matter what the cost.

My lips were gummy with peanut butter as I opened the next letter. Nowhere within William's fantasies was there mention of if and when he might kill me, but the ocean was good for that. He could rent a boat and dump my body in the sea. No one would know until my body washed ashore. There were ravines in the ocean too, places where the seafloor dropped off and all the really scary fish lived. I filled in the parts of the fantasy that he wouldn't, couldn't name.

Dearest Hannah,
There are days that I wish that the trial were over already so at least I could know my fate. I don't think that I ever fully understood the pain of purgatory before this. I understand why people plead guilty if only to end their suffering sooner.
Are you going to stay with me when they find me guilty? I can't blame you if you want to stray. It used to make me angry when people valued me only for my money and not what I had to offer, and now I realize that I valued myself in that same way. I wish I could buy you flowers and diamonds. I

wish I could hold you at night as you fall asleep. I wish that I could make promises that I could keep.

William wrote all the things that I'd wanted men to tell me for years and it left me with the same sensation I had when I finally purchased a food item that I was craving, only to discover that it wasn't what I wanted after all. I wanted him to tell me about his pain, his violence, who had hurt him, and whom he hurt in return.

I knew that William couldn't give me those answers even if he wanted to, at least not until the trial was over. He wasn't going to incriminate himself to satisfy my curiosity and I wasn't going to ask. I needed to talk to the person who had the answers that William was withholding, who knew the trauma of his childhood, the havoc he had wreaked.

I needed to talk to Bentley.

29

Despite telling Lauren that I was going to stop following people, I followed Bentley to the bar that we'd previously gone to together. Though we weren't having an affair, our communication was limited like we were. Cindy was already suspicious of me and I didn't want Virginia to feel the same. I saw the way that she clung to Bentley's arm like he was a balloon that might drift away if she let go. It was okay, I decided, to follow someone if it was for a really good reason.

The trial was almost over, the defense winding down its argument, and time was running out. Soon, I would lose my access to the extended Thompson family and would become one of those women obsessed with the appeals process. I needed to talk to Bentley again before that happened. I wasn't sure what I was looking for, only that there was something there, hidden beneath the surface.

He went straight to the bar after the trial finished for the day. I could tell from the way that the bartender greeted him that they knew each other, meaning that Bentley's early evening drinking was habitual rather than a one-off. I watched him scroll through his phone for several minutes before I approached him.

"Hey," I said.

He jumped in surprise and then relaxed when he saw me.

"If it isn't William's girlfriend," he said in greeting.

We both laughed like it was a joke rather than the truth.

"Let me buy you a drink," he said.

Even though I was the one who had approached him, it felt like he was the one who had approached me. Bentley held that kind of charm, the man who was in control of every situation.

"Do you want to play a game of pool?" I asked once we were both armed with glasses of bourbon.

Bentley grinned.

"It's been a minute since I've played," he said. "You'll probably be better than me."

Bentley was much better at pool than I was.

"We had a pool table in the basement of my fraternity house," Bentley explained. "We played a lot of games down there, beer pong, pool, you name it."

"I was a nerd in college. I spent most of my time studying," I said, taking a bad shot.

"You didn't go to parties or anything? You seem like you would be wild at parties." Bentley winked at me as one of the balls rolled into a hole.

"No, that came later, when I was in my twenties. I had a lot of social anxiety in college. Then I realized that alcohol existed and things got easier."

"That's the truth." Bentley laughed.

After we finished playing pool, we ordered a round of shots, followed by more cocktails. My body had taken on a warm, slippery quality.

"Where's your wife?" I asked.

We were seated across from each other at a small table.

"She's at home with the kids. I had a few things to take care of in the city, so I decided to stay."

"It seems like you spend a lot of time apart."

Bentley looked sad.

"We've been distant lately, yeah. She wants to blame it all on the trial, but it's more than that. It's everything. She's really devoted to the kids, which is great and all—she's a great mom. I just wish that it didn't come at the expense of us. It's hard to find time alone and any alone time that we did have has been eaten up by this trial. She thinks that everything is going to go back to normal after this. I'm not so sure."

"I can't imagine what it's been like for you."

"My father is having a hard time too," he continued. "He won't say it, of course. Mark Thompson would never admit to having any kind of difficulty. He's convinced that William's going to be found innocent and everything will return to normal. He's already talking about suing the state for negligence."

I made what I hoped was a sympathetic face.

"I think that boomer men have an especially difficult time expressing their emotions," I said. "I can always tell when my dad is having a hard time because he'll get really into one of his hobbies. Like one year he got really into bird-watching. Another time, he bought all these expensive oil paints and declared that he was going to 'master the art of painting' and gave it up after two months. I think it might be cheaper and less time-consuming if he would go see a therapist."

Bentley laughed and shook his head.

"I wish that my father would exorcise his demons through bird-watching," he said.

"Maybe his demons are too big for birds," I replied.

There was a still moment between us as we sipped our drinks and thought of our respective fathers. There was a pang of home-sickness in my chest that I didn't realize existed.

"Thank you for listening. I can see why William likes you," Bentley said, breaking the silence.

I wanted Bentley to compliment me more. To tell me how kind, understanding, and maybe even how pretty I was. Unfortunately, there were more important matters to discuss.

"Last time we talked, you mentioned that there are things about William that I don't know. I'm starting to think you're right," I said.

Bentley looked alarmed.

"Did he say something?"

"No, not exactly. It's more about what he won't say. I know that it sounds stupid since we're only writing letters, but sometimes I feel like William and I know everything about each other. I'm closer to him than I've been with anyone in a long time. At the same time, he's keeping secrets from me. He doesn't talk about the trial in any substantive way. He hasn't even said whether or not he's guilty, which feels like an admission of guilt in itself."

Bentley took a sip of his drink and sighed.

"I'm really not supposed to say anything. I don't want to get my brother in more trouble than he's already in," he said.

"Please? I won't tell anyone. I promise."

He looked me up and down as though looking for a wire.

"You're not an aspiring journalist, are you? One of those murder podcast people? They've approached my family, you know.

They think that they're like some secondary arm of the courts now. There's the judge, the jury, and the podcast hosts."

"No, no, I swear."

Bentley sighed again.

"I always wanted a brother," he began. "Even though I was young, I still remember being lonely. I thought that if I had a brother, it would mean that there would always be someone to play with. It wasn't like that though. I thought he would be able to play with me right away and instead, my parents brought home this tiny, screaming thing. He was always crying, day and night. When I had kids of my own, I realized that he had colic, but I didn't know that at the time. Eventually he got bigger, stronger, and didn't scream quite as much. It was still impossible to play together. William was always competitive, even as a toddler. As soon as he could talk, he would tell me that our mother was his mother and not mine. Everything was his and his alone. We used to get into fights—not an ordinary kind of roughhousing, as some people would have you believe, but real fights. There was one time that I remember that he ran after me with a knife and I had to lock myself in our parents' bedroom because I was scared that he was going to try to kill me."

Bentley paused to take a sip of his drink.

"No one ever believed me. I was older than him, so how could he be a threat to me? I used to get in trouble when I fought back, no matter how much he hurt me. I was always supposed to be the bigger person, even when he caused me physical pain. In public, it was like a switch flipped and suddenly, he was charming and articulate. Like a little grown-up, people said. It didn't occur to them that kids aren't supposed to be like little grown-ups, that maybe that was an indicator that something was wrong. The injuries he caused me are just the start of it. There are other ways that he's hurt me, things that are worse than a broken arm."

With that, Bentley swallowed everything that remained in his glass like he was trying to wash the memories away.

"Do you want another one? I need another one," he asked.

I nodded and handed him my empty glass. No matter that I was already drunk.

"My father encouraged it all," Bentley said when he came back. "He thinks that competition is what inspires people to greatness. It was like he wanted us to fight each other. One time, William broke my arm. Snapped it clean in half. I think my father was almost proud of him. He lied when he took me to the emergency room, said that I got hurt playing soccer. There were other instances like that, times when William hurt me and I had to make up a story for cover. He liked to try to pin things on me too. It was a game for him. He'd hide empty liquor bottles, weed, and condoms in my room and our parents would find them and get mad. One time, my room started to reek. I couldn't figure out what the smell was. For a while, I thought it was me. Then I found a dead rabbit hidden beneath my bed."

I put a hand to my mouth.

"Why didn't you say something?" I asked.

"He swore up and down that he didn't know what I was talking about. He suggested that the rabbit had found its own way into the house and died there. My parents believed him too. William's very convincing. He was a great lawyer. It's too bad that he's finally destroyed himself." Bentley paused to take a sip of his drink. "The rabbit's not even the worst thing he did either. There are things that I can't say. That I'm not allowed to say. I know that he's in jail, but I'm still scared of what he might do."

Bentley finished his drink. I looked at him apologetically.

"Sorry," I said. "I know this is a weird conversation."

"Can I ask you a question?" he said.

"Of course."

"What is it that you want out of this? Best-case scenario: Let's say that William is innocent. Either he's found guilty and spends the rest of his life in jail as an innocent man or he's acquitted, and then what? Are you going to settle down? Get married? Have children? Is that what you want from my brother? And what if he's guilty? Do you want to be with a man who's killed four women?"

I looked down at my hands. My nails bitten to nearly nothing.

"I don't know," I said.

I didn't. The future was a gangplank on a ship at the end of the world.

I looked at Bentley. Our eyes met.

"I take it that you think he's guilty," I said.

"If you want my advice, Hannah, I would leave. Get out of here. Go home and find yourself a nice, normal boyfriend. Someone boring, an accountant. Forget about my brother."

I threw back the remnants of my whiskey and Coke, crunching ice cubes between my teeth. I took a breath.

"I'm going to go use the bathroom," I said.

There was a particular type of drunken lumbering that happened between the stool and the bathroom of a bar. A moment when I went from feeling relatively sober to forgetting how to move my arms correctly. I hadn't wanted to disrupt Bentley and thus, I'd been sitting in relative discomfort for quite a while and in that time I'd gotten significantly drunker.

Something stopped me from reaching the door of the women's restroom. There was a tugging at my arm that startled me.

"Bentley," I managed to say before I found myself pinned against a wall, his lips on mine.

That was how I found myself kissing the brother of the serial killer that I was dating.

I liked to think that had I been sober, I would've pushed him away immediately. Instead, I reciprocated the kiss. It was nice to be close to someone after months of physical solitude. I could've also made the argument that kissing Bentley was almost like kissing William. After all, they were of similar build, had the same eyes and hair. But I was conscious, even in that moment, of the differences between the two men. Namely, that one was my boyfriend who was on trial for serial murder and the other was a married father of two.

It stopped as abruptly as it had started.

Bentley pulled away and wordlessly turned, disappearing into the men's room. After a pause, I went into the women's room, my heart pounding. My bladder was still very full and it was a relief to empty it.

The weight of what had just occurred hit me as I flushed the toilet. Bentley and I had kissed. *No,* I wanted to say. *He kissed me.* The guilt in my stomach indicated that though Bentley had made the first move, that wasn't the whole truth. Bentley had kissed me and I had kissed him back.

I've been so lonely, I tried to tell myself.

He's giving me information about William. I'm doing it for us, I thought as I washed my hands.

While my brain rationalized my actions, I considered the next steps. I was too embarrassed to bring Bentley back to my crappy hotel and he couldn't bring me to the rental that he stayed at with his parents. I imagined Cindy's face if I walked through the door. Maybe we could get a hotel room together, something fancy. I imagined us lying in bed while I grilled him about William, a kind of sexual espionage.

It never occurred to me to let things end there, for the kiss to be just a kiss. I was always escalating things with men far beyond what they were meant to be and then wondering why I left every situation with a wound.

I exited the bathroom expecting to see Bentley at our table and found it empty. I took out my phone and scrolled social media while I awaited his return. Meghan had posted a photo of tasting wedding cakes with her fiancé, and Max a series of pictures from a recent punk show, the last one featuring him with his arm around Reese. The baby of another friend took his first steps. Someone that I'd met once several years earlier was vacationing in Italy. I scowled and put my phone back in my purse. Bentley still hadn't returned.

I went to the bar and ordered another drink.

"Do you want to start a tab?" the bartender asked.

"I think I already have one," I told him.

"You did, but Thompson paid for all your drinks before he left."

"He left?"

"Yeah, a little while ago."

"Oh. I guess I don't need a drink, then."

I looked around again like Bentley was going to reappear. He didn't.

The sting of his disappearance didn't hit me until I was in an Uber on the way back to the hotel, leaving my car behind. In a larger sense, it was good that we hadn't left together; he was married and I was dating his brother. In the moment, though, I couldn't help but wonder if there was something about me that had turned him off. I breathed into my hand to determine if my breath smelled bad and opened a compact mirror to examine my face. I looked the same as I ever did and maybe that wasn't good enough. The Uber driver didn't ask what was wrong when I started crying.

I rooted around in my purse for money for the vending machine when I got back to the hotel and came up empty. The hunger was psychic rather than physical, but that didn't make it any less uncomfortable.

I took out my notebook and a pen.

Your brother kissed me tonight, I wrote and then crossed out.

I'm so lonely without you. I wish you could be here to hold me.

~~I wish you would be honest with me. If you were, I would've never been out with him to begin with.~~

I like to imagine our future together too. We could leave the country. I've always liked the idea of being an expat. We could move to a Scandinavian country. Somewhere cold and cozy. Build a house full of reading nooks. Or we could go to the beach. I hear that Thailand is beautiful and it seems like a good place for a person to escape to.

~~I worry that the mystery is what attracts me to you and that if/when I find out the truth, I'll lose interest the same way that men lose interest in me when they find out that I'm an ordinary, boring girl.~~

I'm not sure if I ever want children. Definitely a dog, which is almost like having a child.

~~I think I like it that you're violent. There's a part of me that likes the suspense of being with someone that could hurt me at any moment. I always knew that Max was going to break my heart. It wasn't a physical breaking, but that's semantics.~~

I like big dogs that don't know that they're big. The kind that still tries to sit in laps and takes up half the bed.

~~I have fantasies about being tied up and have always been too embarrassed to tell anyone about it. It's a cliché to want someone to take control because I'm tired of having to be in control of myself, but desire has never cared about literary tropes. Will you tie me up, William? Will you make me fear for my life?~~

No matter what happens in the coming weeks, a future will exist. There are ways to find goodness in even the darkest moments of our lives.

~~Sometimes I think about what it would be like if you killed me. It's about the mourning rather than the death itself, like my life would have more meaning to it in retrospect. Think about all the people that would confess their love for me if I were no longer around to hold them accountable.~~

You've helped me so much, even from afar. Without you, I would still be working my stupid job, living in my shitty apartment. After this, I'm going to do bigger and better things.

~~At least if I die, they'll know for sure who killed me.~~

30

I thought that Bentley would avoid me after that night. Surely, the kiss—though a physical act—was a reflection of emotional closeness, and in my experience men avoided women they felt close to. In my more rational moments, that was how I made sense of Bentley's actions. He had spent months holding everything in while being hounded by journalists and podcast enthusiasts alike before finally confessing his childhood trauma to me. That vulnerability had spilled out from his lips, first as words and then as a kiss, before he remembered who I was, what I looked like, and his wife waiting at home, and had absconded into the night.

In my less rational moments, I imagined that Bentley was so overcome with desire that he was unable to stop himself from kissing me and had to leave to prevent things from going further. Considering that his wife was significantly more attractive than I was, that seemed unlikely.

Either way, I thought he would be as embarrassed as I was.

Instead, Bentley went out of his way to say hello on Monday morning. Virginia was back, their hands clasped together like a couple in love. If she was threatened by me, there was nothing in her demeanor to show it.

"Hi, ladies. How are we doing today?" he asked the three of us.

"Great," Dotty said and batted her fake eyelashes at him.

I barely managed to utter, "Fine," as Lauren replied, "Good, thanks."

I didn't tell them what had happened. How could I? Our entire friendship was built around our feelings for William and I'd betrayed him. The night replayed in my head as I listened to the closing arguments. Everyone looked tired. The female prosecutor's roots were grown out and it gave me some solace to know that she wasn't a natural blonde.

"To fail to prosecute William Thompson would not only be a failure of justice," she said. "It would mean setting a monster loose on the world."

"We're all for justice," the defense responded, "but true justice means knowing that the right person has been sent to prison."

After the closing arguments were finished and the jury left to deliberate, Dotty, Lauren, and I went out to dinner to say goodbye. The weirdness between Lauren and me after I had spied on her coffee date with Mark had seemingly dissipated, if only because of our impending goodbyes. It was easy to like a person when you knew that you were never going to see each other again.

We went to a Mexican restaurant where I put one chip after another in my mouth.

"Do you want more?" the server asked.

In a different time and place, I would've said no. Chips were unhealthy and if I ate too many, it would give me a stomachache. The days, however, had taken on an air of unreality that made health an impossible concern. I licked the salt off the rim of my margarita as I dove into the second bowl.

"I'm going to miss the two of you. It's so good that we had each other through all of this," Dotty said.

Her usage of "this" might as well have referred to an amorphous blob, for all the ground that it was expected to cover.

"What are you doing after this, Dotty?" Lauren asked.

"My husband and I have been talking recently. I think we're going to try to work things out," she said. "Besides, kids need their mothers. I've been away for too long."

I suspected that somewhere inside that had been Dotty's plan all along. She had used William to punish her husband and he'd fulfilled the terms of his sentence.

"What are you doing next, Lauren?" Dotty asked.

"The semester is starting in a couple of weeks. I'm going to go home for a few days first and then drive to school. I'm looking forward to being back on campus. After all those hours at the trial, maybe classes will actually seem interesting."

"Remind me of your major," I said.

"Criminal justice," she replied, the obvious answer for a girl who couldn't stop talking about killers.

"What about you, Hannah? What are you doing next?"

There was a pause. My tongue felt sticky like I'd eaten a mouthful of peanut butter, a feeling that I was all too familiar with.

Earlier in the week I'd called my mother for the first time in over a month. After some back-and-forth ("Why haven't you called?" and "I've been worried about you"), I confessed that I'd lost my job, had maxed out my credit cards, and needed to move home for a while. I couldn't remember ever having been so honest with her, even when I was small and still considered her a poten-

tial confidante. It was worse than stripping down naked in front
of a man for the first time in a room with unflattering lighting.
As soon as the words were out of my mouth, I wanted to reel them
back in and replace them with lies about how great everything
was, how much I looked forward to the future.

My mother got very quiet for a minute, so quiet that I thought
the line had been disconnected.

"Mom? Are you still there?"

"Of course, you can move home," she said finally. "Whatever
you need. We'll support you."

How it crushed me to shatter her idyllic notions of who I was.

"I'm moving to my parents' house in Minnesota," I told Dotty
and Lauren.

Their faces morphed into pity that was thankfully broken by
the server bringing our entrées. I smiled my biggest smile, like I
wasn't bothered at all, and ordered another margarita.

"Do you think they're going to give him the death penalty?"
Lauren asked.

None of us thought that he was going to be found not guilty,
not even Lauren, who was so certain of his innocence. The question was whether they would give him life in prison or sentence
him to death.

"Yes," Dotty said. "I think they will."

Lauren shook her head.

"That's so wrong. Did you know that it actually costs more
for a state to kill someone than it does to keep them in
prison? I mean, I obviously think it's wrong for the state to kill
someone to begin with, but it doesn't even make sense financially."

"At least they don't use the electric chair anymore," Dotty
said.

"Actually," Lauren butted in, "the injections are worse. There are people that they've tried to kill that haven't died. Also, the companies that make the injection drugs are refusing to supply them, so the states have to get them through illegal means."

"I still think it's better than the chair," Dotty replied.

I knew what she meant. The electric chair was a gruesome image that made her feel uncomfortable. She didn't care what the person who was dying felt as long as she could maintain her own ease.

If only, I thought, *people could elect to be killed in the same way that they themselves had killed, and then William could die with a rope wrapped around his neck.*

"It might actually be good to get the death penalty," Dotty continued. "Then he won't have to rot in prison for the rest of his life."

"It's always better to be alive," Lauren told her.

"I'm just saying, prison is really bad. Is that really how William wants to spend the rest of his days?"

"Maybe he can really find himself," Lauren said.

"I think he knows who he is," I replied.

I was going to miss the two of them in a weird, convoluted kind of way. They were the only people who really understood how I felt about William. Their existence implied that maybe I wasn't as messed up as I thought I was—and everyone needed people like that in their lives. Even people who were ordinary. People who weren't in love with a serial killer.

It made me sick to look at my bill, or maybe I'd eaten too much queso. At the very least, I needed enough credit left on my cards in order to make it back to Minnesota, and as it was, there was no certainty of that happening. Ironically, the more anxious I became about my finances, the more money I seemed to spend. I ate every meal like it was the last I'd ever be able to afford.

Dotty hugged me in the parking lot.

"You'll be okay," she said into my ear.

I resented the implication that I wasn't already okay, that okayness was something I needed to work toward in the future.

"See you on decision day," I said.

"Merely a formality," she replied before turning and walking away.

Something I admired about Dotty was her unwavering belief that William was guilty and how she loved him anyway. Lauren and I still played at the possibility of innocence, however minuscule, as though that absolved us of any moral sin we might have committed by being in love with such a man. If I was being honest, on that night I had no doubt about whether he'd done it. William was a killer, and though there were injustices in the criminal justice system, William going to prison wasn't one of them.

When I made the decision to go to the ravine, it wasn't because I was looking for some last-minute evidence to get William released. I went because I was a little drunk and I knew that returning home without visiting the ravine was like going to Paris and not going to see the *Mona Lisa*. It was my way of saying goodbye to William, to the trial, to the person I'd been in those weeks and the person I was going to become after William was locked away indefinitely.

Before William was caught, the ravine had been a popular destination for members of the forum who liked to go and take pictures under the guise of investigation. I held myself back from calling it what it really was: a type of serial killer tourism. The same people, I knew, would shell out money to stay in the Lizzie Borden house, which had since become a bed-and-breakfast.

I drove there recklessly, passing through yellow lights that were very nearly red. It was like the ravine was a grocery store about to close before a storm and I desperately needed a loaf of bread.

I had always pictured it as being somewhere rural. The kind of place where even if someone managed to survive, they would never make it back to civilization again. Instead, the ravine was surrounded by the signs of suburban America. There were mid-level chain restaurants in a nearby strip mall, places that I had never eaten at but were recognizable nonetheless. It was amazing the way that Outback Steakhouse had penetrated my life without requiring me to ever step inside of one. There were several hotels, including another location of the hotel chain that I was staying in. The parking lots were busy with the flows and pauses of vehicles waiting for pedestrians to cross through traffic to get to their own cars.

Any light that remained from the setting sun was immediately blocked out by the trees as I got out of my car and made my way down the side of a hill. I turned on my phone flashlight and chastised myself for not being better prepared. The ground was littered with discarded chip wrappers, half-drunk soda bottles, and the occasional used condom. This was no nature preserve.

At the bottom, the sound of traffic disappeared. I shivered despite the July heat and looked around at the dense brush, a sight that the women themselves had never been able to see because they were already dead upon arrival.

I imagined William driving to the ravine. Unlike me, he

would've driven carefully. After all, it was erratic driving and a stolen license plate that ultimately doomed Bundy. "Drive like you have a body in the back of your car" was as good an appeal to safety as I'd ever heard. He would've already had the spot picked out before he killed Anna Leigh because that was the type of man that he was.

No one would've noticed William or, if they did, they wouldn't have cared. He looked so innocuous. Even I thought that the first time I laid eyes on his picture and dismissed him as a possible killer. He was a man who was welcomed wherever he was, regardless of the baggage he had stored in the back of his car.

It was almost tender the way in which he had lifted the women out of his trunk, like a husband carrying his new wife into their wedding suite. A final moment of sweetness before everything was lost to them.

Once the women were tipped over the edge of the ravine, they would've rolled all the way down. That rolling was likely responsible for most of the injuries that they had sustained after they were already dead. There was nothing gentle about the earth.

By the time they reached the bottom, their transition from women into bodies was complete. Vermin would begin to feast upon them, rendering them unrecognizable. In the world above, life continued without them, their loved ones still unaware that there was anything to be missed.

Fire ants bit at my ankles as I stood there. I should've been grateful to be alive, to experience the ravine as the four dead women had never been able to, but I could only feel disappointment at the lack of answers it gave me.

Bentley was probably right. The best thing to do was to go back to Minnesota and find a nice, boring man. The type of person who got up in the morning, made coffee, shoveled the walk in the wintertime, and whose deepest secret was that he occasionally watched some porn. There were a lot of people who lived that life who were ostensibly happy. Sure, there wasn't the thrilling tickle in their stomach every time they thought about their love, but who needed that when they had someone willing to put ingredients in the Crock-Pot before work?

As I emerged from the depths of the ravine, headlights flashed in the parking lot. I scurried back to my car, suddenly frightened in the way that I sometimes became when returning from the bathroom in the middle of the night, convinced that a monster had materialized beneath my bed in my absence.

I exhaled as I sat in my front seat, ensuring that the doors were locked around me. The headlights that had been pointed in my direction turned and parked in front of one of the chain restaurants. There were no monsters under the bed after all.

I wouldn't learn until morning the danger that I was in that night, at which point my fear would seem like a prescient and precious thing. Perhaps it was better that I didn't know because I wouldn't have run away. I would've embraced it, let the ravine take me as it had taken the other women, my body consumed by vermin and garbage.

31

I woke to a bunch of missed calls and text messages from Carole.

The last time I'd heard from her was immediately after I was fired and I hadn't bothered to pick up.

"Millennials don't talk on the phone," I'd told her once, which she found ridiculous.

She hadn't left a voicemail after that last call, which meant that I never found out what she wanted and I didn't bother calling her back. I figured that I probably took one of her coffee mugs by accident.

It turned out that the reason Carole or anyone else hadn't left me a voicemail wasn't because I was friendless and alone, but because my mailbox was full, which she informed me of in the first of a long string of text messages.

Hannah call me back.

Are you OK?

Please tell me that you're not the body that was found.

My fingers went to the forum before my brain even registered the word "body." It was a reflex at that point, like breathing. My phone already knew where I wanted to go, which at times I resented. Algorithms were proof that there was more to love than simply predicting what someone wanted.

I didn't have to scroll to figure out what happened. The news presented itself to me like raindrops in a downpour.

Another body had been found in the ravine.

In the days after 9/11, I had a friend who repeatedly talked about the vacation her family had taken to New York two months prior to the attack.

"We were right there," she said. "It almost happened to us."

I didn't understand her fixation. There she was, fully intact, half a country away, and accepting comforting hugs like she'd been through trauma. There were enough people who died or who were almost dead or first responders who were still suffering health consequences years later. Why did we need to add to the tally? It was like she needed to figure out her relationship to the event in order to make it mean something.

I understood, in a realer sense, how she felt when I read the word "ravine." I reached up and touched my head and came away with a leaf, which I crumbled into pieces between my fingers. I had the uncanny feeling of being both alive and not, like a cat inside of a box that no one wanted to open.

I was right there. It almost happened to me. There was a twinge of disappointment, even though I was happy to be alive.

The forum was doing whatever the virtual version of screaming was.

"How could this have happened? William's in jail."

"Maybe he's innocent."

"It's probably a copycat."

"What is up with that ravine? It's like a magnet for death."

"This is a failure on every level."

I saw forum users that I hadn't seen in months, people who'd long since lost interest with no new murders to contemplate.

"What does this mean?" they asked. "What do we do now?"

They were upset, but they were excited too, or maybe that was just me projecting my own emotions onto them. That's what was nice about people online. They felt whatever I wanted them to feel, their emotions an extension of my own.

I went into the bathroom and splashed water on my face. There was a smudge of dirt on my forehead that I scrubbed away with a washcloth. I kept waiting for something to happen, a lightning bolt to appear in the blue sky outside of my window. Instead, the world continued as normal around me.

I remembered what Bentley had said that night in the bar, how he was worried that William could still hurt him even though he was in jail. It was too much of a coincidence for the murder to be totally random. Surely, it was connected somehow. One last-ditch effort from William to gain his freedom as though his power was so great that he could now kill women with his mind.

I had to give credit to Carole, who was the first and only person to check in on me after the body was found. She'd woken at her normal early hour to do her meditation practice in the quiet of the morning and, despite her best efforts, was unable to resist looking at her phone before she settled into contemplation. The news of the body caused such a rupture that she skipped meditating in favor of investigating my Instagram page, where she discovered a number of posts tagged in the Atlanta area and deduced that I was there because of William.

I was both touched and impressed by Carole's ability to figure out where I was and what I was doing, especially considering that she wasn't particularly skilled at using Instagram. Her own Instagram was entirely made up of poorly photographed pictures of her dog, Trixie, whom she'd adopted from a local rescue group.

You went to see him, didn't you? she texted.

Carole, as it turned out, knew me better than I thought she did.

It was difficult to get dressed while simultaneously refreshing the forum every few seconds to see if any more information had been released. I texted Dotty and Lauren a single word, **courthouse**, before getting in my car. There was a rumor on the forum that the police were going to hold a midmorning press conference.

The sidewalks leading to the courthouse were chaotic in a way that they hadn't been since the beginning of the trial. Police put up barricades to stop people from treading on the lawn, so people gathered wherever they could find space, some of them holding signs.

KILLERS INSPIRE KILLERS, said one.

LET WILLIAM GO, said another.

I wondered when they'd had time to make them. In times of tragedy, there were always some people who immediately turned to arts and crafts.

Dotty appeared at my side.

"Quite a development," she said.

"Yeah," I replied.

I couldn't decide whether I was a spectator or an actor. Dotty didn't know about my visit to the ravine the night before. No one did. I was the only person who knew how close to death I'd come and I was scared to mention it to anyone else lest I cast a specter of guilt upon myself.

Lauren joined us a few minutes later with a Starbucks cup in her hand. She was cheery.

"It's nice to know that William really is innocent," she said.

"Is that what you think this means?" Dotty asked her.

"Of course. What else could it be? Another woman died. The killer is clearly still out there."

"Or it's a copycat," I said, thinking of the forum.

"Or it's William's partner in murder," Dotty suggested darkly.

Lauren scoffed.

"Why can't you just take this as a good thing?" she said.

"I don't think the dead woman would think of it that way," I replied.

Lauren was silent for a long time after that. She'd forgotten that there was a woman involved, that there was anyone besides William in the world.

The Thompson family was nowhere to be seen. Likely, they were sequestered somewhere with William, trying to wrap their heads around the latest occurrence. Mark was always so certain that William was going to be found innocent. He was probably glowing at this latest body, proof that maybe his son wasn't the killer that everyone wanted to make him out to be.

Please tell me you're okay, Carole texted again, and I realized that I'd forgotten to respond. She seemed like a person from another lifetime, like when a friend from the fourth grade tried to add me on Facebook.

I'm okay, I replied without giving any additional details.

At ten, the police released the available information, which as always was unsatisfyingly sparse. The body was found in the early hours of the morning by an employee who was enjoying an early morning cigarette before his opening shift at a nearby coffee chain. The body hadn't tumbled as far as the others and he'd been shocked to see pale white skin amongst the leaves. The body, I gathered, had arrived sometime after my visit. The killer and I, like ships passing in the night.

The police went through a list of questions.

No, they didn't know if the murder was connected to the others.

No, they couldn't say if it would lead to a mistrial.

Yes, the jury had been sequestered as soon as possible.

Yes, they'd identified the body; it was that of a woman named Kelsey Jenkins.

The forum found out everything there was to know within minutes.

Before she was murdered, Kelsey Jenkins was a bartender. She had the right look for the profession, with big boobs and a tiny waist. There was something retro about her appearance, with her outdated hairstyle and streaks of chunky blond. Kelsey hadn't gone to college. She recognized that she didn't like school, but loved making drinks. She graduated from high school, started waitressing, and as soon as she could, she began tending bar.

It wasn't difficult to figure out who the regular bar patrons were. Drunk people love taking pictures. The beauty of a drunken picture is that it's easy to feel cool while the photograph is being taken, only to look back later and discover that everyone looked like a disaster.

It was reported that a lot of the bar patrons were secretly or openly in love with Kelsey. I wondered if she liked it, all that love.

It was a bar that catered to an older crowd, though young people did occasionally come in. Her admirers complicated things. The more people who were in love with a woman, the more people who became suspects when that woman was murdered.

There was the regular that everyone used to call Lizard, but now that he was sober he wanted to be called Gary. He still went by the bar in the afternoons and drank a Coke and smoked too many cigarettes. Even sober, Gary suffered from a loose tongue and was more than willing to tell anyone who asked what they wanted to know.

"Everyone loved Kelsey. What's not to love? She was hot and we were all drunk," he said in one quote.

There was the guy at the bar who kept a list of women who frequented the bar that he wanted to have sex with, none of whom he'd actually managed to woo, though he continued to show other bar patrons the list like a fucked-up kind of vision board. I knew, without even asking, that Kelsey was at the top of the list.

The longtime divorced guy who at one point was a recently divorced guy and couldn't shake the label of "divorcé." He got kicked out of the bar for spurts of time because he suffered from anger issues that were probably part of the cause of his divorce. He would've been a good suspect if only he wasn't in a period of being banned.

The kid who had recently turned twenty-one and didn't have many friends his own age and so he hung out at the bar with people a decade older than he was and mistook their age for wisdom.

The guy that Kelsey was friends with who stayed at the bar long after closing. They had probably hooked up at some point.

The guy who was still angry that she'd thrown him out and forbidden him to come back.

Her ex-boyfriend who still stopped by sometimes. He reminded me of Max with all his tattoos and his cool punk look. I
hated the way that my jaw tightened at the thought, my heartbreak like the scar on my arm that continued to ache even years
later.

The forum was thrilled with all the new suspects. No one
stated it like that, but I knew because I was thrilled too. If my
life had previously felt like it was ending, this body was a new
beginning.

If Kelsey hadn't been thrown into the ravine, her death never
would've been connected to the murders of the other four women.
She was surrounded by so many men, men with so many motives
and so much liquor. The problem was the ravine, the ways in
which the wounds on her body matched the wounds of the other
women, including details that hadn't been released to the public,
things that the detectives had kept as a gotcha card. It was like
finding a mouse in the house when another mouse was already
in the trap. Things were always more complicated than they initially seemed.

I lamented and cherished my timing. If only I'd stayed in the
ravine longer, I might know the identity of the killer. Conversely,
if I'd stayed longer, then I too might be dead. The deaths of the
women continued to circle around me. William was my boyfriend, yes, but the women were another kind of relationship that
society was reluctant to define. How it ached to be so close to the
truth and yet without resolution.

~~I can't figure out how Kelsey Jenkins is tied into everything.
Sometimes I feel like you're two different people in one; a lover
and a killer, a man in prison and a man on the hunt. The
question is, How can you continue to kill while you're behind~~

~~bars? The question is, Were you ever a killer to begin with? The question is, How do I fit into it all?~~

I showered for a long time, taking advantage of the large hotel water heaters to wash every last trace of the ravine off me.

Of course I will stay with you no matter the outcome of the trial, I wrote William, doubt already starting to set in as I recorded the words.

32

I didn't understand what William meant when he described the torture of purgatory until I had to wait for the jury to finish their deliberations. They carried on their discussions even as Kelsey lay dead, her body dissected by experts and the police questioning suspects.

I began to pack my bags, throwing shirts into suitcases in between episodes of home renovation shows on TV. Somehow, I'd acquired more things during my time in Georgia even though I couldn't remember going shopping. Life was like that, stuff piling up all around whether I wanted it to or not.

In between fits of packing, I did Jill's workout videos and took long showers. It was like waiting for a boy to call me back. They never called while I sat staring at my phone. They could always sense my desperation. No, I needed to be engaged in other activities. A watched pot never boils and a rushed jury never reaches a verdict.

I was wearing my Screaming Seals T-shirt and eating Chee-tos, lazily scrolling the forum, when they announced that the jury had reached a verdict. I screamed and jumped out of bed, scattering Cheeto crumbs behind me.

I dressed like William had received the death penalty and I was the last meal. I wore the uncomfortable bra that made my boobs look nice, a dress that barely passed the standards of court-room attire, and heels that required I bring a second pair of shoes so that I could drive. Whether or not William was convicted had nothing to do with me. It was about the lawyers, the jurors, the judge, and more than anything it was about the women. And yet, I struggled to separate the verdict from myself. Though the dress I wore, my eyeshadow, my hair, couldn't change the outcome of the event, I dressed like they could. I wanted to be more than a footnote in the saga of William Thompson. At the very least, I wanted a chapter dedicated to me in the inevitable tell-all re-leased to the public.

The courtroom was buzzing like a chorus of cicadas just before sunset. Jill's sister was already crying. Her eyes were red and her face hollow.

"She almost looks too thin," Dotty remarked to me.

I doubted that there was any result that could make things right for her. No matter what, her sister would always be dead.

Tripp was surrounded by Anna Leigh's friends. I'd heard ru-mors that he'd begun hooking up with her best friend, but the rumors were unsubstantiated. Regardless of whether it was true or not, I was in no place to judge.

Anna Leigh's parents bent their heads down in prayer, while

Emma's mom clutched a handkerchief like she was attempting to rip it in half. We were a roomful of people who didn't know how to live inside their skin.

William looked as William always looked—handsome, with a tinge of anxiety. I recalled what Bentley had said, that William was a man with two faces, one of a regular man and one of a monster. I stared at the back of his head with the knowledge that it was the last time I'd ever have that particular view. I always struggled with endings, never accepting that something was over until it was really over, and this occasion was no different. I couldn't imagine my life without William—or perhaps it was more that I couldn't imagine my life without the trial, the forums, the letters tucked in my mailbox.

I fantasized about approaching William. Rising out of my seat real casually, so that no one would know what I was doing until it was too late and then, when I got close enough, I would break into a run. William would stand to embrace me, his breath minty and sweet. There would be a moment of euphoria followed by an explosion of pain in my spine as I was shot down by the police officers who lined the courtroom. I would fall to the floor. William would cry out, "Hannah! Hannah!" and my last memories would be of my name on his lips. Paramedics would rush to my side, but it would be too late. I would already be gone.

The vision was romantic. The way that Bella in *Twilight* spent the entirety of the second book trying to throw herself off cliffs for the merest glimpse of Edward. It was possible that I had no idea what love was.

"What do you think William smells like?" I asked.

"What?" Dotty replied.

"I think he smells like one of those manly candles—you know, like pine and cigars," Lauren said.

My foot tapped on the ground. I knew it was annoying, but I couldn't make myself stop. I wouldn't have been surprised to open my mouth and have a trail of bees emerge.

I looked at Bentley. He held Virginia's hand, his posture relaxed. I thought about our kiss and then I deliberately didn't think about our kiss. Bentley was nothing, an aside in the love story of William and me.

Mark and Cindy looked tight, like they were having a contest to see who could hold their breath the longest. Mark, who'd maintained his certainty that William would get off, wore a sour expression that indicated that perhaps he wasn't as certain as he made himself out to be.

None of the friends who supported them outside of the courtroom were present. They could privately support the family of an accused serial killer, but it was a step too far to be asked to do it in public. My willingness to debase myself for William meant that I loved him more than people he'd known his entire life.

The judge called the court to order. Extreme silence either indicated that nothing at all was happening or everything was, and that's what happened in the courtroom when the judge banged her gavel, as we all simultaneously held our breath and left our bodies.

Please, the voice in my head murmured.

Please, please, please, please.

I wasn't sure what I was asking for, whether I wanted him to go free or merely survive.

It was difficult to parse the individual words the jury foreman was saying, like reading an academic text only to discover in the conclusion that I hadn't understood it at all. The law was a language, one that I couldn't hope to know.

Finally, she uttered the words that we'd all been waiting for.

Not guilty.

And again.

Not guilty.

Not guilty.

Not guilty.

There were gasps from the crowd. Someone was audibly sobbing. Was it me? William hugged his lawyers. Mark pumped his hands in the air like his favorite football team had just scored a touchdown. The action was inappropriate, but also fitting. Bentley and Virginia stayed seated, their postures unchanged from before the announcement. I looked at my friends beside me. There were tears falling down Lauren's cheeks and she held Dotty's hand, as she was also crying.

Jill's sister's body was contorted in grief. She bent her bones in sorrow as Emma's friends wrapped their arms around her. People were shouting. I wasn't sure if they were incoherent syllables or if I'd lost my capacity to understand words.

My heart was pounding so fast that my fingers were numb. I realized that I'd never totally considered this as an option. There was a clear-cut script for what was supposed to happen. William was supposed to have been found guilty and I would go back to my life. I would continue to write him for a few weeks or months until I found a new hobby, a boyfriend whose corporal form could be close to mine.

"Well, what happens now?" Dotty said.

"I have no idea," I replied.

33

Dotty and I stayed seated in the courtroom as everyone else began to file out. It was a game of chicken driven by inertia rather than speed.

After hugging his lawyers, William was immediately accompanied out of the room for safety reasons with his family trailing close behind. I watched William leave, followed by Mark and Bentley and their wives. No one turned to say goodbye to me.

I missed the fantasy. When William's freedom was a hut on the sea.

The journalists left to file their stories. Lauren excused herself, saying that she needed to get on the road. I resented her pragmatism in the face of the unexpected, a skill that I assumed came with age that I'd somehow never acquired.

"Maybe find a new hobby," I told her as we hugged goodbye.

Then it was just Dotty, the victims' friends and families, and me. We were frozen with it, the impossibility of the situation. Jill's sister let out intermittent shrieks that were so loud that security told her that she needed to quiet down. Later, she would tell the waiting television crews that she hadn't slept in months.

"I just wanted to go to bed secure in the knowledge that William Thompson was behind bars. Now I'll never sleep again," she cried.

"My wife deserved better," Tripp said, paused, and then added, "from everyone," before leaving to start a weekslong bender.

They would see one another again, the friends and family of the victims, bound forever by the tragedy that had altered their lives. It was a bitter community, one that they would give up in a second if only they could revive the dead. The police would investigate other leads, find other suspects, but the taste for justice would forever be soured by what had occurred at William's trial, like biting into a moldy strawberry and then throwing away the rest of the fruit for fear of repeating the experience.

"He's not coming, is he?" I said.

"No, I don't think so," Dotty replied. She picked up her purse, a leather thing that was more expensive than anything I'd ever owned.

"Best of luck, Hannah," she said.

We hugged and there was comfort in the heaviness of her perfume.

Police officers approached me.

"It's time to go," they said.

I gathered my things and walked outside, confused by the brightness of the sun. My legs wobbled and I sat down on the courthouse steps. It seemed possible that I might die right then and there with the way that my heart ached. I recognized the feeling. It was the same way I'd felt when Max started dating Reese, when a man failed to text me back after a good date, when the potential of something dissipated into nothing at all. An irrational kind of heartbreak, based more off the relationship I'd built inside my head than anything that had existed within the world. I was a widow mourning the loss of a husband who never existed and who didn't have a grave.

After an indeterminable amount of time, I slowly made my way to my car. It hurt to move. My legs mourned the loss of William as much as the rest of me. I'd always understood our relationship to be conditional, predicated on the notion that he would forever be in jail and I was the pathetic woman willing to date him while he was there. In that situation, I was the one with the power if only because I was the one who was free. With William's release, the situation reversed and suddenly, it was like every other relationship I'd ever had.

I held it together for the drive back to the hotel, but just barely. Gulping sobs took over my body as soon as the door of my hotel room closed behind me for the final time. I collapsed onto the bed and cried about William, about the loss of my job and the wreck of my finances, about the dead women and their loved ones who would never get the answers that they needed. I cried about Kelsey Jenkins, both for her death and the way in which she'd messed with my life. I cried about Max and Meghan, all the people I'd become distant from as I aged. I cried about Bentley, how our kiss was a betrayal and his disappearance into the night a second kind of treachery. Tears rolled down my cheeks and snot came pouring out of my nose. Everything, everything, was wrong and I didn't know how to make it right.

As my thoughts grew increasingly desperate to the point where I started to consider ways that I could sacrifice myself to the ravine that would be both painless and memorable, there was a knock on my door. Someone, somehow, had sensed my desperation.

I don't really want to die, I wanted to clarify. *I just don't know how to continue to live.*

I opened the door to find William Thompson standing there with a bouquet of flowers. He was still wearing the suit that he'd worn earlier that day to the trial. He looked handsome, unreal. A mirage of a man in the desert of my love life.

I turned and looked at my reflection in the full-length mirror next to the door. My face was wet and puffy. My hair, once straightened to the best of my ability, had grown frizzy with the summer heat. He wasn't supposed to see me like that. I knew from experience that it was important to be beautiful and coy for as long as possible. Men didn't like women who were a mess. Men wanted women to be calm and stoic no matter the chaos that they wreaked upon their lives.

"William," I said. "How did you find me?"

How strange it was to realize that he had a body, pores and all. My eyes traveled across his face, taking in every freckle, the patch of hair he'd missed while shaving. I wanted to reach out and touch him, but I appeared to be frozen in the doorway.

"I wanted to go to you right away, but they wouldn't let me," he said.

The words were so much what I wanted to hear that they became painful.

"They told me it wasn't safe to talk to you in the courtroom, and then I realized that I didn't have your number. We've only ever written each other. I came here to find you."

"I thought you forgot about me," I said.

"Forget about you? I could never forget about you. I meant what I said, Hannah. Your words kept me going through the worst time of my life. I don't know how I can ever repay you."

He took a deep breath. His hand was shaking. What was

happening? It seemed unlikely that he would kill me right then and there, but it was possible that he was hungry for murder after the months that he'd spent in jail.

"I know this is crazy," he said. "But I promised myself that if I was ever free again that I would do crazy things. I spent months lamenting my loneliness. I can't let this opportunity pass me by. I can't let you pass me by, Hannah."

I was dizzy as he got down on one knee. Snot continued to run out my nose.

"Hannah Wilson," he said. "Will you marry me?"

Somehow, I'd become trapped in one of my own fantasies, but everything was slightly off. Where was the beach? Why was my dress so rumpled? He didn't even have a ring.

I pasted a smile on my face.

How I'd judged those women who went on reality television shows where they got engaged and married to men that they'd never even met. The hours upon hours that I'd spent alone in my studio apartment analyzing the genuineness of their relationships. What I hadn't understood at the time was how enticing an invitation to enter another person's orbit could be. Falling in love was always a risk, I just chose to raise the stakes by falling in love with an accused serial killer. How ironic that I'd been imagining my own death when he came knocking on my door.

"Yes," I said. "Yes."

I would've started crying if I hadn't been crying already. William swept me into his arms, and I was aware of a slight smell emanating from my pits.

That's when I kissed my fiancé. Only time would tell if he'd let me live long enough to become his wife.

PART THREE

34

Undisclosed Location

"Tell me why you killed them," I say.

If I'm going to die, at least I'll know this.

"Do you know why you do the things that you do, Hannah? I'm curious. You make such bizarre choices. You strike me as a person that doesn't really know what they want," he replies.

It seems inordinately cruel that he's trying to destroy me emotionally before he kills me. I console myself with the fact that after I'm dead, I won't have to hate myself for still caring what he thinks.

"I've never killed anyone," I reply.

"But you delight in their deaths. Don't try to deny it. I read a lot of interesting things last night, Hannah."

"You found the forum," I say.

Though the forum is public, this is an intrusion.

As a child, my mother gave me a diary with a tiny lock as a birthday present. The lock made it feel important and I fastidiously made sure that it was sealed whenever I tucked the diary back beneath the clothes in my dresser. After a few entries, I realized that I had nothing of great importance to say and certainly nothing that counted as a secret. I stopped writing in the diary and it was forgotten until my mother cleaned out my dresser a couple of years later and asked if she could toss it.

The cruelty of the internet is that there is no lock. Even posts intended to be private can be found if someone wants to see them enough. It's where people reveal their most secret of selves, right out in the open.

"We were trying to help them."

"Bullshit," he says. "You wanted glory."

I don't attempt to deny it.

"You haven't answered my question," I press again.

"Oh, Hannah," he says. "I wish I didn't like you so much."

My stupid brain is flattered by this compliment. He takes the briefcase and sets it on the floor in order to sit in the chair across from where I'm sitting. I breathe a little more. If nothing else, this gives me a few more minutes to live.

"I know what you're wondering," he continues. "You're wondering if I did this with the others, brought them here and had nice little chats. You want to know if you're special or one of many."

"You don't know what I'm thinking," I reply, though he knows exactly what I'm thinking. I want to be special in death as I was never able to be in life. I wish he couldn't see inside of me the way that he does. I've always been so transparent to everyone around me. The expansiveness of my emotions visible to men even as I've tried to hide them deep within.

"Anna Leigh and I didn't spend much time talking, if that makes you feel better."

"You were having an affair?" I ask.

I wish I could text Dotty. She always suspected something

like this. I've never had better gossip in my life and here I am, tied to a chair without my phone.

"There's always sex involved with a girl that pretty," she had said.

"She thought Tripp was an idiot, you know," he says. "These girls, always marrying men that they don't respect."

"Why did you kill her?"

"I only took what was owed to me. Then, after it was done, I realized that I wanted more."

There it is: finally, a confession. I've spent so much time thinking about this moment and it doesn't feel like I thought it would. It was supposed to feel good, victorious, and instead I'm filled with an increasing sense of self-pity as I realize that this piece of knowledge isn't worth paying for with my life.

He doesn't look remorseful. If anything, he has the same look of glee that I used to get when I told people that I was corresponding with a serial killer. There are people who have spent years in therapy trying to achieve the same level of self-assurance that he has right now.

"Was it worth it?" I asked Lauren once, about her time at the Kris Cooper trial.

"It's always worth it," she said, "if you think someone might be innocent."

I wish she were here with me now, if only I could ask, "What about when you know they're guilty?"

35

After William kissed me, I invited him into my hotel room like knowingly welcoming a vampire into my house.

"Sorry, I don't have much to offer," I say. "Are you thirsty? I can get you some water."

"No," he said.

He looked at me and I lamented my disheveled appearance. It seemed possible that he already regretted asking me to marry him.

He moved toward me and I couldn't stop myself from flinching. Every move was a potential act of violence.

When he grabbed me, it wasn't to strangle me but to kiss me.

"Are you going to kill me?" I whispered between kisses.

William laughed like I was joking and pulled me closer, his hand making its way to the zipper on my dress. I shivered as he slowly pulled it down, revealing my naked back to the air. There was a pause in his urgency as William stopped kissing me to make eye contact as he slid my dress off one shoulder at a time and it fell into a puddle on the floor. He undid my bra strap single-handedly like it was a practiced, simple thing.

I was left in only my pink cotton underwear. William looked at me, his eyes moving up and down my body. I was self-conscious even as I worried that I might be about to die. The women, I knew, were all naked when they were found in the ravine. There was no sign of the clothes they had been wearing before their disappearances. Was this how it began? A slow stripping of the layers like preparing an onion to be cooked?

People always talked about the fight-or-flight response, but people rarely talked about the third thing your brain can make you do when you're afraid: freeze. "Frozen" was the perfect word to describe the stillness of my body as I stood almost naked in front of a man who'd been accused of serial murder. William approached me, grabbed my wrists, and pulled me close. My breath quickened. I closed my eyes. I waited for my death.

It was William's lips and not a rope that met my neck. They moved down my body as he pulled off my underwear so that he could slip his tongue in between my legs. I'd never orgasmed so quickly, my body alert with the fear of death.

William removed his own clothing. Though he was thin from his time in jail, he lifted me up effortlessly and placed me on the bed. I wondered if he'd repeated Jill's workouts while stuck in his jail cell the same way that I'd done them in my hotel room, both of us squatting in memory of a woman who was brutally slain.

"Would it even be possible," the defense attorneys had asked during the trial, "for a single person to move the bodies on their own?"

"Yes," said the expert who was testifying. "But he would have to be very strong."

There was no discussion of condoms or birth control or anything at all.

William climbed on top of me.

The last time I tried to have sex with Max Yulipsky, we'd gone to his favorite dive bar, a place so dark and loud that I spent the evening nodding along to moving mouths that didn't seem to notice that I couldn't hear them. It was a weekday and if I'd been with anyone else, I would've gone home hours earlier than when Max finally announced that he was tired and we trekked back to the house that he shared with his roommates.

True to his word, Max was tired and he stripped down to his boxers and climbed into bed and closed his eyes.

"Max," I whispered, and then kissed his ear in the spot where I knew he was most sensitive. I put his hand on my side to let him feel my nudity. It was important to me that my body was enough to wake him from his slumber.

"Mmm," he murmured.

Max begrudgingly woke up and made an attempt at sex. He struggled to get hard and after a few minutes he said, "I don't think it's happening tonight, Hannah," and rolled off me and immediately returned to sleep, leaving me to lie in bed pondering why I wasn't enough.

In retrospect, that occasion should've been a sign that Max was on the verge of ending things. At the time, I read it for what I wanted it to be, which was a whiskey-filled blip.

William had no problem getting hard, no problem fucking me while pinning my hands back against the bed with such force that I couldn't move. With each thrust, I waited for the turn, when he went from man to murderer.

It never came.

William orgasmed with a grunt and then collapsed on top of me. He lifted his head and kissed my cheeks, my forehead.

"That was amazing," he said.

"Uh-huh," I said in agreement.

He rolled off me and we both lay naked on top of the comforter. I remembered the shabbiness of the room, the clothes still scattered about, waiting to be packed. I was imperfect and William still wanted to make me come.

He rolled onto his side and ran his fingers along the far side of my cheek, turning my head so that I looked at him. His eyes were an icier blue than Bentley's and I chastised myself for making the comparison. I was suddenly self-conscious of my breath.

"I want to give you everything," William said, still stroking my cheek.

"You already have," I replied, though it had been more of a process of removing all the facets of my life one by one until he was all that I had left.

"I'm serious," he said.

We rotated our bodies until we were spooning. I spent five minutes thinking about how perfectly our bodies fit together until my arm started to hurt and I squirmed. I didn't want to break up the moment because I wasn't sure what lay on the other side. Finally, William announced that he was going to take a shower.

"Sorry," he apologized as he untangled his body from mine.

"It's okay, you've had a long day," I replied.

I should've taken the time while William was in the shower to text people and tell them where I was. I didn't need to make the same mistakes that Emma had made in the hours before her death. Instead, I got out my notebook.

William fucks like a man ready to kill, I wrote in the guilty column, *but he hasn't killed me yet.*

36

We couldn't go to the beach, William explained, because he had certain obligations to fulfill to his family first. Once he put the time in, he assured me, we would do everything that we dreamed of doing in our letters.

I didn't point out how much it sounded like he was still serving a type of sentence.

We spent the night in my hotel room, splurging on a variety of food delivery in between sessions of lovemaking. In the morning, he took me out to breakfast after I shoved the rest of my belongings in my car and drove to his hometown, where there was a house already waiting for him.

"Not *my* house," he told me over pancakes. "*Our* house."

I smiled at him as I bit into a piece of bacon. I hoped that he didn't expect me to contribute to the mortgage. Later, I would learn that the house was actually owned by William's parents, who didn't deal, as the peasantry did, with mortgages.

The house was in the historic district in the city that William grew up in. I pulled into the driveway and took in the white single-story home with an expansive porch featuring a swing that looked out over the sidewalk. The door was painted a bright blue as a measure of quirkiness and next to the door was a plaque that declared the building historic.

The inside of the house was modernized, with white furniture on top of refurbished dark wood floors. Pristine couches bordered a rug placed before a wall-mounted television that hung over the fireplace. Behind the living room was a formal dining room with a table that stretched the length of the room.

I dragged my suitcase in behind me. It had been a gift from my parents before my study abroad trip when I was in college. Since then, one of the zippers had broken and the front pocket was starting to come apart at the seams. I'd never had the money to travel extensively, never mind buy myself luggage to take with me. The suitcase looked out of place in the house, the single belonging not curated by interior decorators. I took solace in the fact that there was no mirror in front of me to see if I looked the same.

The kitchen was small and tucked away at the back of the house, though its smallness was offset by an adjoining butler's pantry. The three bedrooms were lined up in a row on the right side of the house with the original bathroom placed between the first two smaller bedrooms and a second bathroom added on to the largest bedroom as a means of creating a master suite. The bathroom was large, taking up much of the space that had formerly belonged to the middle bedroom—now an office—and featured both a freestanding tub and a shower. There were two sinks, one for William and one for me.

William's belongings were already neatly tucked into the drawers of the dresser and hung in the closet according to fit and color.

"These are your drawers," he told me, gesturing to the left-hand side of the dresser. It was the first time that a man had ever offered me a sliver of space within his home. I once asked a man that I was dating if it was okay if I kept a spare outfit at his house and he broke things off the next week, saying that things were "getting too serious." The offer of the drawers and some closet space seemed like an outrageous act of kindness that could be eclipsed only by diamonds.

My belongings looked shabby next to William's, the difference between my twenty-dollar shirts and his brand-name products apparent in a way that they never had been before.

"We'll go shopping," he told me as he watched me hang my dresses in the closet.

I enjoyed the prospect of a man paying for my purchases even as I resented the implication that the things I owned weren't good enough as is.

I kept waiting to round a corner and discover a murder room decked out in a plastic tarp and a wall full of weapons, but there was nothing. There wasn't even a basement or a shed in the back-yard. A true search, I knew, would have to wait until William was gone. A girl couldn't just come out and ask her fiancé if he was a murderer. That was something that needed to be kept private, like how I waited until William was on the other side of the house before daring to take a poop. Until then I marveled at my surroundings. It was the nicest place I'd ever lived, my childhood home included, and all it took to get there was getting engaged to an accused serial killer.

No, I corrected myself. I was engaged to an acquitted serial killer, though I wasn't yet convinced that there was a difference.

William made us dinner on our first night in the house together.

"I've missed cooking," he explained.

In his previous life, before anyone thought he was a murderer, William enjoyed taking gourmet cooking classes. This type of cooking was distinct from what I'd done in my studio apartment, when I grudgingly made food to stay healthy and alive. When William cooked, he wanted it to be a luxury experience.

I sat on a stool in William's kitchen—our kitchen—a wonder to me after spending weeks living off vending machine food in a hotel, and watched as he expertly tied a seasoned pork loin with twine and diced tomatoes for bruschetta.

We swung on the porch swing while the pork loin cooked, drinking red wine and eating melon wrapped in prosciutto. A couple walking by with their dogs waved at us and we waved back. They didn't know they were waving at William Thompson, the acquitted serial killer, and I wondered what it was like to move through the world with such obliviousness.

Inside, William set the table with candlesticks and dimmed the lights in the dining room. He opened a second bottle of wine before cutting into the meat, which dripped with juice.

"Cheers," he said, and we clinked our glasses together.

I'd often claimed that I couldn't tell the difference between cheap and expensive wine, but the stuff in my glass proved otherwise. It was possible that I'd never had good wine in my life.

"Tell me, Hannah. What is it that you would do with your life without any limitations?" William asked.

I took a bite of my salad and chewed thoughtfully. I didn't

know where to start. There were always limitations. It wasn't a real question. It was like asking someone what books they would bring if they were stranded on a desert island. I was too worried about survival.

"I've always wanted to write a novel. Something really epic, you know? I used to love to write when I was younger, but I haven't had time in years," I told him.

William smiled through the candlelight.

"What else?" he said.

"I guess I've always wanted to run a marathon. Is that too cliché?"

"No," he replied. "Nothing is too cliché when you really want it. What else?"

"I don't know. Travel? I've been to a few places in Europe, but never to other continents. I would love to go to Japan."

"Done," William said.

"What?"

"I want you to take this time for you to do what you want. All of it. Write your novel, run a marathon, go to Japan. Don't worry about getting a job." He paused and looked at his plate, a momentary sorrow flickering across his features. "I've let down other people that I loved and I don't want to let you down. You can help me by letting me help you."

I swallowed the food in my mouth.

"I don't know what to say."

"You don't have to say anything," he said.

There was a nagging discomfort from William's offer. I was so used to men giving me nothing that I greeted all kindnesses with suspicion. Later, I would realize that this was the standard dynamic for the Thompson family. The men went off to work while the women entertained themselves with their little hobbies and everyone acted like this was a gift.

We moved on to talking about the books that William had read in prison.

"I thought it would be a good time to read the classics," he said and laughed. "I realized quickly that *Bleak House* didn't provide the intrigue that I needed. I ended up reading trashy thrillers more than anything else."

"You can't beat a good thriller. Sometimes you need to be on the edge of your seat."

"That's absolutely true," William said and topped off my wine.

I was polishing off the side of roasted carrots when my hand bumped the glass, spilling red wine across the table. I froze.

William grabbed one of the white cloth napkins to wipe up the spill and I watched the crimson liquid spread across the fabric.

"I'm so sorry," I apologized.

"It's okay," he said. "Really, it's fine."

I realized that I was still waiting for something to happen, for William to wrap the twine he'd used on the pork loin around my neck, to slip poison in my glass of wine, to grab my hair and drag me across the room for ruining his perfect table. Instead, I had merely grown drunk and clumsy.

William came up behind me in the kitchen as I helped clear the plates. My body tensed as he cornered me against the counter, pressing his body against mine. He spun me around and lifted me up so that I was sitting on the counter, surrounded by the remnants of his cooking.

I thought that it was possible that he might try to kill me until he unzipped his pants and pulled my underwear aside and fucked me like he was a normal man and we were a normal couple enjoying our first night in our new house together.

Afterward, I passed him dishes and we put them in the dish-washer one by one.

I waited until he was asleep before I got out my notebook. I wrote down what William made for dinner and how he'd kissed my forehead, wet and sloppy, after we had sex.

The evening was everything I'd ever dreamed of from a man. The most that Max had ever cooked for me were some drunken pizza rolls. And yet, I could still feel that void inside of me that ached for something more. I'd gotten William the lover, but where was William the killer? Maybe I'd been misinterpreting my dreams all along. It was possible that I'd always wanted vio-lence and not love. Or maybe I'd intertwined those things so closely that it was impossible to separate them.

37

It was four days before I was left alone in the house.

In that time, William and I went to a home goods store and he insisted on buying a print of my choice to hang in the house.

"I want you to make it your own," he said.

I ended up choosing an abstract piece featuring swirls of paint. William hung it in the living room and its colorfulness clashed with the whiteness of the space.

I discovered that William always put the cap back on his toothpaste, put his dirty clothes in the hamper immediately upon taking them off, and made the bed each morning. Dishes weren't allowed to sit out on the counter or soak within the sink, and when we moved the decorative pillows on the couch for ease of sitting, it was expected that they be put back in their place when we were finished.

"Sorry," he apologized. "I'm a bit of a neat freak."

"No, I appreciate it. I could stand to be a little tidier," I told him.

I also discovered the spot on his ear that made him melt when I kissed it. He made me orgasm so hard that I discovered a new universe inside of myself. We got memberships at the yoga studio a few blocks away and William took me to a running store to get a new pair of running shoes.

He didn't try to kill me even once.

On the morning that William went back to work we ate breakfast together, plates of scrambled eggs and toast spread with local jam. Everything was wholesome and delicious.

"You look cute in your running gear," William said. He was back in a suit, a look that I thought of as "trial William." It was jarring to see him in everyday clothes, even if his sweatpants cost more money than my most expensive dress.

"Thank you." I smiled and took a bite of toast.

I had no intention of going running. Instead, I planned to search the house.

"Goodbye, sweetheart," William said, and kissed me on the forehead. The word "sweetheart" felt like it belonged to someone else, as though he'd temporarily forgotten my name.

"I'll miss you," I replied.

I breathed a sigh of relief when William walked out the door and evaluated the space around me. I needed to search the house in a way that ensured that everything looked the same when William returned. The pitfall of having a house where everything had its place meant that the slightest deviation was cause for alarm.

William's underwear drawer was the first place that I looked. This was projection. As a teenager, I'd frequently hidden contraband in my underwear drawer. Things that seemed bad at the time and now were so innocent: condoms, notes passed between friends, and a book about sex that I'd gotten as a gag gift.

When I opened the top drawer of William's dresser, I discovered that William was the kind of man who folded his briefs.

I took out my notebook.

Folds his underwear, I wrote in the guilty column.

The second drawer contained a variety of neutral-toned T-shirts that were equally as organized as his underwear and the last drawer contained several pairs of sweatpants. On top of the dresser was a mug where William deposited spare change, and a display box for his collection of expensive watches as well as several types of cologne that my plebeian nose was unable to fully appreciate.

His bedside table was similar. Whereas my table held a dog-eared novel and a glass of water that was accumulating dust, his was devoid of everything aside from a cell phone charger. I wondered if neatness was a trait that he'd always had or something he picked up in jail like a former military man who made his bed like he was still on active duty.

Fastidiously clean, I wrote beneath the note about his underwear.

Being neat didn't inherently mean that someone was a murderer. Surely, there were just as many killers who left their dirty clothes on the floor and dishes in the sink, as I was apt to do. However, I couldn't stop thinking about the testimony at the trial where they talked about the cleanliness of the killer, how they hadn't left any part of themselves behind.

Looking at William's closet, the rows of button-down shirts, it occurred to me that it could've belonged to anyone. The only thing of note in the closet was a box. I hesitated to open it, worried that I would find teeth or hair or some other remnant of a body. Serial killers, I knew from television, liked to collect mementos from their victims to remind them of their kills.

It was, in fact, a box of mementos, though not ones from dead women. There were birthday cards from people whose names I didn't recognize, wallet-sized pictures from high school, and a packet of handwritten notes bound by a rubber band. I froze when I saw my own handwriting. They weren't all from me. William, it appeared, had kept some of the mail he'd received while he was in jail. I flipped through the letters, looking for anything of interest. All of them appeared to be from women, judging from the handwriting. If any men had written him, William hadn't kept it. *I cannot bear the thought of you being locked up,* one of the letters started. *You fucking psychopath,* began another. *I need to feel you between my thighs,* said a third. It was painful to read them, this correspondence with other women. I wasn't sure if William had responded to any of them, but there were a few notes by the same people, which suggested that they were written as a response.

Writing other women, I noted in the guilty column.

I didn't reread the letters that I wrote. Even though they had only been written weeks or months earlier, I already thought of that version of myself as someone naïve and inarticulate. I didn't want to revisit who I was then, someone so desperate for love.

In my notebook, I jotted down the names of the other women who had written him.

Lily, Cara, Jessie, Stacey, Allison.

I wanted a list, in case one of them later turned up missing, or for the second, less nefarious reason, that I wanted to know their names in case William was still in contact with them and was engaged in a type of epistolary adultery. I couldn't ask him about the letters because to do so would be to admit that I had snooped. Ordinarily, carrying such a suspicion around with me would've been unbearable, but I was already investigating to determine whether my fiancé was a serial murderer. What were a few letters on top of that?

Underneath the letters, I found a key. I took a mental snapshot before returning the contents of the box, doing my best to replicate their earlier placement.

I checked the hall closet, which was empty aside from a couple of jackets and an umbrella hanging on a hook on the wall and the towel closet that contained only extra towels and sheets. The living room was too spotless to hold any secrets and I doubted that he would hide anything amongst the pots and pans in the kitchen, though I checked just to be sure.

The guest room was sterile. It was like entering a hotel room, the bed already made and towels hanging neatly in the bathroom. My decrepit suitcase was stored in the closet next to William's brand-new luggage as well as a couple of prints that William didn't want to hang on the wall but said he "couldn't bear to get rid of for sentimental reasons."

The Thompson family took compartmentalization of their emotions very literally within their interior design.

I checked the office last.

Though I'd never had a home office or even a home of my own with separate rooms, I understood that this was supposed to be a sacred space for certain types of men. Home offices in movies always had mahogany walls and a drink cart full of whiskey. William's office was painted white and light filled, but he did have the drink cart.

The desktop computer was asleep and when I tried to turn it on, it asked for a password that I didn't know. There were no errant papers or Post-it notes containing a possible password and I decided it was best to leave the computer alone. After all, it wasn't like a smart serial killer would open a Word document and type out a confession.

The top drawer of the desk held an assortment of office supplies that were neatly organized in a tray. I didn't know that a desk could be like that. When I had worked, a past that was starting to seem impossibly long ago, my desk had been an avalanche of papers and pens that I would clean off only for the mess to reappear a couple of hours later. Messiness was part of the work for me. William, it seemed, thrived on tidiness.

In the bottom drawer of the desk was another box, this one with a lock. I recalled the key in the box in the bedroom closet and ran to get it. There was immense satisfaction as the key slid into the lock and effortlessly turned.

Inside the box there was a gun.

Gun!!! I wrote in my notebook. No additional commentary was needed.

I stared at it. I'd never seen a gun before, not in person. Where I was from, guns were used largely for hunting, and my family did not hunt. No one I knew casually kept a gun in their desk, at least not to my knowledge. I reached for the gun, the pull almost magnetic, and then I hesitated, my fingers mere millimeters away. The gun could have fingerprints on it that were evidence of some crime, or, worse, my own fingerprints could be transferred and used to incriminate me. Though none of the women found in the ravine had been killed by a gun, I didn't want to make any assumptions.

My desire to pick up the gun outweighed my rational brain. I got a T-shirt from the bedroom and wrapped it around my hand. The gun was heavy, heavier than I was expecting. I wasn't sure if bullets were inside of it and I didn't know how to check. I held it like I was going to shoot and then felt a tingle of discomfort up my spine that told me to put the gun away.

I had been so busy marveling over the gun that I neglected the other items in the box. At first glance, they appeared to be innocuous things, notable only in their proximity to a weapon. There was a gym card, a hair tie, a half-empty pack of cigarettes that had been crushed by the weight of the gun, and a worn paper bookmark.

Upon closer inspection, I realized that the gym card bore the same logo that the temporary pass I'd been given to Jill's gym had. That wasn't such a shock; after all, everyone knew that Jill was William's personal trainer. It was only natural that he had a gym card. Still, the weirdness of its placement gave me pause. I didn't know what to make of the cigarettes or the bookmark. William, as far as I knew, hadn't ever been a smoker. He was the type that valued his health over momentary pleasures, something that he confessed to occasionally regretting while he was behind bars. I opened the pack and next to the cigarettes, there was a green matchbook with a Celtic logo on the front.

Next, I examined the bookmark, which appeared to be from an independent bookstore in Atlanta. That too wasn't unusual as William was a known reader and in the few short days that I'd lived with him, I'd noticed his penchant for shopping local.

Finally, I picked up the hair tie. Hair ties were so ubiquitous in my life that I hardly noticed them. I always had at least two around my wrist in case I needed to pull my hair back. They were also an item passed amongst women in bathrooms, like tampons for a surprise bleed. More than once, I'd gifted desperate strangers the hair ties on my wrist and glowed in their thankfulness for an unreasonable number of hours.

William, however, had no need for a hair tie. He wasn't the

type of man to have a man bun and the careful placement beneath the gun indicated that it wasn't some mistakenly dropped
piece of ephemera. No, it was a hair tie of import. I looked closer
at it and found a blond strand wrapped around the elastic. I got
the same feeling that I did when plunging down the drop of a
roller coaster, my stomach abandoning the rest of my body.

Could the hair belong to Anna Leigh? I carefully ran my fingers over the hair and held it up to my nose to sniff, disappointed
at its odorlessness.

I spread the items out on the desk and took pictures of them
one at a time as well as a picture of the gun. William's office,
temporarily, became my evidence room. I also added comments
in my notebook. Beneath where I'd written *Gun!!!*, I wrote *gym
card, cigarettes, matchbook, bookmark, hair tie*, with a note beneath *hair tie* that said *Anna Leigh's hair???* I placed the items
back in the box, doing my best to re-create how I'd found them.

I went to relock the box and then hesitated. Because I didn't
own anything of value, I'd never been afraid of burglars and thus
didn't understand why people felt the need to leave guns unse-
cured in their homes. That, of course, was before I moved in with
a man who'd been acquitted of serial murder who kept a used
hair tie wrapped with blond hair in a box in his desk. I returned
the box to the drawer without locking it and slipped the key back
into the other box in the bedroom.

When I had finished my search, I made my way through the
house, making sure that nothing was out of place, my mind continually drifting back to the things that I'd found in the office. It
was possible that they were nothing, miscellaneous items that
had made their way into William's office in the haste of the move.
I doubted that was the case. For a man who valued cleanliness
so highly, I could think of only one reason why William would

want to keep things that were essentially garbage: they were murder souvenirs, the type that the police were looking for and never found during their investigation.

My skin tingled when I thought about the way that William and I had made love the night before. How he was so eager that we didn't bother removing our clothes and how he fucked me from behind while moaning about the deliciousness of my body. What items was he collecting off me to put in his little box of gore?

38

Everyone in the yoga class stared at us as we moved through our sun salutations. William was oblivious to it or he relished in it, placing his yoga mat in the center of the room where everyone could see him.

"It's nice to feel like a regular person again," William told me over dinner one night. "I've never liked being the center of attention."

Despite his claims, I imagined it was difficult going from a scenario where everyone spent their days ruminating over the mundane details of his life to one where he was almost treated like an ordinary man. Almost.

The yoga women whispered amongst themselves.

"It's him. It's William Thompson," they said.

I knew they would go home, tell their spouses, their coworkers, their friends about whom they'd seen, because I was once them, gleeful with my little packet of letters that I carried around with me everywhere.

I thought I wanted to be the subject of attention until the yoga women trained their gaze upon me. My new yoga pants were tight and stiff. Unlike William, who moved easily through the poses, I struggled with balance and had to come out of a pose more than once. I worried that they wouldn't think me beautiful enough to be with him.

"I know he's an accused serial killer, but surely he could get someone hotter," I imagined them saying.

Although I didn't manage to achieve any kind of Zen, I left the class with aching glutes and arms from trying so hard to perform like the person I thought the women wanted me to be.

There was little for me to do once William left for work. There were housekeepers who came once a week to clean and he assured me that he didn't expect me to be any kind of homemaker.

"I want you to follow your dreams," he told me.

If only William knew that my dreams revolved around fantasies of him attempting to murder me. A fantasy I justified by telling myself that it would allow me to finally know the whole truth about what had happened to the women.

I went to a coffee shop down the street from the yoga studio with the intention of starting my novel. I ordered a latte and a fancy-looking pastry with the cash that William had given me.

"No strings attached," he told me as he handed over the wad of bills.

What a luxury it was to order food without worrying about how I was going to pay for it.

I got a table by the window and plugged my laptop in. Next to me, there was a group of college-aged kids doing Bible study. I couldn't imagine being so concerned with goodness at their age, a time in my own life in which I'd only wanted to be bad. I wished I could tell them that they were sitting next to William Thompson's fiancée.

I really did intend to write a novel. I opened a blank Word document and waited for the inspiration to come. I always presumed that it was lack of time that interfered with my creative life. If only I were given the time and financial freedom required, I was certain the words would pour out of me.

As a teenager, I started a novel about a vampire who was in love with a human and despaired because he could either turn her, thereby ripping her soul from her body, or watch as she aged and turned ugly and died. I didn't get much done on my vampire novel because it was hard to write scenes about kissing when I'd never been kissed myself. Additionally, much of the book was a rip-off of *Twilight*, a book that I claimed not to like and read in secret beneath the covers.

As an adult, I wanted to write a novel centered around three generations of a single family because that's what all the most serious novels I read did. I looked at my document and wrote down a sentence, deleted it, and then wrote another. How did a person begin? I finished my cup of coffee and got a refill.

I didn't know how it happened, but somehow, I found myself back on the forum. I didn't remember typing in the URL or even logging on to my account. It was like I was possessed. The truth was that I could only ever write about William. Serial killers inspired me more than generational trauma ever could.

I was dying to tell the forum about the things that I'd found in William's desk. The thing that stopped me was that in order to tell them about the things in the desk, I would also have to tell them how I'd gotten access to William's house, which would require explaining that we were engaged and had moved in together. There were several things that stopped me from doing this.

First, my own parents didn't know about our engagement and I didn't like the idea of strangers online hearing about that

particular life event before the people who had raised me, regardless of how distant we were.

Second, to tell the forum about my search of the house implied that it was a strategic engagement, an investigative aid
rather than an emotional act. Yes, it was true that I wanted to
know that truth about William, but it was more than that. I
thought about him all the time, as a lover, a fiancé, and a potential murderer, and to tell the forum about us would be to give
them sway over our relationship, and I didn't want that.

Lastly, I was worried that some of the forum members would
become vengeful toward me. I already knew from the trial the
way that people behaved toward those who were sympathetic toward William, and that was without knowledge of our romantic
entanglement. If anyone was going to threaten my life, I wanted
it to be William. For those reasons, I kept my newfound discover-
ies inside and scrolled the updates of the less knowledgeable.

Because William had been acquitted, the police were looking
into other suspects in the four original murders. They'd had little
success. They found someone who went to law school with Anna
Leigh and knew Emma through mutual friends, but they couldn't
extend the connection to Kimberly, Jill, or Kelsey. Maybe the
murders weren't connected after all. Maybe it was five unlucky
women who somehow ended up in a ravine.

Some of the forum members continued to pursue William as
a suspect even though he'd been found not guilty by the jury.
They figured out that he was working for his father and even
shared the address of the law office, which I found alarming.

"I understand that he's family, but if someone in my family did
that I would disown them without a second thought," someone
posted.

Someone else emailed the office to voice their complaints. In return, they got a form letter that said they "appreciated the concern" but had "full confidence that justice was served" and they "hoped the real criminal" would be found soon.

The forum, thankfully, had yet to find William's home address, though they were looking. I felt a giddiness from having information that they wanted and couldn't obtain.

Other users were investigating the Kelsey Jenkins murder, which they felt hadn't been properly looked into due to the chaos that was the end of William's trial.

"It has to be someone who knows William," one user reasoned.

"If not a copycat, maybe someone that he paid to murder her. You know, to throw people off his scent."

Try as they might, they hadn't yet been able to find a connection between William, anyone he knew, and the bar that Kelsey worked at.

I too was fixated on Kelsey Jenkins, but for a different reason than the other forum users. Kelsey's murder was the closest that I'd come physically to any of the killings. Sometimes, I still thought about being in that ravine, the sky darkening menacingly around me, the tension of the situation increased through my nostalgia. It was almost dying in the same way that having a lottery ticket one number off counted as almost winning the lottery, which was to say that it was mentally close and tangibly distant. The gulf between being murdered and alive was large and passable only a single time. But it made me feel close to Kelsey like we'd known each other or even like we'd been each other.

I started a new page in my notebook that I labeled with *Kelsey Jenkins* at the top and decorated with a variety of doodles as I scrolled the forum.

No evidence that William and Kelsey ever met, I wrote.

By the time that my half-drunk second cup of coffee had grown cold, I'd written only two sentences of my novel: *Katie's mother was a bird-watcher like her mother before her and her mother before that. Katie came from a long line of bird-watchers.*

"I started my novel today," I told William over dinner.

I could feel his support from across the table.

"I'm so proud of you, Hannah," he said.

I wondered if he would kill me if he knew the truth of what I was doing or if he would merely break up with me. I couldn't decide which outcome was worse. At night, I checked and double-checked to make sure my notebook was secure within my purse. I took pictures of inane things so that the photos I took of the items within his desk were hidden deep within my phone. I needed to ensure that he didn't find out what I was doing until the moment I wanted him to know. The uncertainty I had was whether that moment was when I went to the police or if it was an intimate reveal, something that tied us together through life and death.

39

William's family threw a party to celebrate his release. He bought me a new dress for the occasion that cost more than the one that I wore to prom.

"My family can be intense," he said.

We went out to eat at an upscale chain restaurant at the outlet mall.

"I've already met your family," I confessed over a plate of seared salmon.

William frowned.

"At the trial. It wasn't always pleasant for me there. See, there were some girls."

I tried to explain how I was harassed without directly referencing any of the murdered women, whose names made William clam up.

"Your father, he approached me, said that he appreciated my support."

"I'm sorry that happened to you," William said.

I wasn't sure if he was referring to the girls or his father. I didn't tell him about what had happened with Bentley. I read once that people who cheated confessed to their partners not because it was the right thing to do but because it was a way of assuaging their own guilt. Though it was true that I felt guilty, I was more worried about what William would do if he found out. I also didn't mention what Bentley had said about his mother being convinced that I was hitting on his father. He didn't need to know the enthusiasm with which I'd followed Mark Thompson around.

"I haven't told them about our engagement yet. I'm planning on telling them at the party."

I tried to smile with my eyes.

"I can't wait," I said.

I hadn't told my parents about the engagement either. I texted my mother and told her that I'd found a "work opportunity" in Georgia and that I would update her when I got the chance. Somehow, I never found the right moment. I never pictured that telling my parents about my engagement would also involve a discussion about acquitted serial killers and I was unwilling to puncture my vision of their joy just yet.

I was nervous about the party. Having previously met Cindy Thompson, I knew that there was nothing that I could wear that would impress her. I didn't look like her or Virginia or Anna Leigh, women raised within a tradition that taught them they needed to look a certain way. Theoretically, I railed against such conventions. Women, I thought, should be able to look however they wanted and still be considered to be worthy of love. That didn't stop me from judging myself and my inability to conform.

I made an appointment at a salon to get my hair and nails done.

"I want to impress my future mother-in-law," I told the stylist, failing to mention that my future mother-in-law was William Thompson's mother.

My natural hair color was a medium brown with the errant gray that was creeping in faster than seemed possible. I dyed it a honey blond, the lightest it had ever been.

"I want something like this," I said, showing the stylist a photo of Anna Leigh that was zoomed in so closely that it was impossible to identify it as her.

I recognized that it was weird to dye my hair the same color as a murdered woman's. It wasn't that I wanted to be Anna Leigh—though I was jealous of her law degree, family money, and renowned beauty—but rather that I genuinely liked her hair. After all, I'd spent hours upon hours staring at her picture, to the point that I sometimes forgot that we had never actually met while she was alive. It wasn't dissimilar from seeing the face of a celebrity again and again and bringing their picture to the salon.

"I love your hair. You look amazing," William said.

I didn't look as good as I wanted to, but I looked okay.

I could tell that William was nervous. He sprayed on too much cologne and kept apologizing for things that hadn't happened yet.

"I'm sorry for how they are," he said.

Mark and Cindy Thompson didn't live in a house like everyone else. Instead, they lived on an estate, a term that I didn't understand until William's car stopped in front of an electric gate and we drove up a winding driveway lined with trees. Geographically, the house wasn't isolated, a mere fifteen minutes from our own home, but structurally it was a fortress. William put his hand over mine as he steered. I wasn't sure which one of us he was trying to comfort.

The house itself was a cream-colored monstrosity. The front door was actually two conjoined doors and wide porches flanked either side of the house. The size of the house made me nostalgic for my own childhood home and its tiny bedrooms and meager two bathrooms. There was such a thing as too much space.

William handed the keys off to the valet driver like we were at a fancy restaurant. I looked down at my outfit and hoped that I wasn't underdressed.

If the Thompson family status had dropped a notch since William was accused of being a serial killer, the number of people at the party didn't show it. I walked in expecting a crowd similar to that of the gathering I had attended in Atlanta, the one where Bentley and I ended up splintering off in order to have a private chat. Some of those same people were potentially in attendance, but it was difficult to tell with the crowd.

Everyone was delighted to see William. No one seemed concerned that there was an acquitted serial killer in their midst.

"William!" they exclaimed. "So great to see you! I always knew you were innocent!"

William was gracious even as he gritted his teeth. He was nothing if not well trained in social niceties.

We wound our way through the house. William's parents were baroque in their decorating sensibilities, with everything possible gilded and heavily ornamented. The other guests barely seemed to notice me.

"This is Hannah," William said when people glanced my way, without giving me a qualifier. It felt a little like he was ashamed of me, though I knew that he was waiting to make the announcement about our engagement.

Mark and Cindy Thompson were holding court in a formal living room. Mark made a joke that I couldn't hear and all the men around him laughed. Cindy sparkled in a blue sequined dress that she somehow managed to pull off. I hadn't seen their full power at the trial, I realized.

"William," Cindy said and kissed her younger son on the cheek.

She didn't acknowledge me until Mark came up and hugged me, his touch unexpected.

"Why didn't you mention that you and my son were so close?" he said. "I wish we could've gotten to know each other better."

"So nice to see you, Hannah," Cindy said, giving me a smile that was equivalent to an early spring thaw in Minnesota. She still didn't like me, but I could sense something beyond disdain under the surface. If William allowed me to live for long enough, it was possible that she would finally accept me in her world.

I started to talk, but Mark interrupted me to greet William.

"My son is finally home," he said.

Mark directed his attention back at me.

"Why don't you have a drink? We need to get you a drink."

A server with a tray appeared. It was the only house party that I'd ever been to that was big enough to require actual servers versus a dingy little home bar setup in the kitchen.

"I'll just take a pinot grigio," I said.

I suspected that I had more in common with the servers who wandered around the room than I did with any of the actual guests. They probably couldn't wait to go home and tell all their friends that they worked at a party held for William Thompson.

My eyes darted around the room. Both William and Bentley had told me so much about their childhoods that it was strange to be standing in the space where they had spent their youth. It didn't look like a place where there had ever been children present, each room more formal than the last. How did a person grow up in such a house and become a killer? Alternatively, how did a person grow up in such a house and not become a killer?

If Bentley and Virginia were at the party, they were nowhere to be seen. As anxious as I was about the possibility of William finding out what had happened between Bentley and me, I almost wished they were there for the comfort of familiar faces. William kept getting roped into conversations about what it was like to finally be free, conversations that were peppered with jokes about the poor conditions of the prison system.

"It wasn't really like that. I spent a lot of time by myself. I wrote a lot of letters," William said with a glance in my direction.

I excused myself to use the bathroom, grabbing canapés off passing trays of food as I went. The forum had been dying to search the Thompson family estate for months and I wasn't going to let the opportunity pass me by. I wanted to see if I could find more items connecting William to the women, beyond what I'd found in the desk in his office. Though I didn't think that Mark had a role in killing the women, there was something suspicious about him. I still didn't know why he'd driven to all those sites linked to the women on the day that I trailed him. If I'd learned anything, it was that the Thompson family was always more complicated than they appeared to be on the surface.

Walking through the Thompson mansion was like walking through the board game of Clue. I got lost trying to find my way back to the front of the house and briefly wandered into the kitchen, where there was a host of catering staff prepping more platters.

"Excuse me," I said.

That was when I noticed the second set of stairs at the back of the room.

There was a grand staircase in the front of the house, the

kind where girls used to line up on prom night and show off their dresses. The staircase in the kitchen was narrow and unadorned, meant as a passageway for staff to deliver things to the upper floors without being seen. The wealthy's desire to hide their help was advantageous to me in that circumstance because it meant that I could explore the rest of the house without the watchful eyes of the party guests.

The second floor was a long hallway of closed doors. Hanging on the wall in between the doors were portraits of old white men who I assumed were members of the Thompson family. I wasn't sure what I was looking for. A full-blown murder room would clash with the décor of the rest of the house, but it seemed like the kind of place where it was possible to find an errant dead body or a sick child locked behind one of the doors. That was the problem with historical homes. They were beautiful and also desperately haunted.

I hesitated before the first door. I tried to remember the story of Bluebeard. Something about a woman going into a room that she wasn't supposed to and finding the corpses of those who had come before her, but I couldn't fully recall how it went.

I opened the first door to discover a bland guest room, not unlike the one that William and I had in our own home, though the furnishings were more ornate. No corpses at all. I paused in the second room, which turned out to be a bathroom, in order to empty my bladder. Even the soap next to the sink felt expensive.

When I opened the third door, I found the bedroom of a teenage boy. The preserved childhood bedroom was the first and only similarity I'd witnessed between the Thompson mansion and the three-bedroom home that I grew up in, where the posters from my teenage years still hung on the wall. Because there was no financial incentive for the Thompsons to keep their grown children's rooms the same, I gathered that it was a rare sentimental impulse. To destroy the teenage bedroom was to destroy a conception of one's own children, to acknowledge that they were always and forever adults.

I walked inside, closing the door behind me. I wasn't sure if the room belonged to Bentley or William. There was a poster on the wall of a professional football player and a blue flannel comforter on the bed. A large desk was placed before the window with a view of the front yard where guests still streamed through the entrance. On the desk was a signed baseball in a glass case and a framed picture that I picked up for closer examination.

I gasped. In the picture there were two boys, presumably Bentley and William, with blood smeared across their faces. Upon second glance, I realized that they were standing next to a dead deer and the photograph was a memento of a hunting trip. The presence of the deer only made me feel slightly better, though I knew that Mark Thompson was an avid hunter.

I opened the desk drawers. Unlike the neat desk in William's office in our home, the contents were messy. Pens that had long since dried up, old school notebooks and assignment sheets. All of the ephemera that was saved for no reason at all. A red notebook with *William* and *Math* scrolled across the top let me know that I was, in fact, in William's room. There was something reassuring about knowing that William had once been messy, an indication that his neatness was a learned trait rather than ingrained psychopathy.

I riffled through the papers, looking for something that said "future killer" or anything that seemed like it might be related to the women, like the things he kept in his office at home. The only thing of note that I found was a series of handwritten notes with girly handwriting. They looked so much like the letters that

William kept in the box in his closet that I did a double take before realizing that they were the kind of notes that kids passed to one another in school or slipped between the slats of a locker rather than things that women sent to a man imprisoned for murder. I gathered the notes together and slipped them into the clutch I'd brought with me to the party. Surely, no one would miss something that had been gathering dust for all those years.

Too much time had passed. I slipped out of the bedroom, back down the stairs, and back into the party. The crowd was now gathered in the formal living room, their attention on Mark Thompson, who held a champagne flute in the air. William stood next to him, looking less pleased with the situation than his father. I hastily grabbed a glass of champagne from a server to join the people around me.

"This wasn't just a trial for William," Mark said. "This was a trial for all of us. I have never been more grateful for God and the community that we have. We never would've made it through without you. Cheers to the future."

"Cheers" echoed through the crowd as glasses tinkled against one another.

Mark looked surprised when William raised his glass a second time and started to speak.

"Thank you to my family, blood and not. As my father said, this has been a difficult time for all of us. However, there was a bright spot in the darkness."

Oh god. When William had said that he intended to tell his parents about the engagement, I thought he meant in private. As he continued, I realized that he was going to tell the entire crowd of people.

"It was through these traumatic times that I met the love of my life, Hannah. I'm so excited to announce that upon my release, I asked her to marry me."

William's eyes searched for mine and I made my way to the front of the room through the claps and cheers of the crowd. Mark and Cindy clapped along with their guests, but there was something about their enthusiasm that felt fake. I wanted to hide, to run back up the stairs and return to William's bedroom.

"Cheers, honey," William said, and we clinked our glasses together. He'd never called me "honey" before, never mind in front of a crowd of people. The word was sticky, uncomfortable.

"Cheers," I said. I could feel the stares of their crowd as they analyzed what type of woman would fall in love with an accused serial killer and the inverse of it—what type of woman could make a serial killer fall in love with her.

I didn't know whether my mouth had positioned itself into a smile or a grimace.

Bentley was the first member of the Thompson family to congratulate us. He must've arrived while I was rooting around upstairs.

"Congratulations, brother. I can't wait to get to know your bride," he said and winked at me. I took the wink as a sign that he had no plans to tell William what had happened between the two of us at the trial.

"I look forward to getting to know you as well," I said too formally.

"It'll be good," Virginia said, "to have another woman in the family." It was the most that she'd ever acknowledged me.

"I wish you'd told us earlier," Cindy said to William. Despite all the Botox, her face was still capable of frowning.

"I'm telling you now," he said.

She pulled at my left hand without warning.

"Hannah doesn't have a ring."

Cindy looked at me like I was the one to blame for that absence.

"I still need to get her one," William replied. "I was a little busy up until recently."

"Well, I'm thrilled. Who would've thought that this is how William would meet the love of his life?" Mark said.

"I could've guessed," Bentley said, and we all laughed like it was a funny joke.

The sensation of the air around me told me that no one in the Thompson family was as happy as they claimed to be.

I spent the rest of the party being approached by guests who offered their congratulations and then asked intrusive questions about my life.

"Where are you from?"

"How did you and William meet?"

"What do you do for work?"

I did my best to answer even as I was overwhelmed by all the names and faces. I was grateful when William stepped in for me.

"Hannah is a novelist and she writes beautiful letters," he said. The party guests seemed to think that "novelist" was my real career. For the most part, they kept their comments about how we met to themselves, though a few people let things slip.

"You must be an amazing writer if you could land this man through a few letters. I remember high school. All the girls were after him."

"At least William knows that you'll always be loyal if you were willing to stick by his side through all of this."

"When did you know that you loved him?"

I didn't tell them that I'd loved William since the first time I saw Anna Leigh's face.

"Oh, you know, William's so smart and supportive. He really wants me to follow my dreams," I said instead.

The notes I discovered in William's childhood bedroom called to me from my handbag, but since I'd found them, I'd become a known entity and it was impossible to hide. Everyone talked to me like we'd been best friends for years. I noticed that most of the party guests were Mark and Cindy's age. There were few people under fifty and of that demographic, most of them seemed to be related to one of the older guests at the party. The only person I recognized outside of the Thompson family was Alexis, whom I'd first seen having coffee with Mark and again when she'd served as a character witness for William at the trial. It was clear from the way that she slid from one conversation to the next that this crowd of people was familiar to her. Seeing her, I could only think about how much happier Cindy would be if William were engaged to a woman like her instead of me.

Bentley found me in a rare moment of peace that I was using to stuff as many canapés in my mouth as possible. I'd been taking sips of wine to break awkward silences all evening, which resulted in a large consumption of wine on a very empty stomach.

"It's good to see you again, Hannah," he said.

We hadn't had a real conversation beyond the required pleasantries since our kiss. I swallowed the food in my mouth.

"It's good to see you too," I replied.

"How are things going?"

"Great. I'm engaged. Writing a novel. You know."

My plate was empty and I looked around desperately for another server; all of them seemed to have disappeared.

"Yes, my brother mentioned. Congratulations. We're going to be family."

"You're not going to tell him, are you? About what happened?"

Bentley smiled at me. It was the dazzling smile of a man who knew how good-looking he was.

"I don't even know what you're talking about," he said.

It took me a moment to realize that he was agreeing with me rather than that he had actually forgotten our kiss. I hoped that he liked my dress.

"Good," I said, and was grateful when William appeared at my side.

"My dad's business partners want to meet you," he said, placing his arm around my waist as he pulled me away.

I couldn't tell if there was weird energy in the air between them or if it was my own projection.

I approached Alexis Hutchington before the end of the party when William's father pulled him into another room to talk with some older men who were indistinguishable from one another. I wanted to gauge her intentions toward William. She'd claimed that their relationship was platonic, but as someone who had unexpectedly fallen in love with him, I couldn't quite believe that was the whole truth. I'd had my eye on her throughout the evening. From a distance, she looked as beautiful as ever, but up close she looked a little ragged, her makeup smudged around the edges like she'd been crying. Her breath carried with it a heavy smell of liquor and I gathered that she was quite drunk.

"Alexis? I'm Hannah," I introduced myself.

"Ah, yes, the new fiancée," she said, like I was the butt of a joke that hadn't been told yet.

I meant to slide into the conversation. Start with some pleas-antries about the food or the expensive-looking jewelry that dan-gled from her ears. Instead, I asked her if she was in love with William, a question that made her burst into laughter.

"You're not the first person to ask me that. Our parents tried to set us up for years."

"So?" I pressed. "Did you ever date?"

Alexis squinted at me like she was trying to measure my soul and then glanced around the room in the way of a woman who was about to utter a secret.

"At the risk of perjuring myself, there was a time a few years back when something almost happened between us. We went on a couple of dates, or at least I thought they were dates," she said reluctantly. It was unclear whether her hesitation was due to con-tradicting her testimony or if she was embarrassed about having misconstrued the situation.

"There was one night that I thought we were going to hook up," she continued. "But when we got back to his apartment, Wil-liam started crying. He told me that he wasn't good enough to be with me. When I asked him what he meant, he said that he was worried that I would get hurt. He told me that he couldn't be with me because he thought he was going to cause me harm."

She looked down at the floor, her pretty face unable to meet my gaze.

"Why didn't you say something during the trial?" I asked. I wanted to know more, for Alexis to paint me a picture of Wil-liam's face as he cried.

"I didn't think it was going to matter. I thought he was going to be convicted. The lawyers, they coached me. Told me what to say. I guess it didn't really seem like a lie until he got off. I only testified because my parents wanted me to. They don't know about what happened between William and me. As far as they know, William is the nice boy that they watched grow up who just happened to be in the wrong place at the wrong time. And Mark, he practically begged me. I've never seen him act that way before."

The meeting I'd witnessed in the coffee shop suddenly became clear to me. For weeks I'd wondered what Mark had said to Alexis and now I knew. *I need you. Our family needs you. Think about all the good times that we've shared. Do you really want that to be over?* There was something satisfying in knowing that I'd seen Mark Thompson beg.

Alexis stopped talking when William and Mark reappeared in the living room. Later, I would smell cigar smoke on William's suit jacket. That was who these men were, the type of people who disappeared into spaces absent of women in order to smoke expensive imports.

"Thank you for being honest with me," I said and squeezed her hand.

Alexis walked away before William could say anything, heading straight to the bar that was set up in the corner.

Though I hadn't learned anything that definitively proved William's guilt, the conversation with Alexis made the party worth it, even as I fought through discomfort in the rest of the conversations with the Thompson family acquaintances. There had been a burgeoning romance between Alexis and William, a seemingly perfect couple, and he'd ended it over fear of his own actions. Something must've shifted since then that allowed him to get into a relationship with me. Either he trusted himself more or he'd decided to give in to his impulses, the ones that he had warned Alexis about the night that they almost hooked up.

"I'm going to get a ring," William murmured into my ear when we were finally back home in bed. "Any ring that you want. Do you like diamonds? I'll get you a big diamond."

I flexed my fingers and pretended to moan as William's own fingers flicked across my nipples.

I didn't tell him that what I wanted most was immaterial. He could fill my fingers with precious gems and none of them would be worth as much as the truth about what had happened to the murdered women, a gift less like a ring around my finger and more like a rope around my neck.

40

I took the notes from William's room with me to the coffee shop on Monday after our usual early morning yoga session. Already I was becoming stronger, more flexible. I purchased several matching sets of workout clothes that I'd seen Jill wear on her Instagram posts that I'd never been able to afford before I had access to William's credit card. I looked good, like one of those fitness people. The other women in class continued to watch William and me, but I was beginning to enjoy their eyes on me. *Yes, I have sex with an accused serial killer,* I hoped my body said with every pose.

"I'm off to work on my novel," I told William before I left.

I got a croissant with my latte even though William and I had already eaten breakfast, my anxiety about money already dissipating like a snake shedding its old skin. I took my usual table by the window and carefully took out the notes. I wished I had the white gloves of an archivist.

That math test was so hard, the first note began. *I studied so much and I'm sure that I failed it. I swear that Mr. Seager wants us to fail. The questions looked nothing like what was in the study guide.*

There was no response from William. Presumably the sender of the notes kept his responses; perhaps they were even stored in a childhood desk somewhere. It was like listening to a single side of a phone call. I could tell from the handwriting that they were written by a girl. It was popular girl script, letters that were cute and looping.

Did you know that Samantha has a crush on Tommy? Don't tell him. She would kill me if she knew that I told you. She wants him to ask her to prom. Do you think that he will?

The notes were a disappointment, not even good gossip by high school standards. It was a reminder that other people are fundamentally boring. I didn't care who liked whom decades prior. I wanted to know about William and any signs that he showed of being a potential serial killer as a teen. Occasionally, the note writer delved into emotional confessions.

I can't wait to get out of here, she wrote. *I want to go to college somewhere in California. Somewhere as far away as possible where I don't know anyone.*

Mostly, though, she recounted the things that happened in school, the small dramas of each day, and her anxieties about schoolwork. She was hyperbolic, claiming that she had failed nearly everything, only to come back and report straight As. There was no clear romantic connection between her and William, but I presumed that at least one of them was interested in the other due to the longevity of their correspondence. There was a single reference to violence.

I heard about the fight. I don't think it's fair that they suspended you.

You're not even going to get this until you get back, the note said, confirming my suspicion that they were passing them back and forth during the school day.

Other than that, the only piece of information I was able to glean from the notes was the writer's name.

Sometimes I think to myself, god Gracie, you're so dumb.

I tried to remember if I'd ever heard William mention someone named Gracie and came up empty. I spent the rest of the morning refreshing the forum until I exhausted all possible content and went home to watch television for the rest of the afternoon, making sure to clean up before William came home and found me sprawled across the couch.

My investigation stalled after that. I kept waiting for something to happen, but there was little news on the forum and I was certain that I'd searched every corner of the home that I shared with William. Every once in a while, I checked the box in William's desk and found it undisturbed. If the objects truly were mementos of murder, they weren't ones that William liked to look at often. I was eager to get back into the Thompson estate, but William had told me that he saw enough of his family at the law firm and would rather spend his free time as just the two of us.

In lieu of material proof, I hoped that William would reveal something in his actions.

He came home from a run one day with his clothes bloodied.

"Are you okay?" I asked, though I already knew that he wasn't the one that was hurt.

"Yeah," he said through panted breath. "I found an injured dog and I stayed with it until the shelter could come pick her up.

Thankfully, they said that it's just a surface wound and that she's going to be all right."

The story was suspicious, but sure enough, the following week a dog showed up on the "Adopt Me" page that matched the description of the one that William had found.

Another time, I walked into the kitchen to find several bags' worth of equipment from a home improvement store including tarps, bricks, and a variety of tools. I wondered if William was building some sort of murder cave or planned to brick me inside of our home like the villain in an Edgar Allan Poe story.

I spent hours strategizing how to best broach the question of whether my fiancé planned to encase me in brick, only for William to excitedly announce that he planned on building a pizza oven in the backyard. After an afternoon of enthusiastic progress, the supplies were abandoned in the grass, never to be lifted again.

I thought for sure William's dark side broke through when he pulled out a pair of handcuffs one night during foreplay. I prepped myself to die, an emotional state that had lost some of its vigor after doing it so many times—my body crying "Wolf!" only for the wolf to reveal itself to be a man who enjoyed performing cunnilingus. *This time,* I insisted, waiting for my pulse to quicken. *This time he's really a murderous beast.*

"What's this?" I asked.

"I want to try something new," he said and secured me to the bedpost.

"Be right back," he said and disappeared from the bedroom.

In the forty seconds that I waited for him to return, I contemplated all the ways that he might be planning to kill me. There would be strangulation involved, certainly, but I knew from the forensic testimony that whoever killed those women liked to take their time. Before I could make any headway in my halfhearted attempts to escape from the handcuffs, William returned with a can of whipped cream. He smiled deviously.

"I thought we could use a little treat," he said.

I hoped that I was able to properly hide my disappointment.

Other days, he was simply in a bad mood for reasons that I suspected were related to his family.

"It's hard working with my father and brother," he told me over dinner one night. "I was determined never to work for my family. I wanted to make my own way in the world, and here I am, working for them."

He repeatedly brought up his mother's comments about my lack of an engagement ring. He stared at my naked fingers.

"Just wait," he said.

I didn't have the heart to tell him that the ring wasn't the real issue that Cindy had with our engagement. It was because she could smell it on me, the stench of being one of those women, like I was a body already starting to rot even as I was still alive.

"I'm so excited," I told him.

While I waited for him to kill me, William and I settled into a rhythm.

We went to yoga every morning and ate wholesome meals for dinner that included every food group. On Saturdays, we went to the farmer's market and purchased fresh cut flowers to brighten up our home. We took selfies that I wasn't allowed to post online because it was a security risk. William lived with the knowledge that there was always going to be someone out there who thought he should've been found guilty and wanted him dead because of it, and he didn't want me to have to share that risk. What I failed to mention was that the forum had already figured out who I was and spent an entire day in a flurry, posting whatever pictures they could find of me, critiquing every facet of my being, and suggesting that maybe I was the one who killed Kelsey Jenkins before moving on to their next topic of conversation. What the forum didn't know was that I was sitting there reading every word they said about me, chiming in with a couple of quips of my own about my crooked bottom teeth and cheap clothes. Even as their insults wounded me, I felt haughty in my invisibility, pausing only briefly to consider that if I was an anonymous member of the forum, there was no telling the actual identity of the other users. At least in that space, I was able to acknowledge the engagement publicly even if they hated me for it.

I thirsted for the attention I would receive if I posted a photo of William and me together. I wanted the people who didn't know who he was to see his handsomeness. I wanted friends from former lives to search my name and say, "Oh my god, Hannah is dating that guy who was acquitted for serial murder" and tell everyone they knew about it. Because I couldn't post a picture that revealed his identity, I made a point of posting a photo of our fingers intertwined suggestively.

Meghan and Carole were the only people who seemed to take notice.

Are you dating someone??? I can't wait to hear all about it at my wedding!!! Meghan said, texting me for the first time in weeks. My coupledom seemed to reopen possibilities in our friendship that were previously closed.

Carole left me a voicemail that said, "Hannah, I saw the picture you posted online. Please tell me you're not with that man."

I responded to Meghan and said, **Yes!!!** I imagined taking a weekend trip with William to Minneapolis to attend Meghan's wedding. We could book a suite instead of staying at my parents' house and I would parade him in front of all my friends while they whispered amongst themselves about William's identity.

I didn't reply to Carole. I didn't want to hear her disapproval. I couldn't even assure her of William's innocence because I wasn't totally convinced myself.

Still without a ring, William and I started planning our wedding, settling on a local art gallery as the perfect place. We both agreed that a small ceremony was best.

"My parents can make anything a circus," William said.

I made an invite list in my head that included my parents, my two cousins, my aunts and uncles, and a series of question marks next to Meghan's name. I considered inviting Dotty and Lauren and ultimately kept them off the list when I couldn't decide if it was weird to have other women who harbored obsessions over my fiancé at our wedding ceremony. As far as I knew, neither of them had heard about the engagement. Every time I considered texting them, my gut filled with a mixture of guilt and satisfaction that I was the one, me, who had successfully persuaded William to settle down, and I ultimately decided that it was better if they didn't know.

We picked a date nine months in the future, an amount of time that William described as "soon" and I took as evidence that William wasn't going to try to kill me before then.

We set a wedding date, I wrote in the "innocent" column of my notebook.

While William was at work, I either spent my time binge-watching trash reality television or at the coffee shop where I scrolled the forum and played games of solitaire.

"How is your novel going?" William asked occasionally.

"Great," I always responded, though I still had the same two sentences that I'd had since the first day I started writing.

"I hope you'll let me read it someday," he replied.

"Yes, absolutely. When it's ready."

The forum grew dejected. Not only were there no leads on

who killed Kelsey Jenkins, but the truth about what had happened to the original four girls was still unknown. Even as users swore they were committed to finding the killer, conversation lapsed into talking about our favorite true-crime documentaries and books. Things that were already documented were so much more satisfying than things in action because they already had a resolution, or if they didn't, the lack of resolution had become a thing of lore, like the Black Dahlia. William resided in an uncomfortable murky area.

"If only he would commit another murder so we would have more evidence to work with," one user joked.

"Don't say that," said another. "These are real people we're talking about."

The day that everything changed, I was eating avocado toast and drinking a caramel latte while eavesdropping on the Bible study group sitting next to me.

"This passage really spoke to me," a girl said. "I realized that the reason Brett broke up with me is that he sensed we're not meant to be together. We're not soulmates."

I lazily refreshed the forum, more out of habit than anything else. Someone had posted a picture from the bar where Kelsey worked and I started to scroll by when I noticed a bowl of matchbooks sitting on the bar behind her. I zoomed in and though it was blurry, the image on the front looked familiar. I got out my phone and flipped through pictures of the gourmet meals that William had cooked, a cute dog I'd met on a walk, and an embarrassing number of selfies, until finally I reached the pictures that I'd taken of the contents of the box hidden in William's desk from the very first week we moved in together.

"Holy shit," I said loudly, and the entire Bible study table turned to look at me.

The matchbook was identical to the ones in the picture.

I didn't know how to make sense of it. What I'd just discovered seemed to imply something impossible, something that certain users on the forum had been claiming since it happened: that William, from his jail cell, had somehow played a role in the murder of Kelsey Jenkins.

41

I wanted to rush to the bar where Kelsey had worked as soon as I discovered the identity of the matchbook, but I couldn't because William and I had been invited to the Thompson family estate for dinner.

I hadn't seen any of the Thompson family since the party after William was first released.

"They're all very excited about the wedding," William assured me repeatedly in a way that suggested that they were harboring reservations.

The matchbook had to wait. I carried the knowledge of it home with me and began to get ready. It took some searching, but I'd managed to find a dress that Anna Leigh had worn to a friend's bridal shower on an upscale resale site that was perfect for a Thompson family get-together. I paired it with earrings that William had bought me at the farmer's market that looked like a pair that Emma owned.

"You look beautiful," William said when he came home.

I had an irrational urge to tell William about the matchbook, not because I wanted to confront him, but because I'd gotten in the habit of telling him the most mundane details of my day: the things I'd eaten, the way my body felt, lies about the progress I'd made on my novel. That was the pleasure of having a partner. There was always someone to tell things to regardless of how small or stupid those things were. It proved to be incredibly difficult not to tell William about himself.

I watched as William changed out of his work clothes, buttoning up a clean shirt. *Did you hire someone to kill Kelsey Jenkins? I thought. While you were writing letters to me, were you communicating with someone else and giving them instructions to kill? Was she murdered only to draw attention away from you or was it something else? A weak pour, a miscalculated bill, or a rejection of your advances?*

William sprayed on his cologne and smiled at me.

"Ready to go?" he asked.

It was never clearer to me that he was unable to read my mind.

At the Thompson family estate, a maid greeted us at the front door and led us to the formal living room where Mark stood next to a drink cart with a glass of amber liquid in his hand. Cindy sat on the couch, already drinking something out of a martini glass.

"It's my future daughter-in-law," Mark announced when we came in. He hugged me and shook William's hand, a formal gesture from a father to a son.

Cindy eyed me for a minute, taking in my appearance before getting up to greet us.

"Nice to see you again, Hannah," she said.

Everything she said carried a double meaning. Even as she told me that it was nice to see me, her greeting carried with it a stench of disapproval. Her iciness wounded me. Despite myself, I longed for her approval. Even though her son had possibly killed several women, her tone implied that I still wasn't worthy of him.

"What would you like to drink?" Mark asked.

"I'll have what she's having."

I gestured toward Cindy's glass, hoping that she would take my order as a gesture of goodwill. I wasn't usually a martini drinker, but I also didn't usually dine inside mansions.

Bentley strode into the room as Mark handed me my glass.

"Hannah," he said, and kissed me on the cheek, leaving me with the feeling of his lips even as he pulled away.

"Bentley," I said politely.

Virginia and the two children trailed in behind him. The boys wore button-down shirts and bow ties, their hair carefully combed. They hugged their grandfather before sitting primly on the couch next to their grandmother.

"I'll have a glass of milk, please," the older one said.

"Me too," echoed the other.

They were curious children, like adults tucked into tiny bodies, nothing like the rambunctious babies my friends had started to push out. William told me that Bentley's children, much like himself, were primarily raised by a series of nannies. Eventually, they would enroll in the same private schools that he and Bentley had gone to, their admission secured through legacy status.

I sat down on the couch across from them.

"How old are you?" I asked.

"I'm five," replied the younger one.

"I'm eight," said the older one after regarding me with a watchful eye, not unlike his grandmother.

He already looked like Bentley. I could see his entire future like a movie. He would be the rich, popular kid in high school.

He would go to his father's alma mater and rush his fraternity, where he would be a shoo-in. He would meet a woman who looked exactly like Virginia and after an appropriate amount of time they would get married. He would join his father's law firm, which by that point would be Bentley and William's law firm unless William killed me first.

I asked for a refill of my martini. William sat next to me on the couch and placed his arm around my waist.

"What are you learning in school?" I asked.

"I'm learning to read." The younger one beamed.

The older one sneered at me like it was a stupid question and I was relieved when the maid came in and announced that dinner was ready.

"Wine?" the maid asked after we were seated, and I eagerly accepted, downing the rest of my martini.

"So, Hannah, what do your parents do?" Mark asked.

The meal started with a salad served on delicate white plates. I crunched a crouton between my teeth.

"My dad is retired and my mom's a teacher," I replied.

"How nice that she gets summers off," Mark said and laughed.

I worried what my face was doing as I bit my tongue, thinking of how my mother would respond to the comment. My mother still didn't know about the engagement, though she knew I was seeing someone. She tried calling occasionally and I answered every few calls, giving vague responses when she asked about my whereabouts.

"Don't worry, Mom, I'm safe," I assured her.

Even though I could tell she didn't believe me, she never questioned any further. I suspected that she didn't want to know.

"What did your dad do before he was retired?" Mark continued to press.

Mark, I understood, was the kind of man for whom work meant everything and I knew that my answers could only disappoint him.

"He worked in data management. I never totally understood what it was that he did," I said apologetically.

William shifted the conversation to discussing football and I was grateful for the distraction. I excused myself, citing the need to use the restroom. My plea was legitimate; my bladder was uncomfortably full, as the maid had continued to fill both the water and wineglasses and I had continued to drink.

I didn't mean to snoop. I really didn't. I already had the matchbook to investigate, and the results of my last estate search—the notes—had yielded nothing of interest. Somehow, I found myself wandering past the bathroom door that Cindy had directed me to and toward the rest of the first floor.

I didn't care about the living room or the foyer. It was disarming how few personal effects the Thompson family décor contained. One of the affordances of wealth, it seemed, was the ability to erase yourself. Instead, I headed straight for the closed door that I'd noticed at the back of the house, a room that I'd seen Mark abscond to with several of his business partners during the party.

The room turned out to be an office paneled in a dark wood. There was a fireplace on one wall that seemed larger than necessary for Georgia's weather. On top of the fireplace was a taxidermied stag head and I thought uneasily about the picture I'd found in William's room of him and his brother smeared with blood. On another wall was a row of shelves that contained books that were too pretty to be anything other than decorative. The wall across from that was covered in guns.

The guns were mounted like they were precious paintings and

not items whose sole purpose was inflicting death. There were big guns and little guns, which were the only descriptors I knew how to use. Guns that looked like they killed quickly and antique guns that killed slowly. What, I wondered, did Mark need all of those guns for?

"This isn't the bathroom," a voice behind me said, and I jumped.

"Bentley," I said. "You scared me." I was grateful that it was him and not Mark. It wasn't as though I thought Mark would shoot me for my intrusion, but it didn't seem entirely out of the realm of possibility.

Bentley grinned.

"You were gone for a while and I thought I would check and make sure you found the bathroom," he said.

"I found the bathroom. I just—"

"Wanted to see the house? That's understandable. This place is monstrous. Virginia is hoping that they'll pass it down to us, but in all honesty, I would rather sell it."

"That's funny. I thought this sort of place would be your style."

"Nah, I like something a little more modern."

Bentley strolled deeper into the room and looked around like he was seeing it for the first time.

"Why does your dad have all these guns?" I asked, gesturing at the wall. "Does he hunt or something?"

"Something like that," Bentley said.

I raised my eyebrows at him.

Bentley shrugged.

"My father likes expensive, violent things and guns fill all of his parameters. He used to take us to the shooting range when we were kids, but I don't know how much he actually goes anymore."

I looked at the wall and frowned. I thought about the box in William's desk, the weight of the gun when I held it in my hand, and the things stored beneath it; the gym card, the hair tie, the bookmark, and the pack of cigarettes with the matchbook tucked inside—a matchbook that I now knew came from the bar where Kelsey had worked. I wasn't yet sure how Mark's gun collection connected to it all or if it even did, but being alone with Bentley provided another kind of opportunity.

Bentley knew things about William, things that other people didn't or were unwilling to admit. *William is a complicated person. He can be dangerous,* he'd told me the first time that we talked. It was possible that he could help me figure out how the matchbook had gotten into William's desk drawer, how William could be connected to Kelsey Jenkins's murder even though he'd been in jail at the time of her death.

Besides, even if he didn't know anything, I'd been dying to tell someone about the matchbook. The forum was off-limits because it would mean outing myself as William's fiancée, a woman I'd previously insulted under my anonymous username. I couldn't tell William because I would have to admit that I had snooped through his things and in the best-case scenario that made me a bad fiancée and, in the worst, it was possible that admission might send him into a murderous rage. Telling Bentley was almost like telling William. His face, in the dim light, nearly identical to his brother's.

"I found something," I said.

"What?"

"I found a matchbook in William's closet. It's from the bar where Kelsey Jenkins worked."

Bentley stopped his pacing to look at me, his face momentarily dropping its jovial veneer.

"That name sounds familiar," he said.

"Kelsey Jenkins, the woman who was murdered during William's trial," I said, incredulous. Surely, he knew who Kelsey Jenkins was. Sometimes I felt like the only one who remembered the women, their names already lost to William's infamy.

Bentley looked away, his glance shifting toward the wall of guns.

"Are you snooping on my brother?" Bentley asked. He picked up a cigar that rested on the desk and examined the label.

"I wouldn't exactly call it snooping."

Bentley raised an eyebrow. His face was still serious, but there was a playfulness to the movement.

"Okay, fine. Maybe I am snooping. In any case, I need someone to go to the bar with me. Do you want to go?"

I regretted the invitation as soon as it came out of my mouth. If there was anything that a person wasn't supposed to do while engaged to an acquitted serial killer, it was go to a bar with the killer's brother to investigate a murder.

He put the cigar down.

"Yes," he said.

We made the type of eye contact that carried an intimacy with it. The weight of our actions wasn't lost on me, a fiancée and a brother investigating the person that they claimed to love.

Before either of us could say anything else, William appeared in the doorway.

"What are you doing?" he asked.

He had that look on his face, the one that he got when he was upset and was trying to hide it.

"Nothing. I'm just giving Hannah a tour of the house," Bentley replied quickly.

"Dinner is getting cold," William said, like he had made the food himself.

We followed him back to the table. Bentley's older son was describing his part in the school play where he'd been cast as the lead. I watched Mark as his grandson spoke. He was recontextualized for me after seeing the wall of guns. He cut into his steak, smearing it through sauce before putting it in his mouth and chewing aggressively. I thought about when I had first met him and how I'd mistaken him for being friendly because he acted friendly with a lot of people and smiled often. I'd since realized that a smile could be used as a weapon and friendliness used to cover underlying anger.

I made a mental note to write *Father has gun wall* in my notebook as soon as I got a moment alone.

Two things happened during dessert.

The first was that William got down on one knee and opened a box. Inside the box was the biggest diamond that I'd ever seen, which to be fair wasn't particularly meaningful as I didn't spend a lot of time looking at diamonds.

"I'm proposing again," William said. "Properly this time."

I regretted, a little bit, spending the day wondering whether or not he was a serial killer as he talked about how special our time together was and how the longer we lived together, the more he loved me.

He slid the ring on my finger. I hoped that they didn't have any remnants of chocolate on them from the soufflé. It was too big and the diamond immediately slipped to the side.

William frowned.

"We'll get it resized," he said.

The diamond was overshadowed by the second thing that happened.

"Not to steal any of your thunder," Bentley said. "But Virginia and I have an announcement too."

I opened and closed my fist, fiddling with the ring on my finger.

"We're pregnant," Virginia said.

Cindy let out a screech of joy. Their eldest child rolled his eyes. William delivered a strained "Congratulations."

"This is exactly what we needed after the year that we've all had," Mark said.

"We're so excited to bring a new life into this world," Virginia replied.

William was dejected in the car.

"I know that I'm supposed to be happy for my brother," he said. "And I am. It's just, I wanted that to be a special moment for you. For us."

"It *was* special."

"My brother, he has this need to be the center of attention. What were the two of you talking about in the office, anyway?"

"Nothing," I said, staring through the window into the darkness.

"Nothing?"

"He was telling me about the house."

"Oh." His utterance carried doubt with it.

In bed, William fucked me voraciously, the way that he had when he first came to my hotel room and it had been months since he'd last touched a woman.

"I want you to have my baby," he said when he finished. His breath was hot against my face.

"It's something to talk about."

"I'm serious. I want us to have a little baby. I want him to have the kind of life that I never did."

I thought of the Thompson family estate, the maid that waited upon the family hand and foot.

"Okay," I said. I kissed him on the cheek.

I was self-conscious when his cum dribbled out from inside of me when I got up to use the bathroom. There was something constraining about the thought of a child, like being tied up in a bad way. To think about forever monitoring my own progeny to see if they had any signs of being a killer.

42

I forgot about inviting Bentley to the bar until he showed up at the house one morning after William left for work. I was still wearing my yoga clothes. In truth, I planned on staying in my yoga clothes the entire day. When the doorbell rang, I assumed it was a package.

"Bentley," I said when I saw him standing there.

"Do you still want to go to that bar?" he asked.

I paused for a moment.

"Yes."

I let him into the house. Bentley sat on the pristine white couches while I put on a dress and some makeup. My hand shook while I applied my eyeliner and I had to clean it off and start again.

"Ready," I announced as I walked into the living room.

"You look nice," Bentley said.

"Thank you."

I knew that it shouldn't feel like I was going on a date, but it did.

"Aren't you supposed to be at work?" I asked as we pulled onto the highway.

"I set my own schedule," Bentley said, and then glanced at me. "What about you? Aren't you supposed to be working on your novel?"

The way that he said "novel" made me blush, like I was filling in the pages of a children's coloring book.

"I'm allowed to take breaks," I replied.

There were several minutes of quiet and I wished that Bentley would turn some music on. I was too nervous to do it on my own for fear of being mocked for my choices.

Bentley broke the silence first.

"Tell me, Hannah. What have you learned about my brother?"

I knew that William would loathe that particular pathway of questioning, which didn't stop me from pulling out my notebook.

"Quite a bit. He cares about his body. He likes to eat well and stay fit, though he occasionally eats a fast-food hamburger and a milkshake as a treat. He talks about reading books more than he ever actually reads—I think he's quite insecure in some ways— and likes to watch dramas on TV. He's a good cook, but only in foods that he's been trained to make. William likes to stick to things that he's good at, which I guess is true of most of us. He's very tidy and it bothers him when things are out of place. He told me that he can't focus when there's clutter. He likes being a law- yer but wishes that he was at his own practice instead of working for your father."

I paused, flipping through the pages, trying to decide exactly how much I wanted to reveal.

"Oh, and he has a gun."

"I have a gun. Does that make me a murderer?" Bentley asked in his usual flirtatious manner. He was a faster driver than I was and weaved in and out of lanes as he passed slower vehicles.

I thought of Mark's office, his wall of guns. All of the men in the Thompson family had a penchant for weapons, it seemed.

"I mean, maybe. Have you killed anyone?" I replied, matching his tone.

Bentley laughed.

"Okay, so tell me more about this matchbook."

I bit my lip and looked out the window at the passing mile markers.

"You can't tell William about any of this. You have to promise. I do love him, you know," I said.

I worried that I'd already revealed too much. I was a ditch-digger rethinking the hole when I was already too deep in to ever climb back out again.

"Do you?" Bentley glanced at me again. "Can you love someone and think they're a murderer?"

"Keep your eyes on the road," I told him, refusing to answer the question.

Bentley smiled.

"Relax. I've made this drive a million times."

I took a deep breath.

"I looked through William's things when we first moved in together. He doesn't have a lot of personal stuff. It's kind of weird, like no knickknacks or anything. He's very utilitarian in that sense. Anyway, I found a box in his desk with a bunch of stuff in it."

I didn't mention the other things in the box or the notes that I'd found in the desk at their parents' house.

"And in the box, I found this matchbook. I didn't know what

it meant at the time, but I took a picture of it in case it was important. Then one day I was on the forum—"

"The forum?"

"I'm on this forum that's investigating the murder of the women that William might've killed," I said reluctantly.

Bentley let out a deep-throated type of laugh that I'd never heard him do before. It was sincere laughter, the type that couldn't be faked.

"Let me get this straight. You're engaged to my brother and at the same time you're on an internet forum talking about how he's a serial killer?"

"Well, when you put it that way."

"How else would you have me put it?"

I didn't have a good response, so I continued.

"Anyway, someone posted a picture from the bar where Kelsey worked and I recognized the matchbook."

"Wow," he said.

"I know. Wow."

"Wasn't she killed while William was in jail though?" Bentley asked.

"That's what I can't figure out. How is he connected to her murder if there's no way that he killed her?"

"That's the question, isn't it?" Bentley said.

He pulled into a parking space directly in front of the bar. A sign warned that there was a two-hour time limit on the spot and for once, I was grateful for the parameter because it meant our outing had a set end time.

The building was brick with a green awning. The windows were covered by neon signs advertising different types of beer. It looked like the kind of place that Max would go to. Conversely, Bentley looked out of place. His shirt was too nice and he grew too much hair on his head compared to the regulars who lined the bar, a row of matching bald men with beer bellies.

Bentley was unfazed and strode up to the bar and ordered us each a Jack and Coke.

"You like whiskey, if I remember correctly," he said.

The invocation of our previous drunken nights together made me queasy. It might've been a mistake entering a situation in which Bentley was my only way home. I spotted the fishbowl of matchbooks and took one of my own. A memento of my investigation.

We sat at a small table.

"So," he said. "What are we looking for?"

I frowned.

"I don't know," I said.

"You're taking the lead here, Detective Hannah."

It was difficult to tell if Bentley was taking the situation seriously. There was a perpetual grin on his face that mocked me.

"How's Virginia?" I asked, changing the subject.

"She's okay. She's having pretty bad morning sickness."

"I can't imagine that's fun."

Bentley's face wrinkled.

"The whole thing is sort of unpleasant, actually."

"You're not looking forward to being a father again?"

"I thought that we were finally going to get a chance to breathe. You know, with things in our personal lives settling down and the boys getting big enough to be more independent."

"I have to admit that I was surprised when Virginia made the announcement. I was under the impression that things have been a little rough between the two of you," I said.

"Virginia's convinced that a new baby is what we need to make our family 'complete,'" Bentley replied, his tone making it clear that he didn't agree with her.

"Do you need another drink?" I asked. He still had some liquid in his cup, whereas I'd already drained mine.

The smile returned to his face.

"You're such a fish," he said. "Put it on my tab."

The bartender on duty was a middle-aged woman with dyed red hair and large breasts. She looked like someone who had always been behind a bar, who was born for the industry that she found herself in. Kelsey was still young and beautiful when she died, but twenty years down the line she might've turned into the woman who had replaced her.

"Two more," I said.

I noticed a small, framed picture of Kelsey Jenkins on the wall behind her. The frame had a plaque that read **FOREVER IN OUR HEARTS**. I appreciated the memorial to the woman whose death had altered my life so profoundly.

I pulled up a picture of William on my phone, one of us together at a sushi restaurant that we'd had a server take. William looked characteristically handsome and I, regrettably, had blinked at the exact wrong time.

"Do you know this man?" I asked when she returned with the drinks.

She squinted at my phone and shrugged.

"Not that I can recall," she said. "It's hard to say though. We get a lot of people in here. Why? Did he cheat on you or something?"

I wanted to scream. How did she not recognize the acquitted serial killer William Thompson? If society really wanted to punish those accused of being monsters, they would've made them walk around wearing Halloween masks that depicted the crimes they'd committed.

"No, no, nothing like that," I said. "Thank you."

I returned to the table, where Bentley was typing something on his phone. He put it facedown when I returned.

"You look good, Hannah," he said. He looked at me in a way that made me blush.

"Thank you."

"No, really. I mean it. I think it's been good for you—for all of us, really—to get away from the trial environment. People aren't supposed to live like that for long."

When I thought of who I'd been during the trial, I could only picture a jellyfish floating helplessly through the ocean. What a pathetic person I'd been then.

"Yeah, you're right. I think I didn't realize how on edge I was until it was over."

"How is your novel coming along?"

I snorted.

"It's not. I only have two sentences. You know, I always thought that my problem was that I didn't have enough time. Now it's like I have too much time. I can't focus."

"Does William know? He talks about you like you're Charles Dickens."

"No. I don't want to disappoint him. He's been so supportive."

"And look how you've returned the favor," Bentley said, a comment that I resented.

More people began to filter into the bar as it got later in the afternoon. The clientele expanded beyond bar regulars to people getting off work, dressed like professionals. Bentley got us another round of drinks. I began to feel warm as the liquor spread through my veins.

"Why did you kiss me?" I asked Bentley.

It was a question that had been in the back of my mouth since the kiss had happened. In truth, it was maybe why I had asked

Bentley to the bar in the first place. I wanted to investigate the matchbook, yes, but I also wanted to be alone with Bentley somewhere that William wouldn't see us. The thing that everyone forgot when they talked about killing two birds with one stone is that the birds had to die.

I knew what I wanted him to say. I wanted him to describe me as irresistible. To tell me that he had never done anything like that before. I wanted to be special.

Instead, he shrugged.

"Sometimes you just need an outlet," he said.

The response burned.

"Is that something you make a habit of? Kissing women that aren't your wife?"

"Says the woman who makes a habit of trying to reveal her fiancé as a murderer."

I glared at him.

Thankfully, our conversation was interrupted by a guy wearing a T-shirt from a local brewery and carrying three shot glasses full of a clear liquid.

"Hey, man," he said to Bentley. "It's been a while. Where have you been?"

He set the shots on the table.

"I brought these for you and your lady."

I thought he must've been mistaken. As far as I knew, Bentley had never been inside the bar before, or at least, he'd never mentioned it to me.

"Thanks, man," Bentley said. He wore a look that I'd never seen before. A scowl of irritation the man seemed unable to detect.

We clinked our shot glasses together and said, "Cheers," and I threw the liquid down my throat. I coughed with the burn of it, having lost the ability to rapidly consume alcohol after I turned thirty.

"Who was that?" I asked after the man returned to the bar.

"I have no idea," Bentley said.

"Have you been here before?" I asked.

"No. Why?"

"That man, he acted like he knew you."

"He was mistaken. I get that a lot. I've got that look. The everyman."

I peered at Bentley's face. I always thought of him as taking after Mark, but there were shades of Cindy within him too. He had the same penchant for plastering over his true feelings in favor of a transparent veil of lies. As hard as he tried to pass off the recognition like it was nothing, I could tell by the look on his face that he was perturbed. It occurred to me that Bentley had never told me his own motivations for accompanying me to the bar. It was possible that it was a protective impulse, and he wanted to make sure that I was safe during the course of my investigation. It seemed possible too that he wanted to kiss me again. I'd been too wrapped up in my considerations of how Bentley felt about me to stop and wonder why he would want to continue investigating his brother. Was Bentley as obsessed as I was with the women? Had he already been to the bar in order to investigate and that's why the man recognized him?

"What are we doing here?" I asked.

Bentley dropped any remaining pleasantness from his expression.

"You're asking me that? Hannah, you're the one that wanted to come here. Face it, you only fell in love with my brother because you thought that he might be a serial killer and you don't know what to do now that he might not actually be one after all."

"That's not true."

"It is. It's why you sought him out. Don't deny it. It's why you keep investigating even after he was acquitted. You don't care about those women. They're just abstractions to you. You have no idea what it feels like to lose someone close to you like that. Do you even want to marry him or are you just hoping that he kills you first?"

It was so close to the truth that it took my breath away.

"I love him."

"Oh, stop. You love serial killers. You're one of those women. You're a dime a dozen."

"But William loves me."

"Yeah, he loves how mad your hippy schtick makes our mother. He loves that you have nothing, no money, no career, and he can provide everything for you. He doesn't realize that it will never be enough because it's not really what you want from him."

Bentley laughed and shook his head.

"You're exactly what my brother deserves," he said.

"Fuck you," I said and stood up. The world spun beneath me. Shit.

"I'm leaving," I declared.

Bentley's rant was a reminder of why I didn't date men like him. They could be charming and handsome, but they always took a turn when women didn't behave the way that they wanted them to.

"Where are you going to go, Hannah? I'm your ride."

"I'll figure it out," I said and stormed off.

It was dark outside. I hadn't realized how late it was. A ticket flapped beneath the windshield wiper on Bentley's car and I was glad. It wasn't justice for the things that he'd said, but it was something.

I called William. I had no one else. When I spoke, I started to cry. I didn't mean for my tears to be manipulative, but that didn't stop them from being so.

"Will you come pick me up?" I said, my sobs loud and evident.

"Where are you?" William said, his voice panicked.

I gave him the name of the bar. If he was familiar with it, he didn't reveal that through the phone.

"I'll be right there," he said.

Unfortunately, "right there" was still an hour spent outside of a bar where a murdered woman used to work. I expected Bentley to come outside and apologize, but he didn't. I tried to wrap my head around what had happened. Things were fine, flirtatious even, and then a shift occurred. Though I hadn't learned anything more about the matchbook or how it had come into William's possession, I'd gotten a glimpse at the Bentley that William had described in his letters, the one that I'd never fully been able to see before.

I sat down on the sidewalk, not caring how dirty it was or who saw me. The summer heat had finally broken in late September and I might've been cold if I wasn't so drunk.

When William came, he found me with my head on my knees, trying to stop the world from spinning. He glanced at Bentley's car and I could tell by his face that he recognized it.

He held out his arm to pull me up.

"I'm sorry," I said, my tears starting anew.

"Let's get you home," he said. The statement should've been warm, but his voice was grim.

"Are you going to kill me now?"

I meant it to be a joke, though it was clear that William didn't find it funny.

He sighed and shook his head.

"Hannah—" he started to say with an edge to his voice.

Before he could say anything else, I barfed on his shoes.

43

I sobbed the entire car ride home.

"I'm sorry, I'm sorry, I'm sorry," I said, a broken record.

"Stop apologizing," William said, and sighed some more.

"I didn't mean to get so drunk. I'm sorry."

When we arrived back at the house, William dutifully made me a grilled cheese sandwich and then put me in bed and placed a glass of water on the bedside table. I saw him stick his shoes in a trash bag as if there was no saving them after what I'd done.

"Shh," he said as I continued to babble my apologies. "We'll talk about this later."

In the morning, William brought me a latte and a breakfast sandwich from the coffee shop to help ease my hangover. I sensed that he was angry at me, though he refused to acknowledge it even when pressed.

"I know you're mad," I said.

"I have to go to work," he replied.

Although my head was hazy and my stomach queasy, I desperately wanted William to climb into bed and fuck me as a way of apologizing. That he refused to do so made me want it even more.

"I have to go," he repeated as I munched on my biscuit, spilling crumbs across the sheets.

The house became the kind of quiet that was loud again in his absence.

I dragged myself to the couch, taking the comforter from the bed with me. Cozy blankets, I'd discovered, didn't fit the sparse aesthetic that William preferred, which meant that I was often left to freeze in the name of décor. I tried to watch television while lying on the couch and found it made my neck hurt to turn at such an angle to see the screen.

Despite their constant drinking, I'd never seen anyone in William's family, including William himself, manifest any kind of hangover, and this was reflected in their interior decorating. Rooms were designed to look good in pictures and to host parties in, rather than for weathering various states of misery.

I called my mother. Illogically, it seemed like a good time to tell her that I had moved in with and was engaged to an acquitted serial killer. I couldn't hide forever; I realized that now. More than that, I needed her that day, lying on the uncomfortable couch, my mouth dry from dehydration. Though I would never be the daughter she thought I was and she wasn't always the mother that I wanted her to be, she was still able to provide comfort.

My mother's phone rang and rang and rang. When I got her voicemail, I called her back again. Still no answer. Being ghosted, as it turned out, applied to more than just men that I was romantically interested in.

"Hi, Mom," I said to the voicemail. "I'm calling to check in. I hope that you and Dad are doing well. I'm doing good. Really good. Let's talk soon. Love you."

I hung up the phone and wished I had told her the truth. I was always lying unnecessarily to my parents, embarrassed by the reality of my existence.

I dragged myself off the couch to pour a glass of water and rummage through the cupboards for something to eat. The biscuit, though delicious, hadn't been enough to satiate my hangover, which I knew would require several more calorie-laden deposits before showing any sign of easing.

The kitchen proved to be disappointing. William didn't shop in the manner that I was used to. When I lived alone, I dragged myself to the grocery store every Sunday and did my best to buy food that would nourish me, with the occasional bag of chips or a chocolate bar thrown in. It took all of my will to return home and actually cook the food that I'd purchased instead of ordering delivery.

Food magically appeared at William's house. Logically, I knew that he ordered it. When I told him my requests, those things showed up the next week exactly as I had asked for them. The food that arrived was always healthy and fresh. A variety of fruits, vegetables, and whole grains. Nothing that I wanted to shove in my mouth in the midst of a hangover. It felt like cheating, a way around the temptations that everyone else was forced to deal with on a daily basis. I liked it until I didn't. Until I wanted chips so badly that I thought I might die without them.

I was scrolling through my phone, looking at pictures of pizza on the delivery app, when I heard a sound at the door.

"Just a second!" I shouted, and dashed to the bedroom because

I was wearing only a T-shirt and underwear. Bile rose in my throat from the unexpected movement.

It wasn't uncommon for people to let themselves into the house. There were housekeepers and various maintenance people who came in and out in order to keep the house in its pristine condition without necessitating any work on William's part. Two weeks prior, a housekeeper had walked in on me lounging in my bra and underwear, an event supremely embarrassing to us both. After that, I'd made a point of putting on clothes even if those clothes consisted only of sweatpants and a T-shirt, something that I hadn't bothered to do in my hungover state. I missed the nakedness of living by myself, when I regularly pooped with the bathroom door open because there was no one there to see.

The front door opened as I frantically pulled on a pair of yoga pants in the bedroom, which meant whoever it was had a key. My hair was a mess and my teeth unbrushed, but surely maintenance people had seen worse conditions than the one that I was currently in.

I went into the living room to greet the visitor. I dreaded having to say hello, but didn't want to appear unfriendly or as though I thought myself above people in blue-collar positions.

I thought it was William at first, returning to the house to retrieve something forgotten, and then I let out a squeak when I realized who it actually was.

"Bentley," I said.

"Hello, Hannah," he replied.

He held a fast-food bag in one hand and a paper cup in the other. Salt and grease wafted through the air toward my hangover-addled brain.

"What are you doing here?" I asked.

Bentley, to my knowledge, had only been to the house the previous day when he came to pick me up. Bentley and William didn't have the kind of sibling relationship where they stopped at each other's houses unannounced.

"I stopped by to pay you a visit," Bentley said. "I didn't like how we ended things last night."

"Look, Bentley, I know that you mean well, but I really don't feel very good right now. Maybe we could do this at another time? Maybe when I'm wearing clothes?"

I hated that Bentley was seeing me in such a vulnerable state. I was wearing the type of clothing that I ordinarily reserved for several weeks into a relationship when I knew that whoever I was seeing wouldn't leave me because I sometimes wore shapeless clothing and didn't brush my hair. I hated too that I still cared how I looked in front of him, even now, after he'd humiliated me.

"Please, Hannah. I brought you a burger. You're my brother's fiancée. It's important that we get along."

Bentley could've said anything after "I brought you a burger" and I would've agreed with it.

Even in the midst of my hangover, I was careful not to stain the white couch. I made a blanket of paper napkins and took the burger out of the bag. I couldn't remember eating anything so good. I took a sip of the soda. I was never a big soda drinker and had stopped completely when I moved in with William. I didn't remember Coke tasting so syrupy, so overly sweet on my tongue.

"Listen," Bentley said as I ate. "I know things have been weird between us since the trial. What happened—that was wrong, okay? Sometimes when I drink too much, I can't help myself."

I knew he was referencing our kiss without saying "kiss" and it was a relief to finally get it out in the air.

"And what I said yesterday," he continued. "That was wrong

too. I'm sure that you really love my brother. You've stuck by him through so much and I'm grateful that he has you."

The fries were salty and warm. I usually preferred ketchup, but I was so hungry that I didn't care. The food made me sleepy. I was no longer processing the words that Bentley was saying as I consumed the final bites of the burger. My eyes started to close. *Finally, finally,* my body chanted, and I gave in to sleep, never realizing that I'd been drugged.

44

I should've known it was Bentley. All those months of playing detective and I couldn't see what was right in front of me.

Bentley sits across from me. He still looks so handsome, even now. I should be revolted by him and instead I'm revolted with myself for thinking about his handsomeness at a time like this.

The clues were always there; I just hadn't been able to put them together. The way that the murders seemed to follow William around like a grudge. How Kelsey Jenkins died just as it seemed that William was going to go to prison for life. The man at the bar who knew Bentley, like he'd been there many times before. They look so similar, William and Bentley, almost indistinguishable to someone who didn't know what they were looking for.

Still, questions remain.

"What do you mean that you took what was owed to you?" I ask.

"Anna Leigh wasn't as innocent as she made herself out to be," Bentley says. "I'm sure that my brother never told you this, but the two of them were having a little affair long before I entered the picture. I guess he didn't satisfy her or maybe she, like you, was the type of woman that could never be satisfied. Either way, she came on to me when I was sitting in the lobby of William's office, waiting to pick him up to go to dinner. She already knew who I was. 'You must be William's brother,' she said."

"What a come-on," I say dryly.

Though I suppose that it's true that Anna Leigh didn't have to say anything at all to make me love her.

"We went out for drinks so that she could pick my brain. Those were the words that she used. We ended up at a hotel later that night. I asked about her husband and she said that he wouldn't notice that she was gone because he was out drinking with his friends, which he did a lot. Really, I can't blame her for wanting to have an affair. Anna Leigh liked rough sex. Her husband, he was boring, vanilla. All he knew was how to climb on top of her and pound away. She needed something more than that. The fact that she was also involved with William, that was just the cherry on top."

Bentley looks at me while he talks. I think about when he pushed me against the wall in the bar and kissed me, a night that I've thought about again and again. I don't know what he wants from me now. Does he want me to be turned on or revolted? I do my best to keep my face still, unmoving.

"Why did she have to die?" I continue to press.

"I didn't intend to kill her, not at first. I told myself that I wasn't a killer, not like William."

"William's not a killer," I say. "Isn't this proof of that?"

Bentley laughs.

"You and William really don't know each other, do you? Did he ever tell you about Gracie?"

I search the recesses of my brain for the name. As much as I pretend to care about victims, my life revolves around the men who have hurt them.

"Gracie from the notes," I say out loud.

It's Bentley's turn to look confused.

"What notes?"

"I found notes in William's old desk at your parents' house from Gracie to William. I thought they didn't mean anything."

It's the first time that I've seen Bentley look angry, like the way that I think a serial killer should look. I worry that it's enough for him to kill me before I get the whole story. I recognize that there's no good time to die, so I put parameters on it. Not until I know everything, not until I feel satisfied about this one single thing.

"Gracie was my girlfriend," he says. "William killed her."

The statement shouldn't shock me considering that I've spent a year of my life investigating whether William's a killer, but it does. I realize that I've grown complacent while living with him. It's like those people who live with giant cats who are surprised when they're suddenly missing an arm.

"Gracie was a sophomore when I was a senior. She was a lot like Anna Leigh. Very smart, mature for her age. We got to know each other when she came by the house to work on a group assignment with William. I had dated other people before Gracie, but she was my first serious relationship. We were even talking about doing long distance when I went off to college, something that I never imagined I would do."

"How did she die?" I ask.

Bentley stands up and begins to pace the room. It makes me nervous the way that he hovers like a man on the verge of murder.

"There was a party during the summertime. Real amateur shit. William got drunk. He'll say that this isn't what happened, but it is. William got drunk and decided it was a good idea to buy cocaine. He and Gracie snuck off together; that much I know. Gracie didn't do drugs, not like that. She barely even drank."

Bentley shakes his head.

"I don't know what happened in those woods. All that I know is that William called our father in the middle of the night and said that he needed his help. Gracie was found the next day near the house where the party had been held, dead of an apparent overdose. The police never connected what happened to William, but I know that he was involved. He kept telling me he was sorry, over and over again. What a stupid word. He offered to let me punch him and I told him that wasn't what I wanted."

"So instead of punching him you kill four women?" I ask.

"I killed four women because I needed to do something that my father couldn't erase."

"What do you mean that your father couldn't erase? Do you think that he helped cover up Gracie's death?"

Bentley snorts.

"Of course he did. That's what my father does. He intervenes or he pays someone to intervene for him. I think it really rattled him seeing William go to trial. He thinks of himself as having a kind of immunity, like he's the president or something."

I think of the way that Mark drove around to the locations where the women had disappeared. Lauren was right: he had been investigating, trying to figure out how something had slipped through the grasp of his control.

"Look," Bentley continues, "I didn't start off intending to kill them. I thought that I was going to sleep with Anna Leigh, ruin whatever she had with William, and let that be enough. But when I wrapped that rope around her throat—we were just fooling around that time—I could feel William's panic. Her death broke through William's posturing as this sensitive feminist. He's not that, you know. No matter how much he pretends to be. I never thought that I would do something like that, but it's easy to cross a big line once you start crossing little ones. You know that already, don't you, Hannah?"

"Don't compare us. We're not the same."

"I think we are," he says. "We're both bored and looking for meaning. You get off on thinking you're about to be murdered and I get off on murdering. It's not that different."

"What happened after Anna Leigh? Wasn't that enough?"

"It was Kimberly's own fault that she died," Bentley says, and then looks at me. "Kind of like you. She was always talking, asking questions. I went in there a couple days after Anna Leigh disappeared—my brother was distraught, you see, and I went to his condo to comfort him—and I stopped for gas on the way home. She recognized me. I'd stopped for gas there before. 'Remind me of your name,' she said, and I told her. That wasn't enough though; she wanted to know how my evening was and I explained that I'd just been to see my brother, who was upset because the woman he was having an affair with had disappeared. 'I hope she comes back,' Kimberly told me, and I let it slip that she was never coming back because I had murdered her. You don't know how good it felt to say that. But then, of course, I had to murder her too. That really made my brother panic—you should've seen him, drunk and crying, wondering if he was committing murder in his sleep."

"Is that why you killed Jill and Emma? To make him feel crazy?"

"Partially. I could tell that William was interested in Jill from the way that he talked about her. He was right—she was interesting. I found that out on the date that I took her on. Interesting, but insecure. And Emma, well, I wasn't interested in her romantically. She was more my brother's type. I thought it would be fun, though, to see what happened if I pointed the arrow directly at him."

"You led the police to William on purpose."

Bentley shrugs.

"I guess you could say that. We used to do stuff like that as kids, try to get each other in trouble. He should've known it was me right from the start."

"What about Kelsey Jenkins? Surely, you knew that it would be impossible to pin that one on William."

"Listen, I was trying to target William, not put him in prison forever. I thought if someone else died, it might help his defense. You're lucky it wasn't you, Hannah. I know you were at the ravine that night. You didn't think it was a coincidence, did you? That a body was found right after your visit? It would've been so easy for me to kill you right then and there, but I liked our little chats so I decided to let you live. I thought the trial would end and we would never see each other again. Imagine my surprise when you resurfaced after the trial. At best, I thought that William was stringing you along, but then it turned out that he actually liked you. It's a pity, Hannah. We were almost family. If only you had stopped digging, just let yourself be satisfied. Ironic, isn't it, that my brother had the matchbook that ultimately will bring about your death? Almost like he's the one doing the killing. I knew I was taking a risk going to that bar with you, but I needed to know what you found. If only it wasn't for Ricky, that stupid man, always interfering where he doesn't belong. I saw your face when he recognized me and knew it was only a matter of time before you put it all together. It's not all bad though. At least you got to spend the end of your life mooching off my family's money."

"I never asked for your family's money."

"You didn't have to, did you? William gave you everything you wanted because he thought dating a girl like you would make him a better person. He didn't realize how terrible you actually are."

"I'm not terrible."

Even as it comes out it sounds like a lie.

Bentley stands up from the chair. He approaches where I sit and leans over. My muscles brace for death.

"Do you remember when we kissed, Hannah?" he says into my ear.

"You kissed me," I respond. I worry about how I smell, my hangover breath and yoga pants still damp with my urine.

"Only because you wanted me to."

"I love William."

"You thought he was a murderer until today."

"No, I thought that he might be a murderer. There's a difference."

"And that wasn't enough of a deal-breaker for you?" Bentley stands up and folds his arms over his chest. He's looking at me like a person who knows that they're right.

"What about Virginia? Does she know what you've done?"

"I don't want to talk about Virginia," Bentley replies.

This seems like an unfair term of the discussion, but I'm in no position to argue.

"Fine," I say. "Maybe I did think William was guilty and

maybe I did like it when you kissed me and maybe I did take advantage of your family's money. Is that what you want to hear?"

Bentley smiles.

"I knew you liked it when I kissed you. I liked it too."

It's pleasing to me, even now, that a man like Bentley enjoyed kissing me. For all my feminist posturing, I can never fully get away from this desire to please men. I'm not even sure what it would look like to fully please myself. All the moments in which I have loved myself most have been through someone else's gaze.

When Bentley leans down to kiss me, I accept it.

"Did you like that?" he says.

I do like it and I hate myself for that, but I've already been playing this game for months. There is little difference between kissing a man who you think might be a murderer and a man who you know is one. It occurs to me that this might be my last ever kiss. That Bentley will be the last person to touch my body while I'm still alive to feel it. I have so many regrets that they're not even worth counting.

I kiss Bentley again in response. I realize that I've been waiting for this, a resolution to what happened that night in the bar. I just didn't realize that it would likely end in my own death.

"What would you do if you only had twenty-four hours to live?" I posed to Meghan once.

"Eat all the ice cream I could," she replied, and we both laughed.

I have no ice cream. All I have is this man in front of me.

"I'll fuck you if you let me live," I whisper, and Bentley laughs.

"Oh, Hannah," he says. "I do like you."

We gaze at each other as he unties my ropes. I do my best to make an escape attempt, but it feels like playacting as he grabs me and holds me so that I can't move.

"Don't do that," he says.

We kiss again. For a moment, both of us are free and we lower ourselves to the floor, which is cold, but I don't care. Any sensation is a worthwhile sensation when I know that I have so few of them left. Bentley reties the ropes so that my hands are above my head as I lie on the floor. I can tell that he's practiced at this. When I try to picture how I look lying there, I see Anna Leigh's face instead of my own.

He slowly pulls down my sweatpants. I'm briefly embarrassed to be wearing something so obviously unsexy and then I push the embarrassment aside. There's no room left for that in my life.

I don't bother pretending that I don't want Bentley to fuck me or that this is somehow against my will. We will have sex and then he will kill me and I will be memorialized like all the other women who came before me. There's something so logical in this inevitability that it's almost comforting.

He touches my clit and I wonder at the fact that my pleasure still seems important to him even as he's threatening to kill me. I moan and don't bother to parse the distinction between pleasure and pain.

People always think of violent men as having small penises, but that isn't true for Bentley. He pulls down his pants and I gasp when I see it, which makes him laugh. Bentley enters me and I think, *Ah, yes, this is what it really feels like to have a serial killer inside of me.* It's scary and thrilling and I'm able to wholly devote myself to this moment in a way that I haven't fully experienced anything in a long time.

"Are you sure you want to kill me?" I whisper as Bentley ejaculates.

"I have to," he replies, matching my tone.

He kisses me on the forehead. It reminds me of William, a gesture that is more paternal than sexy, and then slowly pulls out.

The sky is pitch-black and starless out the window behind us, as though Bentley and I are the last things to exist in the universe. It's a game of desert island where the human race fails to survive because one of the two remaining people is compelled to kill the other.

There's something peaceful in the knowing. I once read an article online that said the rejuvenating force of a vacation isn't the trip itself, but the anticipation of a break. The power of death lies in its inevitability combined with its unpredictability. We all know it's coming; we just don't know when and that makes it terrifying. Except for me. I know because I sought it out in the body of a man.

45

I've often wondered how people with an impending death sentence, whether it's one delivered by terminal cancer or a verdict delivered by a judge and jury, manage to carry on despite the nothingness in front of them. When it's my turn, a sense of calm that I'd never managed to achieve through meditation sweeps across my body. My jaw relaxes, my neck. My muscles embrace their fate. There's almost a sense of relief; thank god, I don't have to worry about anything anymore.

Just as I've fully accepted my impending death, the door opens with a bang. Bentley is still half-naked, his briefs around his ankles. I've already let go of my mental attachments to the earth: my dreams, my emotional connections, the plans I've made for the weeks and months ahead, and it's painful as they come flooding back in.

"William," Bentley says.

From where I lie on the floor, my fiancé looks like a giant. His face is red as though he's been running. The gun from the box in the office is tucked in a holster around his waist. My sweatpants and underwear are on the floor next to me. I'm aware that Bentley's sperm is slowly leaking out of me, leaving a wet patch on the floor. I'm both a victim and a coconspirator.

"Help," I gasp.

There are, after all, still instincts of self-preservation left inside of me.

William grabs Bentley, who has just pulled his pants up, and slams him into a wall. The sound of it is shocking. It occurs to me that I've never known true violence, only witnessed it on TV.

"I told you to stay away from her," he says.

William swings at Bentley, who is cornered against the wall, his pants finally up and buttoned. William's fist makes contact and he pulls back in order to punch him again. Bentley manages to free his arms and William stumbles as he's shoved backward. It's not yet clear who the victor will be. Bentley is taller than William, but William is stronger due to his obsessive exercising. Because Jill was his trainer, every punch he lands is like a punch coming from her.

Though my legs are untied, it's difficult to move on the floor with my arms restrained behind me, and my half-naked body flails across the floor. It's a stupid, helpless position to be in. I manage to back myself into a corner of the room, out of the radius of their swinging fists.

"Did you call the police?" I ask William.

He doesn't answer me and his silence tells me that no help is coming. My life is dependent upon whoever wins the fight. The motions almost look practiced and I can tell that they've fought before. Both of them are bleeding and William's eye is starting to swell. I've always wanted two men to fight over me, but I didn't want it to be like this.

Finally, William pins Bentley down. He reaches for the gun in his belt and points it at Bentley's head as he kneels over him.

"You piece of shit," he says. "I should've done this a long time ago."

I'm already anticipating the future. William will kill Bentley and we'll put his body in the garbage bags that Bentley intended for me and then we'll dump his corpse into the ravine. Somehow, the police will figure out that Bentley was the serial killer all along and whoever dumped his body in the ravine did it as an act of public goodness. After that, we'll get married in a ceremony that costs more than my parents' house. If murdering a brother and hiding his body doesn't make a couple marriage material, I don't know what does. William will never know how my body ached for Bentley before he came into the room, how I spent months thinking about when Bentley kissed me. How desperately I wanted Bentley to fuck me in those moments before what I assumed would be my death. These will be secrets that I'll keep inside my head forever.

Except William doesn't kill his brother.

His grip around Bentley's throat loosens and William stares down at him, his eyes full of fury.

"I want you to leave," he says. "Leave Georgia, the United States. Go somewhere far away where no one will ever find you and don't come back."

Bentley is abnormally passive. For the first time since I've known him, there is fear on his face.

"You need to leave me alone. You need to leave Hannah alone. If I ever see you again, I won't show you any forgiveness. I will kill you on sight. Do you hear me? On sight. And once you're dead, I'll make sure that everyone knows what you've done. The police, Virginia, your kids. I'll buy a billboard with your name on it that says 'Bentley Thompson is a murderer and an adulterer too.' I can only imagine what the police will be able to find if I tell them about this room. You'll be so hated that they'll send your corpse to prison. Your kids will have to change their name so that no one knows who their father is. Do you hear me? Say that you hear me or I'll kill you right now. Don't think I won't do it because you're my brother. That only gets you so far."

"I hear you," Bentley stammers.

Blood is dripping from William's face onto Bentley's.

"You promise, you motherfucker?"

"I promise."

"I'm going to get up and you're going to leave. I want you gone tonight. If I even so much as hear a whisper of your name, I'm calling the police and sending them straight here. There's not enough bleach in the world to cover your sins. And then I'm coming after you myself, okay? I will make you wish that you were behind bars."

"Okay," Bentley says, his voice so full of fear that he sounds like someone else.

William slowly lifts himself off his brother but keeps the gun pointed at him. Bentley stands, his body stiff. There's a moment when I think Bentley might still lunge, but he stops to glance at William, then me, and finally he turns and exits the room.

Tears are falling down my cheeks. I don't have the capacity to evaluate exactly why I'm crying.

"You saved me," I sob.

William doesn't say anything. He struggles to untie the ropes around my hands and finally uses one of the knives from Bentley's briefcase. I shudder thinking about what remnants of Anna Leigh, Kimberly, Jill, Emma, and Kelsey might remain on those blades.

"Are you hurt?" William asks when I'm finally free of the ropes.

I throw my arms around him and breathe in. He smells like William, only now with blood. It's a comforting, familiar scent.

"No, you came just in time," I say as guilt wraps around my heart the same way that the ropes were wrapped around my wrists.

"Thank you," I say. "Thank you."

There's a part of me that wants to stay here forever. Like when an airplane lands in a new city and I have to anticipate retrieving my luggage from the baggage claim, getting a car, checking into a hotel, and all of those little inconveniences that come with being somewhere foreign. The airplane is uncomfortable, but at least it's familiar.

I know, however, that regardless of what happens, whatever is between William and me in this exact moment cannot last. After all, it was always the killer I wanted and not the savior.

William carefully gathers my clothes from the floor, takes off his shirt, and wraps me in it. I'm passive like a sick child being tended to by their parent. Please, please, reduce my fever.

We emerge from the room and I realize that I'm in the same office building that the Thompson family law practice is located in. This is it, the second location that the prosecution was looking for and never found. Because the offices are in a separate wing of the building, no one heard me when I screamed. The irony isn't lost on me that almost being murdered in an office building is the closest I've ever come to a six-figure salary.

We don't speak on the car ride home. William's face is still red, his jaw clenched. I stare blankly out the window. The world is still here.

Without speaking, I get in the shower at the house and William joins me. We don't have sex. Instead, he kisses me all over my body. I'm still here too.

He looks for injuries and finds none, at least nothing that he can see with his eyes.

After the shower, I cover my naked body with the comforter from our bed and sit on the couch. I don't know how to relate to my skin. It's late at night or early in the morning, depending on one's conception of time. I don't wholly believe that the sun will appear when morning hits.

William sits down next to me.

"We have to break up," he says.

"What?" I say. "I thought you loved me."

"I do love you. I can't trust you though," William replies.

It turns out that he spent the day planning the serious talk we were going to have when he got home from work about what was going on between Bentley and me.

"I knew something was wrong when I picked you up from that bar," he says.

Except I wasn't there when he got home. William knew something was really wrong when he saw that my phone and purse were still there. That's when he found my notebook with all my comments about whether or not he was a serial killer.

"I'm sorry," I apologize, too little too late.

There is nothing I can say to redeem myself. I know by the expression on his face that it is unforgivable to secretly investigate my fiancé of serial murder after he'd so kindly invited me into his home and paid for all my food and shelter.

William doesn't acknowledge my apology.

"I knew you were with Bentley," he continues. "And I knew Bentley was at work because I saw him."

"You saw him?"

"Bentley wouldn't let something like kidnapping my fiancée interfere with his billable hours," William replies. The word "fiancée" is a knife.

William grabbed his gun and headed to the office, where he combed through the maze of the building until he found me.

"I'm just glad I got there in time," he says.

"I can't believe it was Bentley this whole time. I feel so stupid. Why did you have all that stuff in your desk that made me think it could've been you?"

"What stuff?"

"You know, the matchbook, the hair tie, the gym card. The mementos of murder from the women. I found them in your desk in the same box as the gun."

William's face twists into a scowl.

"Ever since we were kids, Bentley has been hiding things in my room to try to get me in trouble. One time, he put a dead rabbit in my room. It was disgusting."

"He said that was you."

William lets out a pained laugh.

"I can't believe that you were with me, Hannah, if that was what you thought of me. It was all Bentley. The rabbit, the murders."

"Gracie too?"

William stiffens at the name.

"What did you say?"

"Bentley told me about what happened with Gracie. He said that you killed her."

William is silent for a long time.

"I loved Gracie," he says finally. "And she started dating my brother. That was painful, to say the least. One night we were at a party and both of us got drunk, really drunk. We snuck off into the woods together and started kissing. I knew it was wrong, but I couldn't stop myself. Bentley did a lot of coke in those days and I guess he got Gracie into it too because she offered me some. There was something wrong with it and Gracie got really sick, really fast. I didn't know what to do. I couldn't call an ambulance because I didn't want to get her in trouble for having drugs. I couldn't call Bentley because I didn't want him to know what happened between us. I sat there and I watched her die. It was the worst moment of my life. It destroyed me. It continues to destroy me. That's why, when I got arrested, I was almost glad. It was like I was finally being punished for what I'd done."

William's posture is slumped, his gaze pointed at the floor. I see him now in a new light. William is a killer, but not like Bentley. His was a murder of passivity. He watched Gracie do drugs and then he watched her die and let his father cover up the evidence. He did, after all, keep souvenirs from his kills; I'd just been wrong about whom he had murdered. That's why he kept those notes from Gracie after all of these years. That's why he moves like a man swallowed by guilt.

"Did you know it was Bentley?" I ask.

The question is heavy. A tarp full of water about to burst.

"Yes," he says finally. "I didn't know for a long time. Women were dropping like flies all around me. Do you know how terrifying that is? There were a few days where I considered the possibility that I was somehow doing it in my sleep or had an alter ego that took over my body. In the end there was no alter ego, only Bentley. Always Bentley."

"Why didn't you tell the police?"

William shakes his head. I wonder if his neck hurts from all that shaking.

"It's more complicated than that. I was already a suspect at that point. I had nothing to tie the murders to Bentley. And besides, he's my brother. I couldn't do that to him, my family. Especially not after the things that I'd already done. I got away with murder once and I lived this whole life. It only seemed fair that he would get to do the same."

"You let those women die," I say.

William shifts uncomfortably with the volume of my voice. I see him as if for the first time. A man so mired in self-loathing that he's willing to let other people suffer if in return he gets to suffer too.

"Please calm down, Hannah," he tells me.

"I don't want to calm down."

"You don't understand my family," he continues.

"I might be the only person who does understand your family," I shoot back. "What about Virginia, the children?"

"Bentley would never hurt them."

"There are ways of hurting people that don't include murder."

"It doesn't matter anymore, okay? He's gone. He's not coming back. I'll make sure of it."

"What are they going to think?" I ask. Is it worse to have a serial killer father living at home than no father at all? Is killing genetic? I think about the baby inside of Virginia's womb. Is each child a new potential murderer? Ultimately, it's impossible to escape the psychic wounds that come with having a family.

"I'll take care of them," William says. I know that he's telling the truth. After all, he's always loved taking care of me. It's a form of penance, I now realize. If he takes care of me, maybe he can make up for Gracie.

I suddenly feel very tired, my wrists and ankles sore from where Bentley bound me.

"Can we go to bed?" I ask.

"I was going to sleep in the guest room," William replies stiffly.

"Please?" I say, I beg. "I just need someone to hold me."

"Okay," William acquiesces.

In the end, he fucks me one last time. He doesn't tie me up or try to kill me and I don't orgasm. Maybe he was never the person I wanted after all.

46

My childhood home is as I left it except for the sewing machine that has taken up residence in my bedroom. Although my mother claims that she's happy to have me home and tells me that I can stay as long as I need, I sense some resentment as I help her carry her collection of fabrics to the unfinished basement.

She left everything on the walls. All the posters from my teen years, pictures with my former friends. They're hard to throw away at first and then, once I get going, there's pleasure in it. I'm so good at ridding myself of the things that no longer serve me.

I paint the formerly lilac walls a sensible gray. My mom looks sad when I show her.

"What's wrong? I thought you'd be happy," I say.

"I kind of liked it the way it was before," she replies without explanation.

We don't talk about what happened with William. While helping unpack, my mother found my engagement ring tucked inside of a box. She picked it up, watched as the diamond flashed in the light, looked at me, and then put it back in the box and said nothing. There are things that a parent doesn't need to know about their child.

I get a job as a barista at a locally owned coffee shop where I used to go to in high school to work on my homework. I get to know the regulars who pass the daily paper amongst themselves like they're sitting at a giant kitchen table. I memorize their favorite drinks and pastries and that information fills space in my brain where other things used to go. The nice ones learn my name and greet me each morning like I'm a friend. I know that I'm not though, not really.

Some days I wish that I had a scar. Something violent that redefines my appearance. No one knows who I am here, which is supposed to be a good thing. I attend a yoga class a few days a week when I get off work in the afternoon and I always place my mat at the back of the room. I've gained some weight and the expensive yoga clothes that William bought me no longer fit. It doesn't matter because no one in the room looks at me, wonders what it's like to be the girlfriend of an accused serial killer. It's fine to be invisible. I didn't love William for fame. I didn't mean to love William at all. It was just something that happened.

I'm thinking about writing a memoir. I don't know where to start or where to finish. I don't know how to tell the story of myself without exposing Bentley, and by extension William, to the world.

I sporadically apply for other jobs. I don't look at the qualifications and send out résumés everywhere. This seems like something a man who was in my position would do. I've decided to let my career choose me instead of the other way around. I've gotten a few interviews, but no job offers. I worry there's something about me, a scent, that keeps employers away.

I hang out with friends a couple of times before I realize that it's making me unhappy and I prefer to be at home streaming television on my laptop. My friends know some version of what happened to me, but they're scared to ask for the whole story. From the alien looks they give me, I presume that Meghan told them I went to Georgia to watch the trial and that I was in love with William. They never acknowledge this; our conversations revolve solely around the weather and things that we've cooked recently, though I can tell the murdered women hang heavy on their tongues. When Meghan texts me to tell me that it would be best if I didn't go to her wedding, I tell her I understand, though it makes me deeply sad.

I call Dotty after I've been home a few weeks. She and her husband have just returned from a trip to the Virgin Islands, where they renewed their vows.

"Things have improved since I got back," she says. "He's different this time, better."

Dotty doesn't say that she is also different and better. Sometimes the standards that we hold for other people are different from the standards that we hold ourselves to.

Dotty has been in touch with Lauren, who's dating a boy that she met in one of her criminal justice classes. Dotty doesn't think that it'll last.

"There's a spell that comes over us in our youth," Dotty says. "We chase after things that we know aren't good for us just so that we can say that we did it. No one wants a healthy relationship when they're nineteen. They only want passion."

We talk briefly about what happened between William and me.

"We got engaged," I say. "But it didn't work out."

I still write William letters. He never responds. I'm not even sure that he's getting them. His absence has left the void that breakups aways leave. Those silly little things that I'm desperate to tell him and can't.

> Dear William,
> I applied for a job as a receptionist at a law firm today. It made me think of you.

> Dear William,
> I've kept up with my yoga practice. You're right, these yoga pants really hold up.

> Dear William,
> My parents are driving me crazy today. I need to get my own place.

> Dear William,
> I tried to masturbate tonight and I can't get my body to feel anything.

> Dear William,
> I've spent a lot of time questioning what I wanted from you since I've been home and I still don't know. I want to reassure you that I only ever wanted love, but I'm not sure that's true anymore.

Sometimes I think about writing Virginia to tell her what happened and to make sure that the kids are okay, but I can't find the words for what I need to say.

I can't stop eating. In the mornings, I eat a bagel smothered in cream cheese at the coffee shop and a sandwich for lunch with chips on the side. I eat dinner with my parents and indulge in the heavy Midwestern casseroles that my mom favors. I ask for seconds because it makes both of us feel good. When I put on clothes and find that they no longer fit, I'm indifferent. I stare at myself in the mirror and all I can think is *Oh*.

I go on dates with men that I meet on dating apps. I don't have any recent photos of myself, so I post pictures from my twenties and they all look disappointed when they see me. I don't care because I'm disappointed when I see them too. I figure that the worst thing that can happen is that they can try to kill me and that's already happened once and I survived.

The men aren't as handsome as William. They don't charm me. They're ordinary men with ordinary jobs and ordinary brothers. I sleep with one of them and the sex is fine, average. Two lumpy people in their thirties banging together. Nobody dies.

I read a lot of books. Mysteries where someone is murdered and it's always the husband who is the suspect. The books become boring as I become adept in my literary detective skills, always figuring out who did it before the end. I keep reading in hopes of finding a book that will truly thrill me.

Underneath it all, the mundanity of my day-to-day, I'm waiting for Bentley to find me and kill me.

I see Bentley everywhere. Out of the corner of my eye while I'm walking my parents' dog, the next aisle over in the grocery store, in the face of every tall white man who comes into the coffee shop while I'm working. It's not really him, of course. Not yet. It turns out when you're looking for one, serial killers are everywhere. I'm not one of those paranoid women though, the ones that look for danger everywhere. Bentley tried to kill me once and he'll do it again. He's not the kind of person to give up on his dreams.

When we said goodbye for the final time, William assured me that Bentley wouldn't try to seek me out.

"He's too scared of going to prison," he said. "If he even enters the same state as you, I won't hesitate to call the police."

I know that William's wrong, that Bentley will come to me eventually, just not for the reason that he thinks.

I consider calling the police and telling them what I know, but the only evidence that I have is my words, and those aren't worth much. Besides, it gives me a little thrill to think about Bentley still out there, biding his time until we meet again. It puts a pep in my step as I walk from my car to the grocery store or as I stumble through the darkness from my bed to the bathroom. Though I know that he isn't hiding under my bed, just the thought of his name makes my spine tingle. I think more than I should about the time we shared when I was tied up. There is nothing sexy about being killed, but that doesn't stop me from turning it into a fantasy.

Max Yulipsky and Reese come into the coffee shop late in March, six months after my return home. They don't see me at first and I watch them as they examine the pastries on display, finally settling on splitting an apple fritter.

They move like people in love, one of them always with a hand on the other. Max and I never did anything like this when we were sleeping together. If I was lucky, one of his roommates made a pot in the decrepit coffee maker.

"Hannah," Max says when he sees me, his eyes widening.

I know from Instagram that Max has gotten a real job for which he wears a button-down shirt and answers email all day. The band is on hiatus. In his posts, he sounded happy about these changes. There was no mention of becoming a sellout, only that it was time.

"Hey, Max." I give him a big smile.

The honey blond dye job has long since grown out and I haven't bothered to dye my hair again. The roots are unflattering, but it's always an uncomfortable process to return to yourself after a brief voyage elsewhere.

"What can I get you today?"

Max orders black coffee and Reese a blended cold drink. Max used to judge girls like that, people who ordered sweet beverages lined with caramel.

"I like girls who can tolerate some bitterness," he said, which led to me attempting to become the type of girl who liked black coffee.

I guess people are willing to put anything aside for the person that they love.

I bring Max his coffee and make Reese's drink. Max hangs around the counter after Reese has already taken a seat at a table by the window.

"How have you been, Hannah?" he asks.

"So good," I say. "I went to Georgia for a few months last year. It was amazing."

"Cool, cool. What are you doing now?"

"Oh, you know. I got this job temporarily. You know, until something better comes along. I've been applying to a lot of different types of places."

"Yeah," Max says, and looks at me again before going to sit down next to Reese. I see him glance back in my direction several times and I ignore it, which makes me feel powerful.

I know what he's looking at. It has become impossible to hide, not that I was ever trying to hide it to begin with. I wear it like a badge of honor, a mark of my almost death and the killer who wanted me.

I put my hand on my belly, my uterus swollen with pregnancy. The baby kicks at my touch. I don't know who the father is, but it doesn't matter much when all the possibilities share a gene pool. It will be up to the child to tell me who he is when he arrives and I will know who to blame if the bodies start to pile up once again.

ACKNOWLEDGMENTS

So many people assisted in the creation of this book.

Thank you to Katie Greenstreet, Leodora Darlington, and Jen Monroe, who saw all that the book could be and helped me bring it there.

Thank you to the whole team at Berkley. In particular, thank you to Candice Coote, Lauren Burnstein, Tara O'Connor, Hannah Engler, Dan Walsh, Emily Osborne, and Dorothy Janick.

Thank you to Brandi Wells, Natalie Lima, Lauren Bingham, Brooke Champagne, Daniel Bernal, Carolyn Browender, Tessa Carter, Darren Demaree, Michael Martone, Amber Buck, Cindy Tekobbe, Kristine Langley Mahler, Amanda Miska, Chad Simpson, Robin Metz, Kellie Wells, Aubrey Hirsch, Lyz Lenz, Jason McCall, Sara Pirkle, Maggie Nye, Megan Bowden, Julia Austin, Kim Caldwell, Theresa Pappas, Easty Lambert-Brown, Elizabeth Deanna Morris Lakes, Krista Ahlberg, Julie Pearson, Elizabeth Blyakher, Blair Jones, Jessica Johnson, Sarah Blake, Shaelyn Smith, Dean Bakopoulos, Patti White, Seth Stewart, Robert Weatherly, Kori Hensell, Julia Ricciardi, Siân Griffiths, Tabitha Blankenbiller, Vikki Grodner, Steven Trout, Natalie Loper, Zach and Susan Doss, Matt Bell, the Whitver family, Marcia Coryell,

Robyn and John Hammontree, and James Eubanks for supporting or inspiring this novel in some way.

Thank you to Monica Berlin, who taught me how to write letters.

Thank you to Split/Lip Press for publishing the short story that led to this novel.

Thank you to my novel-writing students at the University of Alabama who served as my writing companions for many years.

Thank you to my dad and my in-laws for their support.

Thank you to Ronan, whose birth helped facilitate this book in more ways than one.

Thank you to Summer the greyhound for reminding me to go outside.

Thank you most of all to my husband, Brian Oliu, who has definitely never killed anyone.